Newearth Relevance

A. K. Frailey

Hardcover ISBN: 979-8-9998241-3-4

Website
https://akfrailey.com/

Amazon Author Page
https://www.amazon.com/author/akfrailey

A. K. Frailey Books

THE WRITINGS OF A. K. FRAILEY
Books for the Mind and Spirit

https://akfrailey.com/

Contemporary Literary Fiction

OLDTOWN Fly, Sparrow, Fly

OLDTOWN Brothers Born

Historical Science Fiction Novels

OldEarth ARAM Encounter

OldEarth Ishtar Encounter

OldEarth Neb Encounter

OldEarth Georgios Encounter

OldEarth Melchior Encounter

Science Fiction Novels

Homestead

Last of Her Kind

Newearth Justine Awakens

Newearth A Hero's Crime

Newearth Progeny

Newearth Relevance

Short Stories

It Might Have Been—And Other Short Stories 2nd Edition

One Day at a Time and Other Stories

Encounter Science Fiction Short Stories & Novella 2nd Edition

Inspirational Non-Fiction

My Road Goes Ever On—Spiritual Being, Human Journey 2nd Edition

My Road Goes Ever On—A Timeless Journey

The Road Goes Ever On—A Christian Journey Through The Lord of the Rings

Children's Book

The Adventures of Tally-Ho

Wise Home

Wise Home on Lily Pad Pond

Poetry

Hope's Embrace & Other Poems 2nd Edition

Chapter One

Disturbing Force

—Aram County, Relevance's Home—

September, Year 73, Newearth Reckoning

Relevance studied storm clouds as big as motherships progress across the somber sky, dropping rain showers as they went. Crackling, ready-to-be-harvested, corn and bean fields shivered in mute gray and gold, while trees tinged with yellow and red stood silent, waiting. Shiny droplets hung on the edge of pine branches—potential… *What?* Certainly, the crops could no longer receive nourishment for their brittle roots merely snapped, easily giving way when harvesters plowed through.

Wearing dark pants and a cotton shirt, Relevance stood on his porch, his muscular hands clasping the wood railing, watching the sunset. Melodic chords of an ancient composition, Ludwig van Beethoven's Moonlight Sonata, resonated from the glossy grand piano in his living room. Inside, Variant, though only a beginner, played with a neurosurgeon's precision. She had wanted to play this piece above all others, so, in her single-minded way, she had practiced, line by line, this one piece until it resounded with the perfection of an accomplished pianist. Only he knew that she could play nothing else. She did not care to know any other piece.

His fingers still tingled with the vibration of violin strings as he accompanied her a short time before. His musical repertoire was much wider, since *he* luxuriated in the magnificent sensation of bringing mere strings to pulsating life. If he liked, recorded music from a variety of worlds with accompanying orchestras was available, but he preferred the glorifying power of playing an instrument all by himself. He could play nearly a dozen, though only half of those with expert finesse.

The sun broke through the clouds and glowed like an orange ball, hovering just above the horizon. This day was coming to a close, and relief filled him at the thought. Why had he offered to celebrate a day that no one really knew or cared about? In all honesty, he didn't even believe in birthdays. He had no reason to doubt the veracity of *his* parents, such that they were, or his maker, fool that he was, but the day the biomb was cracked open and his body exposed to the elemental forces hardly seemed like a moment to mark with celebration. It wasn't his birthday, anyway. He had turned sixteen a month ago without an ounce of personal interest or celebratory fanfare. Though many people, humans and aliens alike, thought him a man in his prime, mature, and ever so wise. He smiled at that. Men as well as women found him attractive, a trustworthy person who would honor a secret. So very ironic. He kept many secrets. Horded them. But no one knew his secret desires. Well, that would soon change.

A crow cawed as it flew high overhead. He refocused his attention. No revelations today. This was Variant's day. No one knew the actual day of her birth, as no one had cared to record it, as no one had cared in the least about her. She was a product of a woman's egg and a man's sperm, forced together with a few genetic modifications by an obscure scientist who liked to experiment. Once the mottle-skinned, odd baby girl was released from her biomb, only an enterprising Ingot trader saw the slightest worth in her.

She was utilized. That fact kept her alive. Which was good enough for her. Or at least, it had been. Until yesterday, when she bumped into a strange woman who shrank away from her as if bitten. Variant was used to nasty reactions as her mottled skin often reminded humans of snakes, and aliens knew better than to trust her mismatched eyes. But this woman touched off a cascade of childhood memories in Variant, sending her into a violent fit.

Interventionists would have taken her to Bothmal for all the destruction she'd wrecked. But Relevance intervened. Instead of Bothmal, he took her to his new home deep in the woodlands of Aram County and promised her a birthday party.

Using a variety of templates from an ancient OldEarth database called Picturesque, he culled the necessary ingredients for a prime birthday party: balloons, a frosted cake with an abundance of candles, a stack of nonsensical presents, and he even hired six co-workers from a local hospital, where he had acted as an assistant, to stand in as guests: a middle-aged human nurse, the Ingot janitorial manager, a Cresta organ transplant specialist, a Uanyi accountant, and two Bhuaci doctors. Given enough alcohol and a variety of snacks, they were only too happy to party at his home with a woman they did not know.

Gone now, their sloppy, half-drunk goodbyes still rang in his ears. Variant hadn't even seemed to notice them. Or the cake, the balloons, or the presents. All she noticed was the piano. He told her that if she behaved herself and did everything he asked, whenever he asked, she could have it.

No words were spoken. She never agreed in any formal language. But when she sat down, pulled up the musical score for the Moonlight Sonata on her datapad, and began to practice, he knew that she was his. Possibly, forever.

The sun down now, the sky a haze of pink and purple, he pulled out his own datapad and considered the woman Variant had identified as the "disturbing force" that had sent her into such a mindless rage.

Facial recognition identified her as Clare Erlandson, a forty-eight-year-old woman and a longtime member of the Newearth Human Services Department with a nearly spotless record. She had one recorded son: Herson, the first Human-Tabun crossbreed created in a Cresta lab.

The irony smacked of what many would call mystical forces, but Relevance knew better. There was no way that Variant could have known. On a busy Newearth street, she had literally run into the mother of his half-brother. His own mother as well.

Darkness descended, and the weak rays of light faded.

As if a gigantic harvester had roared to life, his mission was set. Relevance knew what he wanted for his next birthday. He smiled, though he had never known an ounce of mirth. It was time to be reintroduced to his family. But this time, there would be no party.

—Vandi, Bala's Home—

October, Year 73 Newearth Reckoning

Bala tiptoed into his warm, golden-lit kitchen and, in one of his sneakiest moves, grabbed his wife Kendra around the waist and hugged her in a warm embrace. Her yelp could have woken the dead in three counties.

"Man-O-Mine, you almost got yourself clobbered with my largest frying pan! You want a big ol' dent in your precious skull?"

Startled out of the romantic moment, Bala stepped back, hands raised. "I didn't know you were armed."

Wordlessly, Kendra lifted her left hand, a cast-iron skillet tight in her grip. She drilled her meaning home with a deadpanned stare.

"Good golly, woman, you could take out an Ingoti invasion force with that thing!" The words were hardly out of his mouth before the ugly memory of a horrific home invasion—one that had left his whole family traumatized for months—rose in his mind. Bala swallowed a lump in his throat and offered a broad smile to move the conversation onto safer territory. “I just wanted to hug the most beautiful woman on Newearth. Is that a crime?”

A twinkle in her eyes, Kendra returned his grin and set the skillet on the stovetop. Then she turned and snatched up a picnic basket and pointed to the door. “Romantic moments were meant for date-night at the most secluded part of the park.” She rolled her eyes as she swept past her husband. “Not the kitchen.”

Chuckling, Bala had to agree, though, as he grabbed the blanket and cooler by the door and headed out into the perfect autumn evening, he secretly defended the kitchen as one of the most romantic spots on the planet. *After all, it's where body and soul are held together with great food!*

—Vandi Park—

Cricket chirpers and a few hardy cicada hummers along with evening birdsong created a lovely backdrop to the orange and red sunset. Bala sighed contentedly as he lay on his back with one arm under his head and the other resting over his happy tummy. “You make the world's best apple pie, Lady-O-Mine. I would have been happy with the veggie noodle thingamajig, the crusty bread with that luscious fruit syrup, and the—I must say potent—spice drink, but that pie was over-the-moon glorious.”

The picnic basket repacked with scanty leftovers sat nestled against the oak tree behind them. With the thick, though rather shabby, old blanket under them, Kendra stretched out next to Bala and snuggled in close.

Bala's heart rate went from somnolent to pounding in an instant. *Only one thing could beat that pie...*

Drying leaves rustled overhead, and a few pink and yellow leaves from neighboring trees swirled to the ground before them, creating a beatific natural shower.

Bala lifted his head and glanced around. No one. They had the park to themselves. *How wonderful!* He turned to face his wife, his arms now encircling her, drawing her in closer.

Kendra lifted her face and stared into his eyes with a searching expression that bespoke deep, turbulent emotions. Not exactly the romantic mood he was hoping for. Shoving his nearly overwhelming desire aside, he allowed concern to step forward. "You okay?"

She nodded and glanced aside. Then she shook her head and scooted into a sitting position.

Bala forced down a groan. He sat up close and nudged her shoulder playfully. "You get in trouble at school? The kids bullying you on the playground? If there's anyone I need to beat up…"

A sad snort and Kendra dove in, unpacking her concerns in quick order. "Something's bothering Seth. He says there's trouble in the north woods—a hidden development just beyond the Amens settlement." She drew her legs up and wrapped her arms around them, shivering. "I have this bad feeling that we've let ourselves get distracted. I mean, we've put all our attention on the kids these past few years, but we have no idea what kind of world they are going into."

Bala considered her words and accepted them. But he didn't fully agree. No one knew what the future held. "I don't know. We've prepared our kids for life with lots of love, solid educations, and some quality off-world experiences. They'll find a way. We can't live their lives for them. Everyone makes mistakes, sure. But once repented, they become learning experiences. It's what you always tell me, anyway." He paused, trying to read her expression in the dim light. "What's really bothering you?"

Kendra rubbed her eyes and sighed; her shoulders hunched. "We need to talk about the penguins."

His stomach clenching, Bala fought frustration that bubbled like an active volcano. "Now? This is our night to relax and spend time with each other without kids and the world crashing in on us."

Kendra's eyes pleaded. "I can't relax. I feel something dreadful is happening, but I can't see clearly. It's like some ol' monster is charging right at our front door, but I've got nothing but a frying pan in my hand."

If his memories didn't include a home invasion, a planet-eating monster, hybrid experiments, and unexplained changes in Newearth leadership, Bala would comfort himself with Kendra's vivacious history as an overanxious mother. But he knew better. "All right, but even Cerulean doesn't know everything yet. We're supposed to meet tomorrow morning. I was going to catch you up afterward, but maybe it's better this way. You can help me organize my thoughts."

A maniacal gleam entered Kendra's eyes, and she sat straighter, her hands beckoning. "Tell all, good sir, and I will do my organizational best."

Succumbing to the inevitable, Bala scootched back against the tree, relaxed, readying himself for a long conversation. "So, okay, I went through every OldEarth record that I could find and discovered some great recipes, by the way, but also a long history of genetic experimentation. Crazy stuff. Most of it went nowhere. But it turns out that those same files have been accessed by others. Namely, the Ingots have reviewed them extensively, probably trying to figure out a way to keep extinction at bay, but strangely enough, so did the Bhuaci. I decided to widen my search parameters and discovered that there has been an Insectine Genetic Improvement Plan in the works for years. Did you ever hear of such a thing? As a race, they want to biologically alter their physical makeup to become more attractive to alien races—especially humans! How wild is that? And then, of course, there is the whole embarrassing Luxonian episode in

Newearth history where they delved into reproductive experiments with human subjects."

Kendra shook her head. Her eyes wide. "Wow, you have covered a lot of territory and haven't even mentioned Cresta studies yet."

Wrinkling his nose, Bala snorted. "Their experimentation on humans is so well known, I hardly needed to check the files." He sighed, the will to live seeping from his body. "Now"—he braced himself—"here's the scary part…"

Kendra swallowed; her eyes as wide as human eyes could grow.

"Relevance's fingerprints are all over these files—and others—that he should never have known about."

Kendra shook her head. "I don't understand."

"Our beloved son, David, has access to interstellar files on the Newearth Docking Bay, and he's been very busy acting as an intermediary. I wouldn't have realized except I saw the code name Goliath. You know how he jokes that, if he had been Goliath, he'd have been a giant with a helmet, a slingshot, and a sack full of rocks."

Horror rippled over Kendra's face. "But we dealt with this already! He's supposed to stay away from Relevance. Barni was going to keep an eye on him!"

Bala pressed his head against the rough tree bark. He looked at the night sky through the swaying branches. "I didn't want to talk about this tonight." He refocused on his wife, sadness filling in the crooks and crannies where fear hadn't yet taken hold. "The penguins are gone forever, never to be replaced. I believe they were experimented on first but not successfully. Somewhere, probably in Aram County—I pray far from Seth—there are other animals being altered and only Relevance knows why."

—Aram County Woodlands—

November, Year 73, Newearth Reckoning

Dr. Anzi stopped in the middle of the woodlands near an oak tree and unfolded the three-legged stool he had carried under his arm. He perched on its solid surface and forced his shoulders to relax. The outdoors always made him feel unhinged. Too much open space. He much preferred a laboratory packed with scientific tools and medical equipment. But, alas, a laboratory was not alive. The woodlands were. Even in autumn in the northern hemisphere, the cold air and crunch of dead leaves could not completely hide the life force throbbing just under the surface and high overhead—the scurrying footsteps of small animals scrounging for food, the pecking of birds searching for the living protein that would keep them alive another day.

He scanned the area, focusing on the details: generations of decaying foliage, fallen tree trunks sprawled like drunken Cresta after gorging on seafood and high-octane Green, shriveled mushrooms scattered on old limbs in remembrance of warmer days, massive boulders wearing patches of dark moss, while tiny mold spores waited patiently in dirt-filled crevices, and round buds on tree-tips insisted that lifegiving sunlight would return soon.

Dr. Anzi sucked in a deep breath and immediately regretted it. The sharp air stung his lungs. Coughing, he stared at the bare branches overhead, pointing toward a sun they could never reach but desperately needed. Despite the cold, his back prickled with discomfort. He had layered on a long-sleeved shirt, a heavy sweater, corduroy pants, hiking boots, and a thick coat. Sweat trickled down his back, and he knew he would not last much longer. Stupid woodlands. Why had he come? He could learn as much from a holoscreen fed from well-placed bots.

Just then, a black crow swooped down and snatched a wizened wild grape from a vine he hadn't noticed. A quick gulp and it seemed satisfied for a moment. Then it cocked its head and stared through its beady eyes right at the good doctor.

Dr. Anzi froze, compelled to see what the creature did next when, suddenly, a massive wing fluttering and a scream unlike anything he had ever heard before broke the stillness. Another feathered body, bigger and far fiercer than the crow, flew onto the scene. An eagle! Into the drift of leaves, its talons grabbed ahold of a squirming snake and, with massive shoulder strength, it lifted off just as quickly as it had come, carrying its prey to a distant tree limb.

Without craning his head to see, Dr. Anzi surmised that it had a nest nearby and would make quick work of the snake. He glanced at the crow, surprised that it still perched on the old log a mere two meters away, staring at him, as if a companion of the deadly spectacle and perhaps just as intimidated but pretending not to be.

Almost in a taunt, Dr. Anzi snorted and muttered at the sleek black bird. "You're not fierce. Not when compared to real ferocity."

As if taking the insult to heart, the bird flapped its wings with a series of angry caws and then flew deeper into the woodlands.

Alone and in silence again, Dr. Anzi felt sadness grip him. Before old memories could take hold, his datapad beeped. A request to meet Relevance as soon as possible flashed on the screen. He rose to his feet, folded his three-legged stool, and turned around. His childhood chased him as he pounded back to the earthen safety of an octagonal structure he had helped to design, a hidden laboratory in the middle of a living microcosm that would provide the life forms he needed to finally rise above the eagles of this world.

Loping over the uneven ground, the image of his father's stern face as they stood shoulder-to-shoulder in a nature preserve rose before his eyes. He quickened his pace. He could feel his father's grip on his six-year-old shoulder as he was turned toward the body of a dead raccoon, its entrails spread revoltingly around its middle, its glassy eyes staring into the distance as if to avoid watching its dismemberment by scavengers. His father's voice intoned in his ears as if the ghost of the man had taken bodily form.

You must face reality, Anzi. Either you master those around you, or they master you. We all die, but only masters choose how they live. He had patted his son's shoulder and nudged him toward home—a haven where his mother would set a delicious dinner before them and then retreat to her private sanctuary of VR travels. She loved seeing new places and cultures though she rarely left the house. Memories of the raccoon and his mother depressed Anzi. He could not explain why.

Once back in the safety of the laboratory, Dr. Anzi divested himself of his overcoat and hustled to the Interview Room—a special space in the third branch where prospective patients could be evaluated before being accepted into the LEAP (Learn-Excell-Aptitude-Progress) program. Ironically, it was also the place where he had first met in person his LEAP primary associate, a deceptively attractive young man named Relevance.

A human-Ingot-Tabunite, Relevance was the first known tribrid to survive gestation. He was also on a mission, one that he could not manage without the trained skills of a dedicated geneticist. The fact that they followed similar visions only made LEAP more possible. Perhaps inevitable. He would say it was part of a divine plan if he believed in such things. But gods reminded him too much of his father, so he eschewed that notion.

Dressed in a simple cable knit sweater over black pants, Relevance stood behind the large steel table in the middle of the room, his hands flat on the surface, his gaze fixed as if studying it.

After taking a deep breath, Dr. Anzi stepped forward and offered his most formal bow. “You called for me? Has there been a development?”

His head rising and his gaze locking onto Dr. Anzi, Relevance smiled. A disconcerting expression if one took the deadly look in his eyes into account. “You have a reputation, Doctor. It’s why I accepted you so quickly, on the recommendations of fellow geneticists from Helm, Ingilium, and Crestar.” He folded his arms over his chest, his legs braced. “Only recently did I discover that your people were never on Lux. No record exists of your family ever being there. Since the human remnant spent seventy years off-world while the planet healed, it is a well-known fact that every example of surviving human DNA is recorded on Luxonian databases. But yours is not there. Nothing quite like it. Very distant relations, possibly. But no direct lineage.” Relevance’s eyes narrowed. “Who are you? Where do you come from?”

Dr. Anzi sighed. It was bound to come out eventually. He wanted to be the one to make the announcement, of course, but that opportunity still lay before him. If only Relevance understood his purpose. “My people did not flee the planet when the rest of the cowards ran. We stayed, hidden in deep caves, and provided for ourselves from the simple ingredients of arctic life. We were survivors before the disaster, and we survived during the disaster. Only my line are pure humans, untainted by the corruption of off-world life.”

His eyes round with wonder, Relevance dropped his arms to his sides. “Where are your people now? How is it that no one has spoken of them all these years? Surely, they would have rejoiced when the remnant returned, greeting them like long-lost family?”

Heat crept up Dr. Anzi’s face. He clenched his hands. “Greet those who ran? The cowards who escaped to foreign worlds? It was us, the true remnant, who kept faith with the planet. But we paid dearly for our loyalty. When we would not accept aliens creeping over our lands, we were killed. Ingots and Cresta murdered hundreds of my kin. Luxonians didn't intervene; they were too busy trying to cobble together the Inter-Alien Alliance to take notice of our decimation." Dr. Anzi straightened his shoulders, standing as tall as his short frame would allow. "Though the planet healed, our fertility did not. OldEarth humanity with their bombs and poisons destroyed my people just as powerfully as Newearth aliens."

Though the fire in his gut diminished, Relevance kept his gaze locked on the doctor. "Are there any of your kind left?"

"All my clan members passed, one by one, through the years; mother died ten years ago and my father five. It's only me, alone, now."

A knock on the door shattered the tension.

Turning to the door, Relevance called out, "Come!"

A lanky assistant in a long white lab coat stepped forward, carrying a small cage. With a grin, he set the framed box on the table. "I found him, sir. The very one you identified. Smart little critter. Lots better than that crazed one that ran away. Took me a while to catch him, though." He peered into the grilled doorway and wiggled his finger between the thin bars. "Thought you were going to escape, too, didn't you? But some things are too strong, and they pull us along no matter what we might wish."

Dr. Anzi crouched down and peered into the cage. A young squirrel stared back through bright black eyes. The doctor whispered, unwilling to further frighten the small animal. "How did you catch him?"

"Caught its mother and put it in the cage first." The assistant smiled in satisfaction. "It worked. Once he saw her in there, he stepped into the cage of his own volition."

His brows furrowed in perplexity; Relevance studied the cage with only one animal. "Where is the mother?"

"Oh, I killed it. No need to carry it along."

Fury filled Dr. Anzi. "You could have let it go! It was a breeder, after all."

The assistant shrugged. "I didn't want this one to try to escape. Now it has no desire to run away."

With a frown and a curt wave, Relevance dismissed the assistant.

His fingers trembling, Dr. Anzi opened the cage door and waited for the squirrel to approach the opening. When it finally did, he gently cupped it in his hands and lifted it free. He stared eye-to-eye with the squirrel who had gone rigid with fear. He spoke to Relevance, though his gaze stayed fixed on the creature. "You want to create animal-human hybrids to discover what makes a human truly human. Not the body, obviously, something deeper."

Relevance stood next to Dr. Anzi, and with a light touch, he stroked the squirrel's soft head. "Yes. Much deeper." He peered at the doctor. "And you? Why should the last pure human want to create hybrids?"

Dr. Anzi chuckled. "It's justice; don't you see? Humanity didn't value their existence on OldEarth. And despite a second chance, Newearth hasn't taught them their self-worth. The human race will lose what little of their identity remains. Once we bring the animal kingdom to sentience, humanity won't stand a chance." He met Relevance's hard gaze with equal intensity. "When I am gone, they will finally realize what they have lost."

His questions answered, Relevance turned away and started for the door. "Then it is a contest between us. I look to discover humanity's value. You plan to prove its demise."

It wasn't until late that night when Dr. Anzi lay down to sleep that he realized that his father's ghost had left him alone all day. Perhaps working with the squirrel, which he now called Squire, was good for him. After all, his father's most powerful lesson had also been his final decree. "Above all, Anzi, master yourself. Only *true* humans are masters."

Relevance's words and the image of the young squirrel following his mother into the cage returned like a knife into his heart. A new thought struck him, one he had never imagined before. Perhaps his father was wrong. He dismissed that thought and slid into a deep sleep.

—Aram County, Cerulean's Cabin—

Clare trudged up the steep wooded path, using every ounce of her frail strength, depending heavily on the integrity of her enhanced leggings, which allowed her damaged body to walk at all. *Lord, I wish they didn't itch so much! I feel like I've got a colony of ants crawling up my legs.* Maneuvering herself onto Cerulean's porch, she huffed her displeasure. This was not how she wanted to spend her free time. Still, when Cerulean called, she was bound to come. He had always been her best friend and ally, no matter the stupid choices she had made.

With a final groan, she smoothed down her lavender sweater, stopped before the kitchen screen door, and pounded.

No answer. Not a sound.

Annoyed, Clare dug her datapad from a pocket and glared at the digital clock. "Yep, it's ten on the dot. I'm right on time." A hint of fear slithered through her mind as she appraised a vintage rocking chair and an arrangement of wicker chairs beside a low table. *It's not like him to ask me to come and then not show up. Unless...* Before her imagination could have its way with her, the sound of snapping wood yanked her attention to the side yard. As fast as her leggings would allow, she hobbled over to the west end of the porch and leaned over, craning her neck to scan the autumn lawn surrounded by fading fields and spent garden to the south.

Cerulean stood between the dying garden and the grape arbor, wearing a sleeveless tunic over rugged brown pants. His muscled arms glistened in the morning light as he wrestled a rotted beam from the arbor frame.

Amazed at his strength and once again wondering why Abbas had turned her friend into a Luxonian-Human hybrid, she marveled at the easy way he pulled the wood free and tossed it aside. After the damage done to her own body in her miserable attempted suicide, she would never again throw a twig as casually as he threw a piece of oak. Suppressing a sigh, Clare dashed away her regrets and called out, "Hey, handsome, you invite a gal over but then leave her waiting on the porch?"

Cerulean's beautiful smile and quick wave set her heart pounding with the indefinable gladness she always felt when she was near him. She smiled back.

He gathered his scattered tools, placed them neatly in a wooden box, and then charged across the lawn. A few light steps and Cerulean stood on the porch, his whole body glowing with strength and vitality.

Unlike me. Clare forced the thought away and braved another smile. "You could at least offer a person a glass of tea or something. It's a tough haul dragging a nearly dead body all the way up here."

Cerulean's bright smile vanished. He merely shook his head as he bustled toward the kitchen door.

Abashed, a sick feeling coursed through Clare as she followed along behind. "Sorry, Cerulean. A regretful return to my former sassy self. I'll be better now. Promise."

Flashing a weak grin, his blue eyes so piercing that Clare's heart nearly melted, Cerulean held the screen door open and waved her inside. "Come in and have some of my best brew. You and those leggings of yours might feel like dancing."

Relief gave way to a burst of joy, and Clare hobbled inside.

Marveling at the picturesque environment that never ceased to amaze her, she couldn't help but wonder for the hundredth time how an alien—a light alien at that—had managed to create such a homey setting. On the east wall, the white freezer and refrigerator units offset the earthy colors of the rest of the room. A thick walnut counter ended a half meter from a handsome old-fashioned stove. The south end of the room led into Cerulean's bedroom and private bathroom, while two guestrooms with a bathroom centrally situated, were conveniently available to everyone. Classic wood shelves and large bay windows took up most of the west and north walls, offering glorious views of golden fields and autumn woods.

Strings of herbs, peppers, and onions hung from pegs interspersed throughout the room, while gourds and pumpkins, from tiny to large, paraded along the countertop. A cornucopia of autumn fruits, berries, and flowers decorated the large central oak table, leaving a smaller unadorned round table and comfortable chairs beckoning from the spacious living room.

Cerulean busied himself at the stove while Clare sighed in blissful contentment. The tea soon made, a steaming cup was offered and accepted.

Clare leaned back on the plush white couch and savored a luscious scent in the air. "Is this cinnamon tea?" She took a tentative sip.

Holding his cup carefully, Cerulean pointed up.

Above their heads hung a dozen or more lacy satchels.

Clare's mouth dropped open. "What are…"

"A gift item from the Amens boutique. I couldn't resist. Nests of herbs create a variety of scents. Spicy cinnamon is my favorite."

The hot tea, pleasant room, and friendly company warmed Clare's insides in a way she had not felt in ages. *This is what I've needed. Me and my good friend…no terrors chasing us.*

Cerulean eyed her as he sipped his tea. Then he placed his cup aside and edged up closer, clasping his hands as he leaned forward.

Warning bells began to clang inside Clare's mind. *Oh, no.*

"We need to talk."

With stiff movements, Clare gripped her cup and set it safely on the table. Her stomach tightened into nauseating knots. *Please, Lord, don't let me be sick.* These days, she never knew how her body would respond to stress. She swallowed hard and braved a tremulous smile. "About what?"

"Relevance." Grief with a tinge of anger filled Cerulean's eyes. "He's back on Newearth, has been for some time. He's behind the penguin extinction."

Dumbfounded, Clare found her voice rising, hysteria nearly smothering her. "Why would anyone, least of all Relevance, want to kill off penguins? That doesn't make any sense!"

His jaw clenching, Cerulean jerked backwards. "He wasn't trying to kill them! He was experimenting on them. And something went terribly wrong."

"Experimenting? To what purpose?"

With a loud huff, Cerulean shot forward from his chair and paced across the room. "I don't know. That's what I want you to help me figure out." He rounded on Clare. "Relevance is *your* son."

Tears burned, and Clare felt her insides revolting. She forced herself to hang on to a semblance of composure. Her voice dropped to a whisper as her gaze fell to the floor. "I know."

Suddenly, Cerulean was at her side, kneeling; he reached out and clasped her hands. "I'm sorry, Clare. That's not what I meant. You've suffered more than anyone. I just need help. Relevance is stronger than anyone guessed. And I don't just mean physically. Somehow, he managed to inherit the best of Human, Tabunite, and Ingot traits."

With a quick swipe at the corners of her eyes, Clare tilted her head and stared at Cerulean. "The *best* of us experiments on penguins, causing their extinction?"

With a sigh, Cerulean climbed back to his feet. He paced to the stove, set the oven to 350 degrees, and then put the kettle on a hot burner. "I can't speak clearly today. Can't think clearly. That's my real problem." He proceeded to grab ingredients from the cupboard: three kinds of flour, brown sugar, salt, oil, vanilla, oats, and a bag of chocolate chips. Then he marched to the freezer, pulled out a bag of what looked like ice and popped it into a pan, poured steaming water from the kettle over it, and then slapped baking utensils on the counter.

Confused but curious, Clare rose and hobbled closer. She leaned on the counter, watching in fascination.

Cerulean proceeded to make multigrain zucchini muffins. By the time he was pouring the chunky batter into the muffin tins, he was ready to answer her question. "Ingots are technologically advanced and put their society's needs above personal gain. They refuse to give up at any cost. Tabunites are naturally sensitive, exquisitely musical, and balance cultural dictates with personal discretion to a fine degree." He scraped the last of the dough into the muffin tin and set it aside. "Humanity's worth you already know."

Clare held in a retort, refusing to betray her race. But the question hung in her mind like a pendulum ready to knock her to the ground, *Do I?*

Wiping his hands on a dishtowel, Cerulean's gaze stayed level with her own. "The *best* of us hope to accomplish some good despite our mistakes."

A bittersweet sensation nudged Clare's soul. She almost smiled. "A happy thought." She tapped the counter. "What do you want me to do?"

After popping the tin into the oven, Cerulean pointed to the teacups. "Rinse those out and get another. Bala is coming over, and we're going to do some planning." Cerulean grinned as he leaned against the counter. “The poor man doesn’t know it, but I have an idea to help save his son and get us the information we need.”

A shiver ran over Clare. “Save his son? Which son? Has Relevance—”

A quick wave and Cerulean put that worry to flight. “No, not that. It’s David. He’s been passing along classified information while working at the docking bay. A risky spy game he’s been playing. Cocky kid thought he was too smart to be traced. Must have forgotten who he was dealing with.” His eyebrows shot up. “Nothing gets by Justine and Max.”

“Oh, Lord…” Though Clare’s tone bespoke her chagrin that Bala and Kendra, aka the most perfect parents on the planet, actually had a troubled child, a part of her heart soared in relief. She squinted at Cerulean, a spark of teasing fun buoying her mood. “So, what are you planning?”

He grinned as he patted her arm. “I’m setting a trap with vanilla tea and hot buttered muffins. David can redeem himself best by becoming a double agent. But we’ll need Bala’s help.”

All fun sensations scattering, Clare tried to keep her voice from squeaking. “That might be risky.” She affected nonchalance. “Maybe he should go off world and get away from Relevance.”

“No, we tried that. Didn’t work. Relevance has some hold on David. And besides, if he stays, he can tell us everything that’s happening. If what I fear is true, Relevance is only a part of a much bigger plan.”

“I thought you said he was behind it.”

“He probably thinks he’s in charge, but you know perfectly well, Clare, those who think they’re running the show rarely are. There’s always a puppet master in the background…layers of them in this case.”

Footsteps hurried across the porch and then huffs accompanied pounding on the door. “Hey, Cerulean, let me in; the wind is howling, and I don't want to get blown into the next county."

"Hold on, coming!"

Bala's voice rose against the wind. "I hope you have something in there to revive me after I risked my neck to get up that prickly vine-infested trap you call a path."

Cerulean tugged on huge oven mitts and smiled at Clare. "Get the tea ready. I'll take care of the muffins. Nothing calms that man better than a good snack." He called out, "Come in, Bala."

Her heart pounding to the beat of new hope, Clare prepared the tea and prayed for the best humanity had to offer.

—Vandi, Dead Possum Pub—

Seth eyed his brother with a cold, appraising stare, but he couldn't keep it up. He loved the guy too much. And he needed to trust someone. At thirty-one, life had taught him a great deal, often more than he wanted to know. He took a sip from his water glass, leaned back on the smooth, conforming chair, and glanced around. The happily chattering crowd, snug in high-polished wood booths and crowded around solid tables, bespoke a substantial business built on a strong community spirit. Seth, as the Environmental Manager of Aram County and still dressed for rough woodland country, was clearly out of his element.

Swaying trees, scampering animals, singing birds in a forest he could walk through for days without meeting another soul was more to his liking. Other than his own family, people made him uncomfortable. Crowds made him clench his teeth. Often in disgust.

Younger by three years, Barni, with dark wavy hair, intense black eyes, and an attractive build, leaned back in a relaxed pose. Ever the professional, wearing a blue cashmere sweater and dark slacks, he chuckled amiably as he motioned for a server. He glanced at his brother. "What on Newearth has gotten into you? You're as jittery as an Ingot in a nudist colony."

Leaning forward, his shoulder-length hair curtaining the side of his face, Seth prepared himself for full disclosure. At the same moment, a Bhuaci serving girl swayed forward in a mini-skirt and clinging top and announced her willingness to get them *anything* they needed. Her eyes danced along with her smile.

Accepting her offer with a grin, Barni clapped his hands together in apparent glee. "You're making my brother blush, an accomplishment beyond measure. Now bring us two servings of sea delights, chips, and the strongest brew you've got." His grin grew to a full-blown smile. "Perhaps you'll cure my brother of shyness tonight."

With a pleased, I'll-meet-that-challenge expression, the server sashayed away.

Unmoving, Seth waited, uncertain whether to make a second attempt at a serious conversation or to simply rise and make a dignified exit.

All hint of a smile disappearing from his face, Barni shoved the napkin dispenser aside and scooted his chair closer to his brother. "This establishment may swing with the sensibilities of its patrons, but I've never seen such a blatant attempt to undermine my good sense. Might just as well print 'Thief looking for easy pickings' in bold letters on her chest."

Wearied by his brother's constant on-stage performance, Seth shook his head. "I've no doubt she *is* offering a variety of services."

Apparently surprised by any astuteness besides his own, Barni raised an eyebrow. "At rock bottom prices, I'm sure." He frowned as he lowered his voice. "What is going on, Seth? You've been away for so long, no scenic pictures or cryptic messages from your latest trip; even Dad is worried. Something at work?"

His hands clasped in a tight grip; Seth took a deep breath before he spoke. He shifted forward so that he was mere centimeters from his brother's face. "Listen, I realize that you can't solve this problem, but I need to tell someone so I know I'm not crazy. I had a very weird experience." He swallowed hard then plunged in. "I…heard…a squirrel talking to himself, nonsense really, but still talking in human speech."

A stunned silence followed by sputtering laughter, and Barni fell backward on his chair. His shoulders shook even as he glanced up at Seth, his chuckles dissolving into an uncertain grin. "You had me going! I really thought something terrible had happened. Wow, I've never thought of you as a funny guy, but you've proved me wrong this time. Wait till I tell—"

His expression unchanged, Seth remained stoically still. Despite his height, he usually found complete stillness to work to his greatest advantage.

Barni sat up; a frown spreading over his face. "What? You can't be serious! A squirrel talking…like reciting poetry or something?" Suddenly his relaxed pose turned professional, assessing, his eyes searching. He feigned an unconcerned shrug that wouldn't have fooled their little sister. "I am a trained counselor; maybe I can help. You hear any other animals…or plants…talking?"

Exhaling a long breath, Seth leaned back and stared at the rough-beamed ceiling. He knew it would be like this. As much as he loved his brother and respected the man's ability to settle inter-alien issues on the Newearth Docking Bay, he'd never been one to accept anything truly extraordinary. Even their parents' ancient faith had been whittled down to historical traditions and community service.

Unmindful of the immediate tension, the serving woman returned with two platters of food and mugs brim full with thick, dark brew. She set everything on the table with swift skill, her gaze darting between the two. "Anything else I can do for you?"

Rarely hampered by an overabundance of social skills, Seth didn't bother to respond.

Barni answered for both of them, "You've saved us from starvation and offered the nectar of the Gods to ease our troubled souls. Thank you, darling."

Apparently satisfied with effusive hyperbole, the woman grinned and spun off to other duties.

Not allowing questions of sanity to spoil his appetite, Barni took a healthy gulp from his mug and then started in on the chips.

Seth listened to the munching for as long as he could stand it, then he dug in. The sea-treats fried in salty batter tasted amazingly good. He suddenly remembered that he hadn't eaten all day. In fact, he couldn't remember when he had eaten last. He took a tentative sip of his drink, liked it well enough, and then swallowed almost half.

"Woah! Slow down, Seth. Unless you've changed more than I know, you aren't used to drinking the strong stuff." Barni scratched his head, a frown growing between his eyes. "What has gotten into you?"

Trying not to burp outrageously, Seth covered his mouth for a polite moment. Feeling a bit better, despite the heady brew, he leaned back on his chair and locked his eyes on his brother. "You're coming to Aram County with me on the next tube out."

As per his usual habit when thinking his options through, Barni glanced around the room. Then he dropped his gaze on Seth, deadpan serious. "Why should I? To listen to a bunch of squirrel chatter?"

Seth poured the last of his drink down his throat, wiped his mouth with the back of his hand, and pummeled the final bit of silliness from his brother's face with cold matter-of-factness. "Because I wasn't joking."

—LEAP Laboratory—

Relevance leaned back on his chair in his top-floor office, surrounded by grand windows, and stared at a message on his datapad. His half-brother, Herson, had reached out to him. How unlikely was that? Suspicion fueled by old envy flooded every pore of Relevance's body, making his cable knit sweater feel tight and hot. He rose and paced across the luxuriously appointed room. He stopped at a large bay window overlooking a wide stretch of woodlands. An image of Herson T. Clare rose in his mind—a frail child with dark eyes in a perpetually scowling face. They had never gotten along, even as children. Their mother's obvious preference for her half-bred Human-Tabunite son rather than her more remarkable child, himself as a tri-bred Human-Tabunite-Ingot, rankled both mind and spirit. Herson's weaknesses and troubles were easily forgiven, while *his* strength and perfection made him an outcast. Clare had wanted a child, but only one. When she was given two, she could not widen her arms to accept the unwanted as her own.

Outside his window, a vulture floated on the last rays of autumn warmth. Its exceptional eyesight and capacity to smell carrion over a mile away were apparently forgotten in its luxurious flight as it rode warm thermals. The bird appeared almost beautiful. Yet Relevance could not forget that it lived on death. A shiver of he knew-not-what ran over his shoulders. Shouldn't he accept nature for what it was and forgive the ungainly bird its disgusting habit?

With a shake of his head, Relevance reread his brother's message.

Dear Relevance,

Just checking in to see what has happened to you. Hope all is well in your world, wherever that may be. I know that we didn't always get along as children, but I've been at the Academy for some time now, and I see things quite differently. More worldly-wise maybe. In any case, I realize that family matters. Mom broke under the pressure of our fractured identities, and it nearly killed her. For better or worse, we either help each other or destroy one another. Since there are more than enough villains in the universe spreading hate and grabbing power, I thought, if you're open to it, perhaps I'll come visit, and we can form a better understanding of each other. I've learned some amazing things you might find interesting.

In all honesty,

Herson

Who is this? Not the Herson that Relevance remembered. Could an off-world academy have changed his brother so dramatically? Or was this subterfuge? Squinting at the failing sun, Relevance considered his options. He would respond, but what he would say would depend on what he discovered. He tapped the datapad to a new page and opened a file on his mother. He'd have to check into her recent movements, where she has been and who she has been seeing. Had Herson and Clare hatched a plot to investigate his experiments? *Very likely.*

A new thought made him sit bolt upright. Was Taug involved? How about his Tabunite father, Gavin? He'd been too focused on his work. "Blast! I'll have to check on them all." He slapped the wall and then returned to his ornate oak desk. "What a waste of time!"

Despite his exterior fury, a flicker of excitement rippled through him as he set his search engines to track down his family. He refused to call it happiness, though he was, disconcertingly, not unhappy at the prospect of seeing his brother again.

—Planet Helm, Sea Shore—

December, Year 73 Newearth Reckoning

Faye, a shapeshifter exiled from Newearth, seeking peace of mind on her home planet, followed the shoreline unconcerned by the mighty cliffs frowning upon her in the brilliance of mid-day. Her entire attention was focused on a black splotch in the distance, that should, upon closer inspection, prove to be an amphibious craft of Insectine origin.

A recent storm had washed mounds of seaweed, heaps of driftwood, and a scattering of shelled creatures onto the shore. She had to watch every step. Her long trailing skirt didn't help matters in the least. With a sharp yank, she dragged the wet, sand-encrusted material from around her feet and bundled it above her knees. If she could have dispensed with clothes altogether, she would have, but given the vast array of fashion photos that the Insectine representative posted on her personality channel, it was clear that this particular personage adored quality clothes.

In a spiteful moment, Faye imagined climbing on board the ship wearing a shapeless bag, but remembering the mission at hand, she shoved that unworthy thought away, scooted over to a dry cave entrance, and reformed her clothing attire into a form-fitting calf length dress with short sleeves. More comfortable and pleased with a few creative touches—a lacy hem dotted with intertwining flowers—she set out once again.

The ship was much as she expected. With arched ribs connecting three massive black orbs, the entire structure resembled an enormous elongated ant with curved windows encircling its middle. Neither as impressed as an Ingot by the technical achievement nor as revolted as humans by the insect-like configuration, Faye waited on shore until the formal welcome ceremony commenced.

She glanced around, fairly certain that she had not been followed and praying that Taug had managed to alter their satellite systems to hide this particular alien encounter. She had never kept anything from Song before, but knowing her complicity in what could be a very compromising situation, she didn't want Helm's most trusted spiritual advisor associated with her actions in the slightest way, possibly branded as a traitor. Her own reputation would be a small price to pay if she could prevent the demise of the universe.

Oh, I'm just being dramatic. Even if hybrids do take over and every habitable planet is overrun with sentient life, from thinking weeds to talking mollusks, the rest of us will still survive. She paused as dread squashed her optimism. *Maybe…*

After rolling several meters onto the sandy beach, the Insectine ship's long bay door unfolded bit by bit.

Faye caught her breath and steadied her racing mind. *I must remain calm. She's not the enemy. At least, not yet.*

A beautiful Mantis figure dressed in a sumptuous flowing gown emerged from the ship with the graceful steps of a seasoned ballerina. With a narrow green face, unusually large black eyes with pink brows, delicate antennae, a surprisingly plump thorax, and slender wings folded over her back, she represented the classic perfection of her kind. Even her dainty back legs set off the muscular power of her front legs, which were clearly used as arms.

Faye tried not to imagine the imposing figure clutching squirming prey and then taking a big bite. She fought down nausea.

A gentle voice rose along with a gloriously spicy scent. "My name is Walking Flower from the Mantis Tribe, though I come on behalf of all Insectine kind. You are Song, most renowned spirit guide of the Bhuaci?"

Flustered, Faye tried desperately to remember if she had mentioned Song in her urgent message, calling for a private meeting on their northwest shore. *No, I wouldn't have...* Fear raced over her. Had *they* contacted Song?

Dizziness rampaged over nausea, and Faye stumbled, nearly falling.

Her arm shooting forward, Walking Flower steadied her. The tall figure tilted her head to the side and seemed to evaluate Faye for several silent moments.

Faye tried to free her arm but discovered that the grip held firm. She'd have to dissolve and reform to escape; panic rose with the thought. Then she looked up and met Walking Flower's steady gaze. No deceit, anger, or ruthlessness there. Mild curiosity and perhaps a tinge of concern etched the elongated face.

Despite having been trained to lie, her survival depending upon guises and utmost secrecy, the truth tumbled out of Faye faster than she could monitor her words. "My name is Faye, once a spy but now simply a Newearth citizen with a terrible secret. I haven't told Song about our meeting. No one can know! There are forces at work that might destroy us all, and I don't know who to trust, but I must trust someone." Horrified by unbidden tears, Faye fought back a choking sob. "My dearest friends have made terrible mistakes, and I fear that we have let loose a horror no one can stop." She shook her head and clenched her teeth against any further weakness.

Walking Flower released her grip, then stepped back with her hands clasped in a prayerful stance. "Would you prefer to talk while strolling upon the shore or discuss matters inside?" She gestured to her ship.

Gratitude flowed like an elixir through Faye. As if waking from a nightmare, she considered the open shore line, broken only by the gentle waves. *No one is watching, and even if Song knew, she would understand. Probably...* "Let's walk. I will tell you what I know, and you may share with me what you will."

Her steps graceful upon the sand, where each foot seemed to hardly leave a print, Walking Flower stayed close to Faye's side, her head bent, her eyes nearly closed as if in deep thought.

Faye gathered the scattered shreds of her presentation and began at the beginning: Clare wanted a baby, and Taug wanted to help…

Hours later, the sun near setting, Faye sat on the edge of a rocky outcropping and faced Walking Flower, waiting for a response. *What must she think of us? Probably hates Taug. Thinks Clare is stupid and weak. I'm probably no better than a brainless slug.*

Her hands clasped in prayer-fashion, Walking Flower's straight back never bent, even while leaning against a boulder three times her size. The lids of her eyes were lowered to half-mast, a low hum from her chest bespoke a meditative mode.

Faye waited in silence, her legs aching and her mind exhausted by the effort of retelling nearly seventeen years of drama leading up to this moment. The whole question revolved around Relevance—What was he doing? Who had he become? And how was Insectine society involved?

Finally, Walking Flower's lids rose, and her eyes focused on Faye, penetrating with laser brilliance. "You told your story well. In truth, I am surprised. I expected lies to be woven through the fabric of your tale, various excuses to escape blame."

Horrifying thoughts clashed in Faye's mind: *She already knew about Relevance. I am not testing her; she is testing me!*

Walking Flower pushed off the boulder and started back in the direction of her ship. "Your illuminated leader, Song, sent me a gift some years ago. It was a puzzle of sorts, pieces of information about each of the people you mentioned. Nothing to explain what had happened or the danger we all face but an opportunity to investigate and see for myself what my people were heading toward." She glanced aside as Faye caught up and jogged at her elbow. "You see, we were on the same path as your Taug but for different reasons. *We* wanted to improve ourselves, fit into the larger universe without prejudice against our Insectine appearance. Our bodies repel even the most advanced societies. A select medical community followed every hybrid laboratory success and failure in the hope that we might alter our physical state and make ourselves more attractive."

Nauseous with the implosion of her plans and worrying about the lasting damage she may have done to her relationship with Song, Faye trudged through the sand, her head aching and her soul encased in misery. "It's all so sad."

While the ship bobbed on the surface of the incoming current, Walking Flower stopped and gripped her hands together as if in earnest prayer. "Yes, terribly sad. To think that we were so deluded as to believe that mere appearance would halt the travesty of hate." She shook her head and stepped lightly over the wet sand toward the open bay door. "You have done your best, Faye. Your love for your friends, different as they are, has ever been true. How many can make that claim?" She reached down and caressed Faye's arm. "Song must be very proud of you."

Tears sprang to Faye's eyes, but the ache in her throat kept unspoken words locked in her mind.

As she stepped onto the threshold and the bay door began to fold, Walking Flower turned and smiled. "I would be honored to be your friend, Bhuac Faye. Perhaps—together—we can prove our worth by being our honest selves?"

After the door closed, the ship slid across the water, then rose and flew in an arc across the dark sky like a shooting star.

Faye let her tears fall freely.

—Newearth Docking Bay—

David decided that he didn't like Justine in the least. Max the robot-human was a joke, and hybrid-Zara was absurd, but android-Justine really didn't know her place. *Crosses personal boundaries all the time!* Even Barni had commented on it, how she flagrantly ignored human comfort zones whenever it suited her. *And she thinks she's human! Ha!*

Shoving down the memory of his mother's instant disapproval of anything smacking of prejudice, David returned to his console on the Newearth Docking Bay upper deck. He had to retreat to the highest levels and burrow into the furthest corner to get any privacy these days. Justine was always coming along, asking ridiculous questions, as if he didn't know how to do his job. *Stupid—*

A strange flicker caught his eye—mottled skin and a flash of red skirt. *Variant?* David's heart pounded as heat washed over his body. *What is it about that woman?* He knew as well as anyone that most people found her repugnant. But some odd allure sent his hormones into high gear. Dreams involving things his parents would insist only "concerned married folks" left him breathless and out of sorts for days afterward. *Why can't she just leave me alone?* But he knew with the same clarity what an alcoholic knows: it isn't the woman or the wine, it's the intoxication he craved. And no one else intoxicated him quite like—

"What are you doing, hiding way up here?"

All one-hundred seventy centimeters of Variant's luscious form stood before him. As he was twenty centimeters taller, they were a perfect match. His gaze roved her body, enjoying afresh the contrast between her fair and dark skin, mottled like that of a Crestonian sea creature but without the routine regularity. The intensity of her eyes—one bright blue, the other dark brown—mesmerized him. Her long, flaxen hair fell in soft waves over her shoulders. The perfect symmetry of her features: almond eyes, sweet upturned nose, and perky mouth, nearly took his breath away. He had to force out his words, "I'm not hiding. I'm working."

Though she didn't shake her head, he knew that she knew that he was lying.

A teasing smile and Variant reached for his hand. “Come on. Relevance wants us.”

Well aware that she never allowed anyone to touch her except Relevance and himself, David accepted her small fingers in his, honored by the privilege. Still, the image of Relevance’s stern expression held him in place. “I haven’t finished reporting—”

Variant tugged his arm. “He knows. This is more important.”

“What could possibly be more important than maintaining good relations with the Ingot High Command and the Cresta Ingal?”

Tightening her lips into a hard line, Variant yanked harder. “Keeping your parents from getting involved. Now let’s go.”

David’s mind smacked into the word “parents” and refused to budge another step.

“Bala is on a rampage—sent messages everywhere—he and Cerulean plan to search all over Aram County to discover what Relevance is doing.”

Stunned by the image of his father confronting Relevance, perhaps even finding out about his own role, left David without an ounce of resistance. He let himself be pulled to the lift, and when the doors swished open, he simply followed her inside.

Variant wrapped her arms around her middle, as if she had taken a sudden chill. “Don’t be scared. Relevance won’t blame you. He knows all about your parents.”

David swallowed hard and met her sideways glance. He didn’t say anything. He couldn’t.

Chapter Two

Beast, Hybrid, Human

—Aram County, LEAP Laboratory—

Three Months Later, March, Year 74, Newearth Reckoning

Squire stood firmly on his back legs in the stark white LEAP Laboratory and faced the tall human figure with all the attention of a devoted servant, though today, it felt more like love. Freedom! What a small word to encompass so great a meaning; his slender squirrel body trembled at the thought of it. He would finally be free to roam the wild woods to his heart's content, a dream he had long imagined but only through backward glances as he was led into the confines of his master's world.

Dressed in his usual lab coat over a dark-sky sweater and earth-colored pants, Relevance stared down at him, one hand resting lightly on the cold steel table, the other hand stroking his manicured beard. "Are you listening to me, Squire?"

Rubbing his forelegs together and dearly wishing he had an acorn to twiddle about, Squire forced himself to meet his master's firm gaze. His speech, though far from fluent, allowed him to bluster his way through his nervousness. "Yes! Yes! Certainly, sir. I listen and obey."

A nod and Relevance seemed ready to move on. "It's time now. I want you to remember what I told you: this is a test to see how well you can manage in your native environment Long-Term. It won't be for just a few days like you've done before."

"I will do my best, sir. My very best!" Squire wanted to say more, but words tended to get jumbled up in his mind when he got excited. His heart pounded, and his ears twitched.

In his frantic desire to see the outside world again, he almost leaped off the table.

"Oh, no, you don't! You must say goodbye first." Relevance scooped him into his arms and began to parade him around the room.

His euphoria crashing, Squire remembered, with something of a shock, that he was leaving everyone he knew and entering the wild world all by himself, a dark danger as much as a privilege. He may have worked harder and advanced faster than any of the others, but a certain amount of what his master's colleague, Dr. Anzi, had called "dumb luck" factored into his early release.

Cages and miniature homes lined three walls of the room. The native beasts must be contained with strong bars, while those awakening to their developing nature—their hybrid human genetics—were allowed incremental stages of personal comfort.

The bottom row of rude cages twisted Squire's stomach as he glanced at the uncomprehending eyes of two calico felines, a trio of foxes, a very young deer, and a small murder of crows. A sour taste rising in his throat, he shifted his gaze upward.

Open sided compartments with a variety of food selections, waste canisters, and even rudimentary learning tools took up the middle level. There were a greater number of small animals, including a hedgehog, an armadillo (which Dr. Anzi insisted was a mistake, but Relevance would not send away), owls, a large rat, and two possums. Their heads lifted as Relevance carried Squire through the gauntlet of their stares, their eyes following with interest but little understanding.

It was the top tier that Squire could hardly face. Instead of cages or cubicles, each premise matched the native habitats of the origin species. He stared with morbid fascination at the tree top nest he had occupied for nearly two seasons. Would he miss it? He hardly knew since he had never been away for more than a couple of days at a time. Another nest, larger though messier, belonged to Tyto, a fierce owl with a cold, calculating personality. Tyto said little, but when he glared, he practically pinned Squire in place with his mesmerizing gaze.

Averting his head, Squire shifted his attention to the next nest where Branoc—a huge black crow—resided. He was the only one who had treated him with real kindness after he had broken his foreleg in a bad fall last winter. Branoc even slipped him a few dainties from the master's table when no one was looking. They had chuckled over that achievement for weeks. Squire offered a shy wave. Branoc dipped his head in respect. It seemed unfair that he, a young squirrel with uncertain capabilities, was allowed to taste freedom, but Branoc, who had a far better vocabulary and a quicker wit, was forced to stay behind.

As if reading his mind, Relevance stopped before Branoc's nest. "You'll go next, Branoc, though Chiara has been complaining nonstop that she should be chosen."

A cackle of annoyance and Branoc ruffled his feathers in disdain; his sharp eyes peered across the room at Chiara's nest. "Dramatic creature that bird!"

Snorting in agreement, Relevance grinned. "OldEarth records show that Killdeers were known for their acting abilities, drawing threats away from their young. Even Dr. Anzi didn't take much convincing to include her in our studies. Though personally, I believe larger birds offer a greater range of possibilities."

Tyto hooted in agreement with such force that Squire jerked back, wrenching his neck.

With a shake of his head, Relevance headed for the exit. "Settle down; we're leaving. No need to rush off without a proper goodbye to your soulmates."

The expression "soulmates" didn't make sense to Squire, though he never dared ask about it. He had learned through painful experience that Relevance could be patient and understanding with an animal just coming into awareness but certain questions, or what he termed "over inquisitiveness," could make him angry enough to return an animal to cage-life for days.

Just before the large bay door, Relevance stopped and knelt at the entrance of a makeshift cave. Two small deer and an immature elk nestled in abundant piles of hay. The deer's large brown eyes roamed aimlessly as they chewed in mindless abandon. The elk was another matter. Squire shivered. There was a being in there, but not a nice one; he was sure of it.

Once out the door, Relevance carried him through the dim tunnel to the outside entrance. All Squire's senses went on high alert. The very first time he had left his master's laboratory behind and experienced the bright rays of the sun on his tawny fur, he thought he had lost his wits. Perhaps eaten a bad nut and was suffering what Dr. Anzi called "a relapse." But after many such explorations into the surrounding woodlands, Squire finally came to accept that this was the real world, and the laboratory where he had awoken was, in fact, a manufactured place, never meant to last. Not like the woodland, which seemed to have always lived and would go on living beyond any countable measure.

Though Squire longed to scamper down Relevance's arm and leap into the ripening foliage, his master kept a firm grip and carried him deep into the sunlit woods.

At long last, when the sun had perched at the very top of the bright blue sky, Relevance stopped before an ancient oak with a purple line painted around its trunk. A curved door with a central knob bespoke a small room at the base of the tree. A tiny shed was situated to the right of it. A matching squirrel-sized bench and table were positioned to the left.

Relevance set Squire on the ground. "This is your tree, Squire. I expect you to use it well. It produces bountifully, and you should find plenty of nuts and berries to last you through next winter. Plus, there is dead wood scattered about, and various useful tools are in the shed. The same ones you practiced with in the lab, you remember?"

Remember? How could he forget? Woodworking classes were his favorite and what led to Dr. Anzi noticing his extraordinary abilities—the very reason he was released early.

"Yes, certainly. I will use them devotedly." He frowned, uncertain whether he had said what he meant. With a shake, he gazed up at his master, and the odd sensation returned, the one he thought might be called love. "Thank you, sir. I am grateful and hope to prove you right."

Suddenly, Relevance's gaze fell from the heights and landed hard on Squire. "What do you mean, prove me right?"

Fear rippled over Squire's skin, sending a quivering sensation down his spine. "What you want, that hybrids can be true. We're not equal to a human, certainly, but we can be relied upon. I am your faithful servant."

The shocked stare that locked onto Squire sent his paws to twitching. It would only take a few seconds to scamper into the upper reaches of the tree. *I'd be safe there.* The fur at the back of his neck rose. "Sir? Is anything wrong?"

Relevance swallowed; his gaze still fixed, but his voice had fallen husky. "I am not a human. Or not completely. I'm a tribrid."

A cold wind rushed in, and dark clouds banked the horizon. Wild black birds cawed as they soared across the sky. Unbelievably, the scent of a foreign squirrel tickled Squire's nose. He tried to retreat into his ancient origin. Sensations of a damp cold front rising and the scurrying of tiny feet in the underbrush alerted his mind to the largeness of what he had entered. He was no longer sure what he was leaving.

Yet, despite everything, even against his native will, he found himself speaking, "You look human, like Dr. Anzi. He is human. He told me so. From OldEarth stock—Aleut genetics, he said." Squire tipped his head to meet Relevance's cold stare straight on. "There's no animal in you. Why develop human in us?"

Unaccountably, Relevance threw back his head and laughed. Loud and bellowing, his laughter grew until the budding leaves overhead seemed to shake in harmony with his mirth.

An owl hooted in the distance, perhaps disturbed by the naked abruptness in a forest of hidden, slinking, shuffling sounds.

Finally, out of breath and leaning against the tree as if supporting himself from sudden weakness, Relevance wiped wet from his eyes.

Squire sniffed. The spring rain was still a distance away. He frowned at his master; the question still stood between them.

"There is animal in all of us, Squire. You will soon find that out. Beast, hybrid, and human, we all rise in glory or fall to wretchedness."

A native squirrel, a female, he was certain—though he did not know how he knew—scampered down the tree and froze, its black eyes fixed on Relevance.

Squire wanted to shout, "Look at me! I'm a squirrel like you!" But the silly thing merely twitched its tail in warning, as if that would do any good.

Relevance shot a stone at the intruder, and it darted into the branches overhead. Then, with a deep sigh, he started away through the budding leaves, his hands hanging limp at his sides.

Trying not to feel the emptiness of his unanswered question, Squire scrabbled up the tree, finding the rough bark easy to navigate. He perched on a low branch, facing the direction Relevance had taken.

Relevance stopped and turned back. He called up, "Show us what human means, Squire. Our bodies do not define us. Help us understand what does."

Squire sat perched on the limb of the old oak tree as his master disappeared from sight and the sun slipped behind the hills. Night would soon close the day. Only when he heard the soft chatter of the female squirrel close by did he stir from his spot in search of an answer even bigger than freedom in a woodland he had dreamed about for so long.

—Planet Helm, Sea Shore—

Taug, Faye's best friend, despite the vast differences in their race and temperament, swam vigorously in the warm sea, his tentacles working in perfect harmony with his powerful legs. He rejoiced in skin-tingling freedom from his bio-suit, headgear, and those blasted boots. An unwary blue-spotted eel tried to slither behind a rock formation, but he sucked it in without hesitation and so enjoyed the nourishing sensation, his whole body wiggled with pleasure. No words formed in his mind. He was well beyond conceived thought, joined instead with elemental nature, swimming, slurping the soupy sea, his body tingling at the touch of every frond and creature he brushed against in his liquid flight.

Faint vibrations tickled his ear, rubbing against his mind, disturbing the free-flowing water.

"T-Au-G!"

At first the vibration made no sense, so he ignored it. Perhaps a bird in the air above was fighting for a fish, calling raucously as they sometimes did in their excitement. He slurped in a small school of minnows.

"TAU-G!"

With a shock, his mind returned to the present world. He was not at home on Crestar enjoying a swim in the Crestonian Sea. He was on Helm, a planet of shapeshifters who accepted him with the benign gentility of an ancient race who have suffered persecution often but ardently wished for peace. The home of his dearest companion, Faye, the kindest soul in the universe. Unless you made her angry…

Bubbles fizzed against his ear holes as he rose rapidly toward the sunlit surface. He broke the surface of the murky water and swished wet from his eyes as he paddled, trying to maintain his position. Swiveling his head, he attempted to clarify the sounds he was hearing.

"He-rrrr! O-vv-er Heeer!"

With a firm shake, he scattered the water from his ear holes, and, suddenly, all became clear.

"Taug! Can't you hear me? I'm right here."

There, on a fallen log that stretched out into the sea, stood his beloved friend. The dearest creature that ever lived.

Splash! A stick struck the water by his head, splattering his face. Taug blinked. "Faye? What's wrong?"

The elven form with almond eyes, perky nose, and cherubic lips radiated high anxiety. "We have to go. Now!"

A part of Taug, clinging to the hope that he could swim a little longer and hide on Helm for—perhaps—the rest of his natural existence, battled with his dutiful Cresta nature and his guilty Newearth identity. He knew perfectly well that actions have consequences. Dread filled him at the realization that he might be forced to face fierce consequences soon.

Even as his tentacles began paddling toward shore, his voice rose in an admonishing plea. "I hardly think a little swim will matter in the grand scheme of things. Couldn't we wait until—"

Her hands perched on her hips, a scowl marring her pretty face, Faye glared through narrow eyes. "Cerulean is gathering everyone at his home in Aram County, and we need to be there. Things have gone a great deal further than we imagined, and time is running short." Her voice rose to a hysterical pitch. "What if they start breeding?"

Taug had no definite idea what Faye was talking about since he had refused to speak of experiments, hybrids, reproduction, and even deleted the word genetics from his vocabulary while on Helm. He had needed an escape, a rest, time to resettle his mind after the shock of having his experiments grow up into real people with minds of their own.

Dragging his full-figured body, dressed only in a modest bathing suit, from the comforting sea left him feeling cold and miserable. He barely slid his gaze over Faye as he passed her and plodded his way across the sandy shore. "Breeding…don't talk to me about breeding. I have nothing to do with that anymore." An image of Relevance as a youngster happily playing in his laboratory, pretending to experiment on one of the hapless lab assistants, gripped his heart and squeezed. *He rejected me. I can't help him…never again.*

Scampering ahead, Faye cut him off before he reached her seaside home. She grabbed two tentacles and stood up on tiptoes, her eyes locking onto his. "Relevance has crossed the barrier between animal and human. Bala's son Seth heard a squirrel talking to himself, so he and Barni searched for it all winter but couldn't find it again. Turns out that Bala's other son, David, had set up a warning system for a secret society involving Relevance, a Dr. Anzi, and a variety of scientists from Ingilium, Sectine, Crestar, and even a couple of Luxonians. He's been hiding out in some secret location, eluding everyone's best scouting efforts.

Taug's interest rose. *Well, if nothing else, a mystery is always a bit of fun.* He started to plod across the sandy shore toward Faye's beach house.

Faye kept in step, her small hands punctuating the air with dramatic gestures. "Cerulean finally met with the Inter-Alien Alliance. Though they took their time coming to an agreement, they're now supporting a full investigation." She scowled as mounting conflicts confused her mind. "Why has the Alliance been so slow to act? I'd have thought, after everything Newearth has been through, they'd recognize a threat before it got out of hand. And I can't see why *light beings* should be interested in human-animal hybrids in the first place; nothing makes any sense!"

A brilliant hot sun heated Taug's fair skin, evaporating the water at such a rate he felt prickles all over his body. He shook his head as Faye marched along at his side. "Luxonians are guardians, remember. They need to know everything going on everywhere all the time. It's their way. Being in the know makes them feel safe." He swung a glance her way. "You know how they are."

Faye grabbed his tentacle and sped up, towing Taug behind. "You started this when you created Relevance. The courts declared that you were as much his father as Gavin. You may not be his biological father, but you certainly helped to bring him into being." She stopped, halting Taug in his tracks. "So, you have a responsibility. You must help."

A black horror swept over Taug, nearly blocking all coherent thought from his mind. A small corner of his intellect stood back amazed that he could feel so terrible, that an emotional reaction to an old drama could still have so much power over his wellbeing. Trying to rid himself of further tragedy, he jerked his tentacle free of Faye's grasp and swung it wildly in the air. "I tried to help Clare. That's what got me into this mess. I'm not helping anyone anymore. They all hate me, as I deserve, I suppose, but there's not a thing I can do in any case. It's over!" He swung around Faye and pounded toward the sand-colored dwelling on the edge of the sea.

Faye stood her ground and called after him. "It'll be over when minnows sing and plankton play in the waves. What in the universe will you eat then?"

Taug stopped. He turned, his gaze merely sliding over his shape-shifting friend. Ocean waves undulated upon the shore as if they played a frolicsome game for their own amusement. He knew, without a shadow of doubt, that the only way for laughter to remain would be if that wonderful, terrifying possibility never came true.

—LEAP Laboratory—

Relevance raced across his office, practically ran into his desk, and scooped his datapad into his hands, fumbled it, righted himself, and then pressed the message tab. *Gavin.* The one he had called Dad so long ago. Warm memories of swimming in the buoyant sea with the strong, quiet man and his many relatives swept over him. The embrace of soothing waves as he rested on the current, watching cousins gambol and play fight warmed his soul. Long-ago-laughter bubbled in his ears making them tingle. Gavin. *Dad.*

A fresh wave of fear weakened his knees. He slouched onto his chair, the datapad limp in his hands. It hadn't been hard to track his father. Gavin had never left Tabun. A leader, though more retired than active, he still garnered great respect among his own people. Tabunites did not write and publish their news. In their primitive way they remained in touch with each other far better than the average Newearth community. Luxonian and Bhuaci reports furnished all he could want to know about the planet and the thriving society living upon its surface.

But what Relevance wanted to know, no other being in the universe could tell him, except Gavin. His father had promised to hold onto one datapad and to check it regularly, no matter how many years passed, in case Relevance or Herson ever desired to reestablish contact. That had been his last message to his sons. At the time, Relevance had not taken him seriously. Once he had been sent away from Newearth, he had blocked all further contact from his mind.

Until recently.

He had to know the truth. So, he had sent a simple message to Gavin.

Hello Gavin,

How are you? Has Herson contacted you?

I received a strange message and grew concerned. Perhaps you can enlighten me as to Herson's whereabouts and what has happened to Clare and Taug.

Respectfully,

Relevance

Below his message, Gavin had responded just as simply.

Hello Relevance,

I am well. Thank you for asking.

Yes. Herson said he would like to see me. I invited him to visit whenever it was convenient. I have no contact with Clare, Taug, or anyone on Newearth.

Respectfully,

Gavin

A choking sensation forced Relevance to his feet. He had no idea why his heart was pounding or why his gut felt like it had twisted itself into knots. *What's wrong with me? Am I afraid that Herson will try to unite the family against me? What family?*

He paced to the bay window and leaned against it, his head pressing on the invisible surface. A shadowed image of his face stared back at him. His own cold tone had been echoed in his father's voice, twisting his heart.

Unlike his absence of desire to respond to Herson, his fingers itched to tap a message back, to ask Gavin details about his life and relieve the bitter chill between them. The grief of a young boy being sent far from home bubbled to the surface, and he was shocked by how much it hurt.

—Aram County, Cerulean's Cabin—

Cerulean stood before his bedroom closet and chose carefully; a tan shirt with brown pants would blend with early spring colors nicely. As a hybrid, he could travel invisibly, though it took more out of him than it used to, but with Bala, Seth, and Barni trailing along, he doubted that an unseen companion who spoke from thin air would help them concentrate.

He checked his reflection in the full-length mirror that Kendra had given him as a Christmas present three years before. He had averred that a mirror did not reflect the spirit of the season, but she had merely crossed her arms, glared in her mock-angry-face way, and insisted that since the rest of the universe had to look at him, a presentable appearance was a gift to many.

It was a useful tool, he had to admit. The previous morning, before another meeting with Seth and Barni, he had discovered that he had put his shirt on backward. Things would not have gone so well if they thought he had lost the ability to dress himself. A few pointed hints from Barni might ruin his reputation forever.

Those kids grew up too fast, know too much, and think far more of their abilities than is good for them. He rolled his shoulders, trying to get his mirrored image to appear relaxed. Ancient memories of himself standing before Supreme Judge

Sterling, with much greater life experience than Bala, Kendra, and all their kids combined yet being treated as an ignorant child, sent his blood pressure rising. Being Luxonian, physical signals weren't usually alarming, but being human, his reaction warned him to corral his thoughts.

Stick to the matters at hand, Cerulean. He grimaced. *Remain polite but firm. No matter what happens, don't let them jump to conclusions that'll start an interplanetary war.*

A firm knock on the door and Cerulean abandoned his mirrored image without a backward glance. Pacing himself, he strode through the kitchen and stopped. A deep breath, a quick swipe through his hair, and then he opened the door for his guests.

Barni stood first in line, Bala slightly behind, and then, trailing in the back, Seth stood taller than his brother, towering over Bala. Unexpectedly, it was Barni who commanded attention. His brilliant black eyes weren't dancing today. Concern pinched his brows as he waited, a bulwark before his family.

Cerulean swallowed a sigh and stepped aside. "Come in and take a moment to rest before we start out."

With a tinge of expert privilege, Barni made his first declaration. "Thanks, but no. Seth heard the talking squirrel again. Let's just get this over with."

Cerulean looked from Barni to Bala's placid expression and finally up at Seth, who merely nodded in stone-faced agreement. *Might as well face the monsters sooner than later…* Cerulean grabbed a walking stick leaning in the corner and then led the way down the porch steps and onto the path that would take them deep into the woodlands of Aram County.

It was only after the morning waned and Seth took the lead, tromping over miles of hardpacked earth, wiggling between two narrow rock outcroppings, climbing countless inclines, and splashing across three streams—one an easy hop-skip-and-a-jump, the others muddy and treacherous—

that Bala beckoned from the end of the line with a weak, huffing voice, "Hey, guys, think we could take a breather…perhaps make a plan…that doesn't involve hiking to death?"

Cerulean turned around and, to his surprise, it wasn't Seth who went to his father's side but Barni.

Seth stood back, clearly bewildered. Apparently, after years of outdoor living, he had forgotten that his dad took an autoskimmer to work and rarely lifted anything heavier than a spoonful of his wife's vegetable stew.

Barni assumed the professional role, checked his dad's pulse, and then pulled a flask from a deep pocket and offered it as an instant pick-me-up.

Covering his wide-eyed surprise with a chuckle, Bala accepted the cure-all, took a large swallow, and wiped his mouth. He lifted the flask. "Want some, Cerulean? Not that you need it but as a new human experience?"

Before Cerulean could refuse the honor, Seth took off running. Cerulean motioned for Bala to stay put and Barni to stay with him, but Barni wasn't going to miss out and, despite his exhaustion, Bala rose with renewed vigor. They took off together after Seth.

It didn't take long before Cerulean spotted Seth kneeling by a large oak tree with one hand pressed against the door of a small shed. With one finger against his mouth in a universal signal for quiet, he, Bala, and Barni sidled nearer.

Seth leaned forward and whispered, "I've got him. It's the same one; I'm sure of it. Extra-large body and knowing eyes. Looked terrified when he ran in here and shut the door."

Nearly bent double, Barni crept closer, his gaze fixed on the shed. "A squirrel shut the door? From the inside?"

Cerulean stopped by the tree and scanned the area. Nothing was moving. Even the birds were still. Four people running through the underbrush had probably warned every critter within miles of their arrival. Odd that this creature had been surprised. Then his gaze fixed on a small wooden table set to the left of the tree, stained and smoothed to a fine polish. A matching armchair stood nearby, and an assortment of miniature woodworking tools lay in a neat line on a rough slab attached to the table.

Something between a hysterical groan and rational curiosity fought inside of Cerulean. He stepped closer, bent low, and picked up the small hammer—a perfect jewel of craftsmanship in its own right.

Barni stomped over, frowning furiously. “What’s all this?”

Bala stopped at his elbow, touching nothing, his eyes roaming. “Fairy folk must live here.”

Seth hissed, “It’s no fairytale, Dad! Be serious for once.”

Shocked silence pounded against Cerulean’s ears.

In slow motion, Bala’s entire demeanor changed. His face hardened, his eyes narrowed, and his mouth drew into a tight line.

Relief began to flow over Cerulean like rainwater in a desert. *Bala is back.*

Though he didn’t grow taller than Seth or affect the authority of Barni, Bala stepped forward, his face set, and with a jerk of his hands, he motioned both of his sons to step back. “You, too, Cerulean. No offense, but we’ve been inexcusably rude, and I think it’s about time we started acting like decent human beings.”

With confused annoyance in his eyes, Seth let go of the door, rose to his feet, and stepped back.

Though Barni’s glare announced his expectation that his father would soon learn from his mistake, he stepped to his side and crossed his arms.

Bala dropped to his knees and shuffled closer. He stopped when he got within range of the small door. Then he reached out and knocked lightly. “Uh, hello, Mr. Squirrel, but we didn’t mean to intrude. We’re strangers to these parts and…well, let me be honest, my son saw you talking to yourself the other day and that concerned him. We came to investigate. Personally, I just want to know that you are all right." He glanced aside at the table, honest longing on his face. "I must say, I always wanted a set of tools like yours, though my wife won't let me use anything sharper than a butter knife."

Bari rolled his eyes.

Seth's jaw clenched.

Cerulean realized that he was holding his breath.

His hands clasped before him; Bala held his pose like a penitent before a judge's bench.

A soft shuffling sound and the door cracked open. A twitching nose poked out, and then black eyes in a small, pointed face gazed at Bala.

Bala bowed respectfully.

Then, to Cerulean's unexpected joy, the door opened and, after stepping forward, a large gray squirrel returned the bow.

—LEAP Laboratory—

Relevance stared at the wall screen as it faded from Squire's face to black. His stomach knotting, he turned away from the monitor and flung himself down on his chair. *What will happen now?* In a surprising twist, jealousy churned his stomach. The image of Squire chatting amiably with Bala rose in his mind. *Why does that bother me? So what if Bala, one of the few humans with a moral code, befriends one of my creations?*

A ping demanded his attention. Relevance slapped on the intercom. "Yes?"

Dr. Anzi's assistant, a bland fellow with no personality beyond what was required, spoke evenly, "The deliveries arrived early this morning. Kitchen staff has the buffet ready, and I've finished the new cages." A hesitation and then the assistant continued, "Can I leave early today?"

Relevance sat up; his interest piqued. "Why?"

"I've got a headache, thought maybe extra rest might help."

Not believing the excuse but without an ounce of proof, Relevance saw no reason to deny the request. "Yes, go ahead. But be sure to have the tools locked away before you leave. We don't want a repeat of what happened last time."

A light chuckle. "Had no idea that squirrel could even lift a hammer. Lucky the killdeer was such a tattletale." A sniff and throat clearing. "Thank you, sir. I'll finish up and be off then."

The mention of the buffet sparked images of a hot soup with a thick sandwich. Relevance switched off the intercom, rose, and headed for the door. *Just hungry; that's why I'm out of sorts.*

His mind settled, Relevance headed to the lift and took it to the central diner on the second floor. A busy attendant packaged special orders for each of the developing animals' nutritional needs and new culinary experiences, while another attendant, jokingly referred to as "The Chef" by Dr. Anzi, arranged a buffet area for the staff. A variety of offerings, including human sandwiches, Bhuaci pasta dishes, nutritionally packed Ingot drinks, and spicy snacks, satisfied everyone, even the Crestonian advisor who usually stayed hidden in his subterranean laboratory studying the effects of the Dumplix enhancement drug on sea creatures.

Relevance grabbed a tray with a deep inset section and made his way around the options. He chose a comforting potato soup and multi-cheese sandwich, which would please his palate and not set off any gastronomical upset.

Once seated, he dug in and ignored the array of Newearth and off-world migrant workers who selected their meals and then sat in groups, chatting amiably. Alone at his table set apart, he ate in silence.

A woman dressed in overalls nudged a muscled worker next to her as they made their way around the central bar. Her voice, though not raised, was clear as a bell. "Did you watch the live bot-cam when that Bala guy practically bowed down before Squire? I'd never have humbled myself before a critter like that. Either he's as dumb as an Ingot slave or as sly as a Crestonian diplomat."

The worker snorted as he filled his tray with a heaping pile of spicy rice and lentils. "Bala's got a great reputation. I looked him up. Just wait; he'll have Squire eating out of his hands before long." He shrugged. "You can infuse smart genetics but can't make anyone wise."

His sandwich halfway to his mouth, Relevance watched and waited for the woman's response.

"You think Bala's going to cause trouble?"

A glance around and the worker shrugged. "Sentience is trouble. You know free will—we all, eventually, make some terrible choices."

The woman frowned in unshielded sadness. "Poor Squire. Such an innocent. Doesn't stand a chance, does he?"

His appetite gone, Relevance rose from the table and headed back to his office. He had no idea what he would do when he got there.

—Newearth Docking Bay—

Justine, as a human-android, didn't technically have a heart and, for the first time in her life, she was glad of it. She sat on the edge of her daughter's bed in a room filled with colorful plants, miniature figurines from every race known in the universe, imitation Sectine cities, Bhuaci villages, Luxonian towers, and even a model Ingoti business district, and watched her daughter sleep.

An unnamed disease had crept over the lovely young woman so slowly that no one had noticed until the symptoms were out of control. Given Zara's history as the first Human-

Luxonian hybrid created by a Mystery Race, now known as the Eternals, she had been gifted to Justine as recompense for Justine's sterility as a hybrid. Only a child when Omega sent her to Justine, her uneven development into a woman was reflected in her body, shaped according to how she saw herself. Omega did much to right the wrongs of his youth, but giving Justine a daughter was more than justice, it brought the Android-Human's whole existence into alignment and made her life meaningful.

What she would do without her daughter, she could not say. She could not imagine it. She didn't want to.

Max, another of Omega's Android-Human experiments, had joined the family as Justine's husband and Zara's father, forging a unique role in their world. Discovering that his humanity involved more than the joys of life, he had struggled to balance justified fury with mercy and faithfulness. As he stepped into the room carrying a large OldEarth picture book, Justine looked over and considered his eyes, for they never lied.

Using his typical throat-clearing signal as an entry point to the conversation, Max stopped beside the bed and peered down at Zara. "She's quiet now. Let me take over, and you can follow up with other matters."

Unmoving, Justine watched Zara's chest rise and fall in regular intervals. The nearly translucent eyelids closed over pale blue eyes that were nearly blind now. "Other matters?"

Another throat clearing and Max dragged a chair from across the room to the bedside. He sat down and opened the book. "Though she is sleeping, I believe that she hears every word I read aloud. She always loved this one." He lifted the cover of the book displaying a water rat, a mole, and a toad linked arm-in-arm, wearing human clothes, and standing beside a sprightly river. "I'll keep her entertained while you find out what Bala's son, David, has been up to."

He dropped the book back onto his lap, a very human-sounding sigh escaping between his lips. "No one has been able to find him since he left the Docking Bay six months ago. Our last records show him working in his secret place on the upper deck, sending reports to various districts—some work related, others written in code. A woman identified as Variant—she has mismatched eyes and mottled skin—quite literally dragged him to an interventionist scooter, though that later proved to be fake, and they were last seen entering a tube bound for Aram County. Somehow, they managed to leave the tube without being traced. This morning, Bala sent an astonishing report about a sentient squirrel that he, Seth, Barni, and Cerulean interviewed yesterday. The creature appears to be harmless but insists that there are many more like him, sentient animals—birds even—in a laboratory run by Relevance. They believe David has been hiding there. Naturally, Bala wants to see David as soon as possible. I told him that you would find him."

Still staring at her sleeping daughter, Justine did not budge. "I'm her mother, Max. I can't leave."

Max leaned forward and placed a hand on her shoulder. "You know as well as I that no one can find a missing person better than you. Bala and Kendra are counting on your help. Cerulean needs you, too."

No heart to break, blood to freeze, or nerves to jangle, yet Justine understood the feelings better than most. Like a blind person reveling in the glory of a warm sun on her face or the embrace of a good friend, she knew well what the body could only hint at. Joy and despair lived beyond the physical realm. In her disabling grief, she wasn't sure that her mechanical body would obey her command, as she was not sure if she could live a moment longer than her daughter.

She looked over at Max and met his steady gaze. "Does our daughter's impending death not kill you, too?"

Laying the book aside, Max shifted from the chair and sat beside his wife on the edge of the bed. He wrapped his arms around her.

Justine let herself be held, resting her head on his shoulder, one hand still reaching back, touching Zara's fingers.

Max's deep, whispered voice respected the silence of the room. "Death is a doorway. That's what Abbas always said. When I asked Omega, he nodded, but then, he explained that the veil over death is there to protect us. We are not ready for what lies beyond. Not yet. Not until we are called." He placed his hands on Justine's shoulders and gently straightened her, their eyes meeting. "She will live in a new way, in a new world. Someday, we will be together again."

Justine wished she could cry. "How can I leave her, even for a moment, when it might be her last one here?"

"If Zara could speak now, what would she say?"

Justine's heart splintered into countless fragments. "She'd tell me to find David and bring him home."

Max picked up the book and repositioned himself on the chair.

To her surprise, Justine found that she could stand. She walked to the doorway and looked back.

Hunched forward, Max held the picture book before his daughter's unmoving face and spoke the words he had memorized long ago.

Without another word, Justine tapped the door, and it slid open. David's picture and every bit of profile information available in Newearth databanks rose before her eyes. *You had better be worth saving, boy.*

—Aram County, LEAP Laboratory—

Relevance strode into LEAP Central and stopped short, his disbelief warred with outrage.

He had left David and Variant in a quiet room in the fourth branch of the octagonal structure with strict orders to stay put and keep out of trouble. They were directed to organize incoming reports, earning his appreciation and perhaps an exotic dinner with him and Dr. Anzi at the end of the week. Once he had explained the danger they faced for breaking regulations now that the Inter-Alien Alliance was involved, they had seemed cooperative enough.

But, now, here they were, sitting before the training holopad with Tyto the owl, Branoc the crow, and a new member—a hedgehog he'd playfully named Urchin—relaxing on decidedly plump cushions, watching the exterior woodlands as if it were family entertainment.

He stole closer and then cracked his voice like a whip. "What is going on here?"

Variant scrambled to her feet and ran to him—an exuberant student who wanted to explain why she was the best one in class with special privileges. David, he was sorry to see, hadn't moved a muscle.

Variant grabbed Relevance's arm. "Come and see! Dr. Anzi told us to keep watch and let him know if there are any developments. We brought in Tyto and Branoc because they won't miss anything." As her eyes strayed toward Urchin, who had waddled in close and seemed absorbed by the scenery, she shrugged noncommittally. "He just showed up." Her face brightened as she tried to drag Relevance forward. "Bala is talking to Squire." She pointed at Branoc. "He told me everyone's name and their history. Dr. Anzi seemed to think that David would learn a lot from watching them. She leaned in and dropped her voice. "He's just using David to better understand Bala. David told me that his dad is so honest, he's transparent." Her eyebrows rose knowingly.

Relevance stopped just outside the circle and considered the three specimens. A new and dangerous thought struck him. *Sentience doesn't evolve into wisdom.* He raised his eyes to the holoscreen, where strategically placed bots created a multidimensional view of woodland events, now playing before their wondering eyes.

Bala, appearing unusually relaxed, leaned against a large scaly tree trunk, while Squire sat on a smooth stump shoved up close to the table, one tiny paw holding a long, thick piece of wood in a firm grip. With the other paw clutching a small chisel, he carved what looked like an ornate walking stick decorated with fierce animal faces. Or, maybe, it was a fancy cudgel.

Swiveling his gaze back to the matters at hand, Relevance scanned the room for Dr. Anzi. Nowhere in sight. Lucky for him. Clenching his hands, Relevance felt a familiar flush, a human weakness he had not yet mastered, as he considered his position with the doctor. *Am I his pawn, a tool to be used like all the rest? This whole laboratory was my idea!* The doctor's smug face rose in his mind along with the desire to smash it with his fists.

Suddenly the screen lighted with live action, catching Relevance's attention. Bala climbed to his feet, one hand rubbing the small of his back. With a serious expression, he bowed formally to Squire, who returned the courtesy. "I don't know when I've enjoyed an afternoon more, Squire. I still have grave doubts about Relevance's work but, I must say, you are the most companionable creature I've ever met."

With a hint of humor in his eyes, Squire smiled. "I could say the same."

Bala laughed. "I bet you could. I'd best be off. I promised to meet the others for a confab this afternoon." He leaned in and dropped his voice to a conspiratorial whisper. "I didn't tell anyone I was coming back. My idea." His eyebrows bounced playfully. "Sometimes a person just has to think things through for themselves, without rash opinions smacking him in the face all the time."

A thoughtful frown shadowed Squire's furry face. His whiskers twitched. "Little of your kind makes sense to me. Being so advanced, aren't humans more unified than the animals?" He rubbed his chin and stared into the distance. "What do humans care about?"

Bala held his pose, his gaze locked on Squire.

The entire laboratory seemed to hold a collective breath. Even Relevance waited for Bala's response.

"I wish I could tell you, Squire. But I'd like you to ask that question again when this issue is brought before the Inter-Alien Alliance Counsel. No single judge can appraise this case—it's too important. Your question proves that."

Squire tilted his head. "It does?"

"You're an animal after my own heart, Squire." With a wave, Bala turned and started away, calling over his shoulder, "I'll be back, bringing a bunch of aliens with me and maybe together we'll be able to answer a question or two."

With a thoughtful expression, Squire repositioned his chisel and started carving his stick again, one end growing quite sharp, almost like a spear.

Relevance hit the "End Monitor" button. The hologram dimmed and then disappeared.

A sad sigh escaped Urchin's lips as he curled up on the pillow.

The show over, both Branoc and Tyto flew off to their respective nests.

Relevance refocused on Variant. He pointed to the hedgehog. "Take Urchin back to his nest and stay with him. He's too new to comprehend what is happening, and I don't want him unduly upset."

Pleased by sudden responsibility, Variant swiveled without a word and scooped the yielding animal into her arms. Humming a nonsense tune, she carried him off.

David stood up and ambled over to Relevance, his shoulders rounded in a permanent slouch. "Some guy, eh? Dad has a way with people. Even animal-people it seems. Everyone likes him."

In no mood to disguise his anger, Relevance chipped his words like shattering ice. "Except. You."

Shocked at the apparent heresy, David found his backbone and stiffened. "I love my dad! I'm not helping you in some kind of rebellion thing, if that's what you think."

"So why have you kept secrets, lied to your parents, passed along sensitive information, and broken at least a dozen Inter-Alien Alliance laws?"

Flushing bright red, David clenched his jaw and spun on his heels apparently ready to march stiffly away from any confrontation.

"No, you don't!" Though younger than David, Relevance had twice his strength and body weight. Using a maneuver he had learned from a formidable Ingot warrior, Relevance strode forward and, after a sharp smack to the head, shoved David from behind, knocking him to the ground. Without hesitation, he jumped on the young man's back and yanked his arms up and back, eliciting a cry of pain. Not finished, Relevance increased the pressure and held it.

David screamed again.

Before the man passed out, Relevance released the pressure on his arms though not on his spine.

David's face lay squished against the cold floor, his breath coming in pants, terror in his eyes. "W-what!"

"Answer my question, David. Why did you assist me against the wishes of a man you profess to love?"

His breaths coming in heaves, as if he might vomit any second, David huffed. "Dad-wouldn't-understand. I had-to-help."

Crouching and getting into David's visual line, Relevance spoke with pronounced care, a deadly calm pervading him. "Why?"

"Variant."

Relevance froze, his brain uncomprehending. "Variant? What has she to do with it?"

"She's so…so exotic! Please, let go! I'll explain."

Recognizing the intoxicating flush of beating an opponent, even one as unworthy as David, Relevance had to force his muscles to relax. He released David's arms and stood up.

After a few moans and an anguished squeak as he balanced on his knees, David finally climbed to his feet. His dark hair disheveled and with a snarl of disgust, he faced Relevance. "Maybe you can't see it, but Variant is special. No one treats her right, but she keeps on going—studies and works and helps out where she can. She might have a bit of a temper but that's to be expected after everything that's happened to her. She wanted to help you, so she asked me to help, too. No one was supposed to know; it was just a game we played. I got the information, and she passed it along." He shrugged. "It wasn't a big deal. Just some stupid info about hybrids. It's all on Newearth News anyway. No secrets these days."

The side door, leading to Dr. Anzi's private laboratory, slid open, and the doctor himself stepped into the main room.

After an instantaneous assessment of the doctor's demeanor, Relevance refocused his attention on David. "Despite the fact that you were using Newearth Docking Bay databases when you've been trained explicitly on the laws regarding information security, you still felt comfortable betraying Max and Justine's trust?"

David's eyes narrowed. "What are you? An Interventionist? A Docking Bay spy?"

Amazed at the lack of self-awareness in the man before him, Relevance shook his head. "Tell me the truth, if you are capable of that."

"I got the information for Variant. She asked for my help, and I gave it to her. If that put Max and Justine in a tough spot, so much the better. They seem to think they are so advanced. Perhaps now they'll—"

Dr. Anzi stepped forward. "I do believe you've said enough, David. It's time you went back to your quarters to await further instructions."

Rage filling his eyes, David stepped toward the smaller man. "Don't tell me what to do! I came here"—he shot an apprehensive glance at Relevance—"to help Variant." He glared at the doctor. "Since I'm no longer needed, I'll leave." His head high, David stalked toward the door.

Relevance didn't bother to stop him. There was nothing more to say.

His gaze following the young man as he marched through the main doors, Dr. Anzi seemed to speak to the air. "Never should have trusted him. Too young and inexperienced. But no matter. He did his part well enough."

Relevance ignored the fact that he was nearly five years younger than David and refocused his attention on Dr. Anzi. "You told Variant and David to watch Squire and Bala. Why? What did you hope to accomplish?"

As if deigning to give his attention to an inquisitive child, Dr. Anzi beckoned Relevance to follow him as he started across the room. "Progress is unpredictable. Some experiments stall to the point of utter uselessness. Like the penguins. Who'd have thought that a simple change of polarity would spell their utter demise? While others…" He pointed to a small gathering in the corner of the lab near the elk bed of straw, surrounded on three sides by bushy plants.

The large black crow Branoc, Tyto the owl, the Killdeer Chiara—quiet for once, hedgehog Urchin, and Elch the miniature elk, had gathered in a tight circle. Ostensibly, they appeared to be playing cards—Old Maid apparently—but their darting glances spoke of a secret discussion.

An initial ripple of horror gave immediate way to pride. Obviously, his vision had worked. These were not the humble servants of humankind anymore. These beings no longer belonged to the same class that could be hunted and stripped of their skin, their flesh set on the table for consumption like so many Nutra-pellets. Here, gathered together, were sentient beings, animal-persons with thoughts, considerations, expectations, fears, and perhaps, dreams. His heart pounding with exhilaration, Relevance waited for the doctor to answer his question.

"Though we knew that animal development was far faster than human, they are growing independent quicker than expected. We must send them out and hurry the separation process along. Variant and David were never capable of helping us progress beyond the initial stages. They served best as conduits to the larger universe. I let them watch the interaction between Bala and Squire to inform them of possibilities." He stroked his chin. "Bala is an extraordinary human. I wish I could claim him as one of my own." He shrugged, dismissing the thought. "Now they must go out and share what they've seen, spreading the news far and wide."

A clutch of fear gripped Relevance, tightening his gut in a stranglehold. For a moment, he understood what David had felt, helpless in his grip. "It's too fast! Our specimens need to grow accustomed to the larger world in light of their abilities. Squire has only just begun his adjustment. Now Bala will bring—"

Dr. Anzi broke in. "We started a process that won't stop with us. In the channels that David developed, I dispersed my experimental process to every laboratory interested in such research. I'm hailed as a hero in every sector of the universe. Even the Inter-Alien Alliance Committee can't halt progress now." He turned and faced Relevance. "Despite their limitations, David and Variant fulfilled their purpose, so they are released from service. But these animal-humans—Animans, will make history. They must be sent out as soon as possible, and as each of our other cases comes to sentience, we will send them out." A grim smile spread over his face. "Then our experiment will flourish in ways we cannot yet imagine."

Relevance's hand twitched at his side. "But what if they aren't ready yet? Look at Chiara—she's a nervous wreck at the best of times. Do you really believe that she can handle the emotional burden of her original nature with human sentience without proper preparation? It might drive her insane. That's hardly what I would call a successful experiment."

A frown and Dr. Anzi let his disapproval be known. "Sanity was never an issue. As your idea of success was never my concern. These early ones can die within the year for all that matters. The purpose, as I told you from the first, was to prove that sentience is not valuable in itself. Only the true human, the uniquely self-contained human body, spirit, and mind, was ever worth anything." He thrust his chin a directional gesture. "They'll go out into the world and prove my point in abundant variety." His shoulders back, the doctor started toward the card-playing group. "I hate to break up their game, but it's time they were made ready. I'll arrange their new home locations, and you can be the one to take them out if you'd like." He glanced over his shoulder. "If not you, I'll have someone else see to it. Most of the assistants are insensitive fellows, but I'm sure they can manage."

Relevance stood frozen in place, wondering when he had lost control of his laboratory, his vision, and the purpose of his existence. Taug's face floated into his mind. He wished he could banish it forever, but suddenly, he felt he understood the Cresta as never before.

Chapter Three

We're Not Done

—Aram County, Woodlands—

April, Year 74, Newearth Reckoning

Squire shivered as he raced over drifts of old leaves. He didn't really mind the spring chill. His fur coat did wonders to protect him from the wind, but the lack of provisions was an issue. Certainly, Relevance and Dr. Anzi knew that he didn't have a personal store of nuts like other squirrels. It hardly made sense that they would send him out only to starve. *They must intend greater things.* The image of the female squirrel he had befriended rose in his mind. She was beautiful, and once he accepted her natural limitations, he discovered a source of companionship like none other. Plus, she had plenty of nuts and was willing to share. Bala's grinning face rose in his mind, and Squire's pounding heart rate immediately slowed to a more reasonable speed.

He scrambled up the trunk of the ancient oak, perched on a high branch, and scanned his environment. Once he figured out a way to increase his food supply, the wide world and his new life would content him completely. After all, likely he'd be a father soon enough.

A shuffling of leaves and murmured conversation caught his attention. In the distance, Relevance and Dr. Anzi's assistant clambered between two boulders. The assistant towed a black wagon packed with cages. Behind the wagon, an elk tied to a lead rope followed with uncertain steps.

Squire's heart picked up speed. *Elch?* Suddenly everything made sense. *They're bringing help! We're supposed to form a community of animal-humans and work together.* A warm feeling invigorated Squire's whole body. He prepared to scurry down to meet the new arrivals.

With a shouted command, "Stop!" Relevance glanced around, his gaze sweeping over the landscape. "No one. We'll release them here."

Confused, Squire stayed perfectly still, though he felt certain that Relevance was aware of his location. They had come here often enough in their introductory rambles through the woods. An odd feeling prickling his insides, Squire waited, not making a sound.

Grunting, the assistant, wearing a thick sweater, paced over to Elch and tugged the lead from around his neck. "Here ya go. There's fresh clover in the field ahead. Get your bearings before nightfall." He slapped the elk on the rump to start him moving.

Elch bellowed, then snorted, "I'm not an idiot!" as he trotted off.

Turning away from the scene with a grimace, Relevance opened the cage door on the wagon and drew Branoc forward.

The huge bird climbed onto Relevance's arm and peered into his eyes. Unspoken understanding passed between them.

A fresh shiver rippled down Squire's back. *What is happening?*

Relevance lifted his arm high. "Make a new life for yourself, Wise One."

The assistant snorted. "It's only a crow. Sentience doesn't make it wise. Just aware of its stupidity, maybe."

It was a good thing that the assistant had turned to another cage when Relevance glared at him. Squire couldn't help twiddling his paws; the situation was driving his nerves into fits.

With an impatient grab, the assistant pulled Tyto from his cage and, without the slightest concern for feelings, thrust the heavy owl into the air.

Relevance cupped Urchin in his hands and watched Tyto right himself and then flap into a low tree branch.

Shifting the small animal onto one arm, Relevance smacked the assistant on the shoulder. “Barbarian! What did you do that for? You wouldn’t throw a person off an autoskimmer, would you?”

The man straightened his shoulders, pulling himself to his full height—at least twenty centimeters taller than Relevance—which made him as close to a giant as Squire ever hoped to see. “I would if it was getting late and I’d missed my last meal because of him.”

Relevance glanced from the assistant to Tyto, who glared down from the tree branch. “How’s that?”

“Stupid bird said he wasn’t ready to leave the laboratory. Flapped all over the place before I could cage him. I was ready to shoot him with a dart, but Dr. Anzi laughed and said he expected great things from that bird and the angrier he got the better he would be.”

Tyto’s wide-eyed glare never wavered.

Squire wondered if his heart would thump right out of his chest.

Urchin squirmed in Relevance’s hands, so Relevance set him on the ground at his feet. “Are you going to be all right out here all by yourself, Urchin?”

Urchin lifted his head and looked around. He nodded at Tyto in a formal salute. Then his gaze swept over Squire as if unseeing. He sniffed and wiped his nose with the back of his paw. “I’m not alone. I’ll be fine.”

A new voice rose from the back of the wagon. “Well, if you’re done worrying about everyone else, perhaps you can spare a moment for me, the one squeezed into the smallest cage, having a panic attack?”

With a gasp, Squire slapped his paw against his forehead. *They brought Chiara? What were they thinking?*

A mad gleam in his eyes, the assistant thrust open the cage door. Before he could snatch the frail bird, Relevance darted forward and cupped the creature in his hands and drew her out.

For a moment, Squire thought that the assistant was angry enough to slap the bird from Relevance's hands, but one look at Relevance's face, and the larger man backed down. Squire almost chuckled. *Size isn't everything!*

Relevance opened his hands, and Chiara immediately began screaming complaints. "I'm not built for this kind of treatment! Sensitive and artistic, that's my nature! Buffoons! I studied the dictionary and know more words than the two of you put together. And here you stuff me unceremoniously into a death trap, then yank me out while hyperventilating, during a full-blown PTSD attack! Squawk!"

Little Urchin's shoulders shook. It took a moment for Squire to realize that he was laughing behind his paws, not falling into emotional ruin.

With a snort, Elch bellowed in the distance. "Hurry up, and let's eat before it gets dark! We've still got to find a place to bed down tonight."

A huff and Tyto lifted off from the low branch. He swooped between the trees like the expert flyer he was created to be and landed on a pine tree a few meters from where Elch stood.

Branoc dropped to the woodland floor and hopped over to Urchin. "We'll go together." He glanced up at Relevance. "Chiara, you can hop at my side or fly over to Tyto and Elch and keep them company till we get there."

Relevance opened his hands wide and Chiara flew up and promptly smacked into a tree branch.

She fell to the ground with a scream. "See what you've done? I'm out of sorts being raised in that egregious laboratory." After fluffing her feathers and a realigning shiver, she hopped to Branoc's side. "You've got more dignity than the rest of them." Her head high, beady eyes darting, she squawked. "You may escort me to the other outcasts."

Squire could hardly wait to ask Branoc what he thought of Chiara. But first, he held his place while the assistant turned the wagon around and started his return trip with plodding steps.

Relevance stayed in place a moment longer, watching Branoc and Chiara—Urchin waddling between them—head toward the open field where Elch and Tyto waited in huffing impatience.

Relevance called out as if addressing a crowd of departing students, "I'll check on you soon. We're not done with each other, no matter what Dr. Anzi may have said."

No response, except perhaps in the secret minds of the first Animans ever to be released on Newearth. Or anywhere, so far as Squire knew. There wasn't much he could say since there were no words yet invented for such an experience.

As soon as Relevance was out of sight, Squire raced down the tree toward his new woodland companions and hoped that they knew how to find some nuts.

—Vandi—

Justine started to run and knew that she could overtake David in a matter of seconds, but she didn't want a confrontation on a busy Vandi streetside, so she slowed her pace and followed at a discrete distance until he turned down an alleyway, leading to his favorite smoke shop.

A disgusting habit he favored since becoming friends with Variant. They both liked to smoke "Blandish," a rare flower that grew in the mountains on Helm. The plant was said to have supernatural properties, allowing the smoker to see into the future and manifest dreams. Justine didn't believe any of it, though she wasn't the least surprised that David and Variant did.

Finally, at a quiet, isolated spot, Justine sped forward and grabbed David by the shoulder. The way he jumped made her wonder who else had accosted him recently. No matter. His personal life was hardly her concern.

"We need to talk."

David spun around, wrenching himself free from Justine's grasp. Fury and a hint of terror were reflected in his wide-eyed gaze. "I'm done talking! I've had enough of you, Relevance, and everyone on Newearth!"

Justine held her ground, ready to pounce but not appearing so. "Except Variant. She has feelings for you. Mutual, I'd say."

If David's face grew any brighter, he might spontaneously explode. Justine didn't want that mess on her hands. She leaned against the stone wall that lined the alleyway and considered the young man seriously for the second time. Only once before, when she had agreed to hire him, had she dedicated any real thought to him. At that point, she had seen an eager kid who wanted to please his parents and prove his worth to the world at large.

He had proven himself but not in the way anyone had hoped. Dark hair, brown complexion, black eyes, and only a hundred-seventy-five centimeters, definitely shorter than his brothers, but about the same height as his father, his slight build reminded Justine more of Bala than Kendra. *If only he had Bala's honesty.*

David crossed his arms and huffed like a child. "Don't talk about Variant. You can't possibly comprehend what she's been through."

Well aware that a smirk was playing on her lips, Justine decided to ignore his staggering ignorance. The direct approach was the only way to reach this kid. "Your parents are worried about you. Max sent me to find you and send you home before interventionists take matters into their own hands. You've broken several protocol laws that the Inter-Alien Alliance Commission will not take lightly. You could be facing serious time on Bothmal."

His face blanching of all color, David shifted nervously, his hands twitching at his sides. "You're exaggerating! It wasn't that big a deal. Relevance wanted hybrid info from various databases, and after Dr. Anzi added his part, he asked me to disseminate his findings back into the data pool." He shrugged nonchalantly. "It's the same kind of stuff that Newearth News reports on all the time. No big deal."

Justine shook her head. Rarely amazed by human blindness and stupidity, this man before her had sunk to a subterranean level. "Big deal when we have sentient animals running free in Aram County, and the process to achieve such a dubious goal has been given to a universe with no moral guidelines."

Rather disarmingly, David smiled. "I thought the talking squirrel was kind of cute. I can't see what you'd have against an animal getting what you've been given." His face twisting, his words taunted with gleeful malice. "Jealous maybe? Now, you're not so special?"

An explosion of fury propelled Justine forward; she grabbed David by the throat and smashed him against the stone wall. The desire to break this stupid arrogant human into pieces filled her.

A sudden cry pierced her rage; Zara's voice called out, "Mama!" Instantaneously, Justine's priorities changed. Spitting her words, she released the boy. "Go home. I'll deal with you later." That done, she spun on her heels and raced back to the Docking Bay. Not sure who she was praying to, she begged, "Please! Please let me see her alive one last time."

—Newearth Docking Bay—

Justine was just barely too late.

Max lay on the bed with his arms around Zara, rocking her lifeless body, now faded to the shimmering glow of a young girl. He could manufacture tears if he wanted to, but there was no need. His face expressed his grief.

No tears slipped down Justine's face either. She didn't miss them. Her soul was wrenched as never before, and she repented of ever desiring a full human body. If this was grief as a sentient android, she didn't want a body that could proclaim such pain throughout every cell.

Max looked at her, his gaze a wordless plea.

With silent care, Justine climbed onto the other side of the bed and lay beside the shimmering, yet still physical, form of her daughter. No one knew how a Luxonian-Human hybrid might experience death. No one had ever wanted to know.

Max's words rose like a whisper in church. "I sent word to Cerulean. He's coming. Bala and Kendra, too. They'll be here soon. But we have this moment together."

Justine nodded. Nothing would replace the loss of her child. Yet friends would offer comfort. Eventually. She wrapped her arm around Zara and a tingle of warmth filled her. Zara's voice, calm and serene, spoke, *I'm not gone forever*, and echoed louder than the cry that had called Justine away from murderous desire a short time before. "Was that you, who called me, Zara?"

Max's head jerked up; he stared at his wife.

No response needed; Justine knew.

Max reached over and clasped Justine's hand.

She accepted it, and together they held their beloved child between them one last time.

—Bala's Home—

Bala hated funerals. He avoided them whenever a suitable excuse presented itself. He looked at David, sitting slump-shouldered on the couch. *I'd say I've got a suitable excuse all right.*

He pictured Zara's lithe figure three days before as she lay softly glowing on her bed. *I was there when they needed me, when I could do the most good.* Standing beside Max and Justine along with Faye and Cerulean as the funeral attendants took the body for preparation was the hardest thing he had done in a long time. It had demanded every ounce of formal training and multiple prayers ascending to maintain his composure. *Kendra and the other kids will help them now.*

He considered his youngest son, and his heart wavered. Bracing himself, Bala marched to the couch and faced the young man. "While everyone is at the service, you and I have a few things we need to discuss."

David stared at the floor and mumbled.

The emotional rollercoaster Bala had been on in recent days did not prepare him to meet resistance with a calm, well-ordered mind. He immediately tensed up, his hands balling into fists, though he had no intention of using them. "Speak up, David. I'm not lying at your feet, so I don't know why you're staring at the floor."

David lifted his head. His voice rose high and petulant. "I said I don't care!"

Shocked by the despair in David's eyes, Bala immediately sat down and put his arm around his son. His voice grew husky. "I don't understand, David. What's happened to you? What is going on?" He squeezed the boy's thin shoulders, his breath nearly choked. "Don't shut me out, please."

Stiff and resistant, David refused to be comforted. "It's all your fault. You and Mom pushed me into that Docking Bay job because you thought it would score points with the Inter-Alien Alliance, and since they rule this planet like the tyrants they are, everyone wants to be on their good side." He stabbed his father with a piercing stare. "Especially you."

Bala swallowed. His mouth had gone so dry he wondered if he hadn't inhaled a desert somewhere along the way. Though his mind could barely comprehend the words, he understood David's aim all too well. The boy wanted to hurt him, to deflect responsibility for his actions onto someone else. Anyone else, apparently. Guilty people did it all the time. Bala had just never imagined that one of his children would do such a thing *to him*. He rose from the couch and forced his hands to unclench.

"You were given a position of trust, which you betrayed. Cerulean wants you to act as a counteragent, to work for Relevance and then tell us everything that is happening." Bala shook his head. "Once, not long ago…a few minutes ago, in fact, I would have agreed to such a plan. I was going to offer you the chance to redeem yourself."

David snorted, "Ha!" He jumped to his feet. "Redeem myself? When it's all of you who have made this planet the hell it is for so many innocent people! Just because someone is different, doesn't fall into a proper category, she becomes expendable, a worthless creature who can be used by others as a toy or tool until she's tossed away!"

An image of Variant's face popped into Bala's mind, and everything clicked into place. He stepped closer and peered deep into his son's eyes. An odd glint—suspicious paranoia or the tell-tale marks of mania—shone in their depths. "Are you taking something? Has your new friend, Variant, given you—"

A shoulder shove and David pushed his father out of his way. He stalked to the door. "Go to Bothmal! Variant is innocent. You're always so ready to condemn an alien you don't understand. Well, you'll have to condemn your own flesh and blood first; how does that feel?"

As the door slammed behind the son he had rocked to sleep, jiggled on his knee, raced in the backyard, and hugged more times than he could count, Bala felt as if his heart had fallen out of his chest and splattered on the floor. For the first time in his life, he wished he had gone to the funeral instead.

—LEAP Laboratory—

Relevance wiped sweat from his brow as he raced at top speed. As he dodged around ancient trees, the springy soil absorbed the pounding of his feet. His lungs burned with exhaustion. Only the scream of a hawk overhead caught his attention and slowed his pace. He glanced up. It was just a wild bird, no one he knew. Dr. Anzi had insisted they begin experimenting on domesticated animals, thereby altering farm and pet industries forever. Just this morning, the doctor had leaned forward, his hands propped on the steel laboratory table, and chuckled over the prospect of Newearth citizens discovering that dogs could converse, horses demand wages, and hens refuse to give up their eggs.

A pain in Relevance's side throbbed. He hobbled to a fallen trunk and plopped down, his breath coming in gasping heaves.

Despite the rest, he could not get the ache in his chest or burning tears in his eyes to relent. He pulled out his datapad and stared at the saved page, the one he had been reading before all thought fled and he had raced outside.

Newearth News Obituary

Zara, daughter of Justine Santana and Max Omega, managers of Newearth Docking Bay, died Saturday, March 30th at her home. Her illness, like her existence, was a mystery. Her funeral service on April 9th is open to the public, though the family asks for privacy and restraint from public intrusions.

Despite celebrity status as the only other Omega creation, besides her parents in the known universe, Zara suffered through the usual tribulations of youth as she adjusted to her hybrid nature as a Human-Luxonian. During a particularly troublesome period, it took the advanced skills of Crestonian scientists to adjust a dangerous tendency toward violence. Her final years were marked by enormous personal development and what her mother called a "sensitive moral integration." Her adoptive father, Max Omega, said that he has become a better person for knowing her and only wished that they could have grown more human together in the future.

Memorials are to be sent to the Newearth Orphans' Fund, where children from every race are adopted into loving homes. As Zara told her mother shortly before she passed, "Love knows no boundaries," so she would like to be remembered in love shared with others.

Memories of Zara as she aided him in his first explorations filled his mind. Justine had not approved of their association, but Zara knew her own mind. She was nothing like David, always trying to impress. She had a personal goal in mind, to learn more about her own unique nature. Relevance had felt an attraction to the strange young woman he could not explain and refused to acknowledge.

She's gone forever. I'll never get to know her or unlock her secrets. The ache in his chest suggested a greater loss. Unlike Variant, Zara was an old soul, a tested spirit who had come through a dark passage and found self-discipline and introspection possible. *I could have talked with her and learned something.* Stomach twisting grief sent alarms through Relevance. *I must get hold of myself!* But the idea that he would never see her again felt like a broken promise, a chance missed.

The words, "No boundaries" sent a shaft of hope through his heart. *Maybe*, he swallowed hard, *Justine and Max know something, an ancient, well-kept secret they shared with Zara. Maybe they expect to see her again.*

Relevance pushed away from the dead tree and started to run back to the laboratory. *That's what I need to discover.*

—Aram County, Cerulean's Cabin—

Bala sat at Cerulean's kitchen counter, ready to take a sip of spicy Chai tea, when one of Supreme Luxonian Judges, Roux, appeared out of thin air. Bala nearly jumped out of his skin. He also spilled his tea. He knew that Luxonians did that to each other all the time, but he considered it rude beyond measure. Cerulean didn't seem to mind, and Roux didn't appear to notice Bala's irritation, which vexed him even more.

With a much too hearty chuckle, Roux stepped over and slapped Cerulean on the back. "So, you've finally found a deferential audience in the animal world, eh, Cerulean?"

The joke fell on the hard floor and never recovered. Bala figured that Roux deserved it. Clearly, he had been away from Newearth too long.

A tapping sound caught Bala's attention. Leaving Roux to try to dig himself out of his most recent blooper, he strolled over and opened the screen door. On the front porch stood the most fascinating creature Bala had ever seen. At nearly two meters, the Mantis figure towered over Bala. He knew perfectly well that as a member of the Insectine race, she could've been from any class imaginable. *Thank goodness she's not a stink bug. I don't think I could've handled that.* He tried on his most welcoming smile and swept through a dignified bow. "Please, come in. You must be Walking Flower."

The large Mantis stepped lightly into the sunny kitchen, took an appraising look around, and then, with hands folded, returned the bow in a formal manner. "You are Bala, Newearth's most trusted host?"

His face reddening, Bala spluttered, "Good Heavens, no! I'm just a Human Services Detective who got himself into a mess by volunteering to organize a committee of alien representatives to consider this matter of animal-humans."

Loud throat clearing directed Bala's gaze back to the porch. Faye stood there in her adorable elfin form and, right next to her, waited Helm's most revered spiritual leader, Song. *Lord, help me now.*

Faye cleared her throat noisily. "You're going to invite us in, right?"

Nearly tripping over his feet, Bala backed up. "Yes! Please, come in. Cerulean is right over—" He cast his gaze over his shoulder in time to see Cerulean leading Walking Flower to the restroom. His brain froze by the myriad possibilities he had never considered before—whether a Mantis person would need…be able to…manage…in such a human setting.

In a shimmering robe over a white outfit, Song hummed as she crossed into the country-style kitchen. "I always knew that Cerulean had good taste; I just never imagined it was this charming."

With an I-know-my-way-around attitude, Faye pranced through the kitchen into the large, open living room. She dropped down on a white couch with a relieved sigh. "Thank goodness! I was afraid we'd be late and have to chase you through the wilderness."

Song found a chair to Faye's right and sat with dignified repose.

Cerulean stepped near and bowed formally. "Welcome to my home, such as it is."

Roux stayed by the kitchen counter but imitated Cerulean's bow, looking as serious and dignified as Bala had ever seen him.

As befit company manners, Faye grinned and Song smiled.

A quick glance at the restroom and a prayer that Walking Flower was finding everything to her satisfaction, Bala finally took notice of his growling stomach. He had spent the night in Cerulean's guestroom, missed his wife dreadfully, couldn't find a decent midnight snack, and woke up too late for breakfast. In frantic haste, he searched the cabinets. To his joy, he found a large bag of potato chips. After ripping it open, he poured the crispy delights into a bowl, clasped it lovingly in his arms, and, feeling exceedingly unselfish, started back to the living room to share.

Pounding on the door halted him in his tracks. He glanced at Cerulean who was introducing a refreshed Walking Flower to Roux. *All well there.* Bala changed his trajectory and swung open the door yet again.

Lang, an Ingot Universal News reporter in her usual cyborg techno-armor, wearing her most enticing form-fitting suit, stood on the porch with Riko, a Uanyi in his trademark white uniform over his rubbery exoskeleton. Neither smiled.

Uncertain what else to do, Bala ignored Riko's enormous insect-like eyes and pointed to the living room with one hand and held out the chip bowl with the other. "Join the others. Here's a snack. I can make tea or coffee if you want some."

With a shake of the head and a curt wave, Riko dismissed the silly chips. Lang took a handful and munched as she made her way forward.

After a swift rotation around the room, offering chips and anything else he thought Cerulean might have handy in his cabinets, Bala returned to the kitchen.

Cerulean joined him. "We aren't here to socialize. It's time we headed out, or we'll lose the sun. There's rain forecast for this afternoon."

Bala stuffed the last chips from the bowl into his mouth and chewed as rapidly as he could while nodding agreeably.

Faye scurried forward and tugged on Cerulean's sleeve. "Where's Taug? I thought you were going to invite him as the Crestonian representative?"

Trying to ignore a bit of chip caught behind his teeth, Bala cleared his throat. "I contacted him, and he said he'd come in his own way and in his own time, whatever that means."

Riko strolled closer and chimed in. "Knowing Taug, and I do know him quite well, it's best we leave him to manage his own affairs." He glanced at his datapad. "I can't be gone for long. Jayla can manage the café with Wendell's help, but the kids are a handful. I need to get back as soon as possible. Can we get this over with, please?"

Cerulean nodded and clapped his hands together. "Let's find out what the animal-human world has to say for itself."

—Aram County, Woodlands—

Bala tromped along the slim path he was beginning to know better than he had ever imagined. The oddity of leading a proxy of Inter-Alien Alliance Committee members discombobulated him beyond words. Still, it was better than staying home and trying to talk sense into Kendra who was searching relentlessly for David, a son who had made it quite clear that he did not want to be found. Bala sighed. Kendra knew what she was doing. David did not.

Plodding at the end of the line, Cerulean followed Roux with his head down, his mind seemingly elsewhere.

In front of Roux, Walking Flower stepped daintily, never hesitating, or disturbed. The two Bhuaci, Song and Faye, ambled on either side of Riko, the Uanyi representative, their words as measured as their steps. "What a pretty bird, reminds me of..." their voices fell to gentle murmurs.

Marching with determined steps, Lang strode shoulder to shoulder with Riko; his exoskeleton and bulbous eyes had ceased to bother her long ago. Neither seemed unduly concerned with the fact that they were not actual Inter-Alien Alliance representatives. As far as Bala could decipher, his suggestion was accepted by the upper echelon, and when Riko and Lang were asked to informally investigate and report the matter back to their consulates neither had refused, though Riko had probably rolled his enormous eyes. As she navigated the narrow path, Lang managed to show off pictures of her foster kids, which drew forth candid shots of Riko's clan. At the sound of their shared laughter, Bala's heart twisted. An image of David's furious expression haunted him. It certainly didn't reflect any version of love, even unrequited love, that Bala recognized. *What's going on with that boy?*

Suddenly, Faye started to jog ahead.

Startled, Song and Walking Flower tried to keep pace and shoved past Bala in their haste.

Before he realized what was happening, the whole assembly had started to run. And, just as suddenly, they stopped.

Sprawled on the ground, Taug's tentacles were splayed at all angles from his body, his feet, free of boots, were limp and relaxed. Not quite naked, he was as close as a Cresta could get without upsetting delicate feelings.

An arrangement of animals surrounded and sat upon the prone figure. An elk reclined to the side with his legs folded under him, a large owl perched on Taug's shoulder, a crow rested comfortably on his middle, a hedgehog standing on his hind legs appeared to be studying his eyes, and a killdeer crisscrossed the area in grand sweeps, screaming as she went, "Bigger isn't better, ya know!"

As the arriving assembly arranged itself around the scene, Bala scanned the area. *Where is Squire?* His heart began to pound. *I can't believe I need the advice of a squirrel, but...* In all honesty, he hadn't a clue what to do next.

Wonderfully, Squire raced down from an oak tree, ran right to Bala, and then, without warning, scurried up his body and onto his shoulder.

So shocked by the swift maneuver, Bala hardly registered the tickle of Squire's whiskers on his neck.

Squire whispered into Bala's ear. "Don't worry. The Cresta is safe. We're just studying him."

Bala attempted to look at Squire's face to determine if the quadruped was pulling his leg but that proved impossible.

Cerulean stepped forward and crouched at Taug's side. "You want to explain, or shall we ask the Killdeer?"

A harrumph and Taug started to rise. The animals positioned themselves to the side.

In a matter of moments, two distinct lines had formed: Bala, with Squire riding his shoulder, stood with Roux, Walking Flower, Faye, Song, Lang, and Riko. A short distance away stood the elk with all three birds perched on his back and the hedgehog leaning on his front left leg.

Cerulean and Taug stood between the two groups.

For a moment, no one spoke.

Finally, Taug swept his tentacles out as if embracing the divided assembly. "This is all my fault, and I wish to make amends." He turned toward the animals. "I created Relevance to support a friend and satisfy my scientific curiosity. Now, apparently, he is doing much the same thing. I don't know anything about his associate, Dr. Anzi, beyond his public profile, but I suspect that he has hidden motives for engineering animal-human hybrids. I wish I could say it was all to the good, but I have my doubts." He dropped his tentacles to his sides. "I never asked Herson or Relevance this question, but it's an important one, so I ask you all now: why are you here?"

In bewildered silence the animals looked at each other, confusion in their eyes. A tremor shimmered over Squire, putting Bala more on edge than ever.

Cerulean flapped his arms in apparent annoyance. "That's a great question, Taug, but one that we could all ask ourselves! Why are aliens on Newearth? Why humans? What makes it right that we are here?" He shook his head. "No one can answer *why* we are here. We are. That's what matters."

Suddenly Squire piped up, "But that's not completely true. Before he freed me, Relevance said, 'Show us what human means. Our bodies do not define us. Help us understand what does.' Relevance wants to discover true humanity." Bracing himself against Bala's head with one arm, Squire rose on his hind legs. "Dr. Anzi is a remnant of the original human race that was abandoned by those who went off-world. He thinks that Relevance's dream will prove his nightmare, that there haven't been any true humans since his people lived on OldEarth, before they were decimated by disease and invaders. When he dies, the last of the true human lineage passes away. So, we"—he waved to the animal assembly—"are here to prove that human identity exists beyond our physical form."

Bala exhaled a low whistle. So many pieces fell into place that his knees felt weak with the weight of it all. No words formed on his lips, but David's troubled expression rose again, sending cold shafts through his body.

Song clasped her hands together in prayer and started to withdraw, pacing away.

Faye called out, "Where are you going? We need your wisdom and advice."

Song shook her head as she proceeded to the open field. "I must spend time in prayer and deep thought. There are no quick answers; we will have more questions before this matter is resolved."

Her face contorted, Faye pounded up to Cerulean and glared at him. "This question has already been resolved! We are shape-shifters, remember? Our bodies never defined us. No one thought we were less because we could appear as an arachnid or an elf. Our spirits make us who we are."

Walking Flower lifted one slim hand. "Oh, but your shape-shifting did help to define you. You've been hunted mercilessly for your special abilities. Your pacific nature, probably because of your physical freedom, nearly spelled your doom."

Lang stepped forward. "She's right, Faye. Ingots have been trying for years to improve our physical condition, changing the heart of us, nearly destroying any hope of decency within us." She shrugged. "For our foolishness, we nearly went extinct…remember?" She jutted her chin at Taug. "If it hadn't been for people like Taug, despite his wanton disregard for personal rights, we would have been decimated to the point of no return."

Riko snorted. "Never ceases to amaze me how even the worst crimes can lead to some measure of good. Look at me. I'm Newearth's best cook because a civil war sent me far from home."

Bala felt his heart squeezing like a vice in his chest. His words rose like a murmured prayer. "Even the most bitter fruit can be sweetened." *Takes a hell of a lot of sweeteners sometimes…*

The elk stomped his foot, sending the birds into flight. "I am Elch, and I live free. In the woodlands, we make our home. Go away and leave us alone!"

The owl landed in a pine tree and hooted, "I am Tyto, and I live free."

The crow squawked from another branch, "I am Branoc, and I live free."

The Killdeer dove in low, swooped over Cerulean's head, and then landed on Elch's back. "I am Chiara. Leave us be!"

Bala gazed down at Urchin who seemed to hesitate between the two assemblies. All eyes focused on him, waiting.

Finally, Urchin rose on his hind legs and lifted one arm. "I am Animan—from both worlds. Do not leave me alone."

In a startling move, Squire raced down Bala's body and scampered over to Urchin. The two animals stood together, apart from the rest. Squire's bright eyes glittered in the morning light. "Like you, we have free will. That is what defines us and answers your question, Taug. We are here to make something of ourselves."

Bala felt tears building in his eyes. *If only…*

In unspoken agreement, the assembly broke up.

Faye and Walking Flower joined Song in the distant field; Elch galloped deeper into the woods, with Chiara, Branoc, and Tyto flying alongside.

Riko announced to the air, “I had better be going. Jayla’s going to have my head if I don’t help with rush hour.”

Lang patted him on the shoulder and followed him back to the main path.

Roux stepped up to Cerulean, rubbing his chin thoughtfully. “This is one for *all* the Supreme Judges to consider. I’m not sure of our part to play. We’ll just have to see what happens.” He glanced over his shoulder and lowered his voice. “They’ll probably die out soon enough. And who would want to repeat a dead-end experiment?”

When Roux blinked away, Bala sighed in relief.

Taug stood chatting with Squire and Urchin, a strange sight considering their height differences.

Cerulean met Bala’s gaze and held it a moment, seeming to comprehend the wretchedness twisting Bala’s gut. After an understanding nod, Cerulean strolled over to the small group and clapped his hands, forcing a cheerful demeanor. “Who wants a bracing cup of tea?” With an amazing lack of formality, Cerulean scooped Urchin in his arms, and Squire climbed onto Taug’s shoulder. In quiet conversation, the foursome headed back to the path.

Alone, Bala waited till all was quiet in the woodlands. He looked into the bright blue sky and asked the only question that really mattered to him, “In this crazy mess, what will happen to my son?”

—Vandi, The Breakfastnook Café—

Kendra sat in a red vinyl booth near the front door and patted Justine’s hand, pity and gratitude pouring from her soul, though her eyes kept glancing at the doorway. Her heart yearned for David to walk through. "Thank you for arranging this, especially considering everything..."

Justine nodded, her fingers playing with the napkin dispenser. "I had to chase him down three times, but when I got Variant involved, he finally capitulated."

Kendra was pretty sure that her heart stopped beating at Variant's name, but she covered her confusion with casual indifference. "The crossbreed with snakeskin?" She shook her head. "I can't imagine what David sees in her."

Frowning, Justine shoved the dispenser back into its proper position and sat up. "I've never known you to be cruel, Kendra."

Her vision blurry with tears, Kendra started reciting the multiplication tables in her head, anything to regain control of her emotions. "I'm not, normally." She almost murmured, "Wait till you have kids," but caught herself just in time. Deflection was often a good option. "How are you doing…handling things, I mean."

Justine's jaw hardened; her words became clipped. "Things? Like my daughter's death?"

Oh, Lord, where do I go now?

Just then, the door chime tinkled, and David edged his way into the diner, followed by two heavily armed Interventionists.

Kendra's heart pounded back to life and nearly burst through her chest. She glared at Justine. "What's going on? I thought we were going to talk with David alone, make him see sense so he could turn himself in?"

Her gaze as direct as a laser, Justine slowly shook her head. "There's no talking sense to someone under the influence of Blandish." She craned her neck to peer beyond the incoming assembly and frowned.

Kendra jumped to her feet and turned around just in time to see her eldest daughter, Rachel, a doctor at Vandi Medical Complex, step in behind the Interventionists. Uncertain of where to direct her words, Kendra focused her attention on the one who needed her most. "David! You're worn out." She lifted her arms, beseeching a hug.

His shoulders slumped, eyes red-rimmed and unfocused, hair matted and clothes filthy, David looked as if he had been sleeping under a park bench.

Rachel slipped past the well-placed Interventionists and positioned herself between her brother and her mother. Only a quick glance acknowledged Justine. "Mom, David's here to make one request. Then he's going into custody at Louie Medium Facility."

After a total blank out of about thirty seconds, Kendra's mind fell into sharp focus. "All right. I understand." She let her arms drop to her sides and stepped forward, ready to take charge of her son and lead him into a better future.

Rachel laid a firm hand on her shoulder. "Mom, let him tell you what he wants to say, then the Interventionists will do their jobs."

Her throat threatening to choke all life out of her, Kendra merely nodded.

Rachel nudged David.

As if speaking aloud took the last bit of his energy, David swung his gaze at his mother and let it waver on her face a moment. Then he forced out his words, "Let Variant go. She's good. Okay?"

The only image Kendra could draw from pictured a sly face wearing cat ears at some kind of costume party posted on an online public site. Whether it had anything to do with Relevance's new pet project or was just a weird coincidence didn't matter. The image had revolted Kendra then, and the memory of it disgusted her now. *Good? The girl with the snake skin and sly smile?*

Rachel's assertive shoulder tap forced Kendra to refocus on her son. His drooping figure and vacant stare bespoke a boy…a man…she didn't know. "What's happened to you?"

David's face crumpled into angry folds. "Just say okay!"

So low she could feel the vibration in her throat, she knew, in the dread of her soul, that actions have consequences. "Okay."

"Okay!" David swung his body around, a wobbly puppet on strings, and faced the Interventionists. "Let's go."

Kendra stood silent as the towering figures with her skinny son between them hustled out the door. When the door shut, Kendra turned and glared at Justine, fury frothing over the edge of her control. "What have you done? I could've talked to him, given him advice, gotten a good lawyer to see that proper protocol was followed. God knows what will happen to him now!"

Her eyes filled with pity, Justine slipped from the booth, stepped up, and placed her hand gently on Kendra's shoulder. "You lost your son over a year ago; we just didn't realize it. You're right, only God knows." Her back as straight as ever, Justine followed the established pattern and strode out the door.

Frozen in place, uncaring that a room full of customers stared with gaping curiosity, Kendra could not decide what to do. Stepping out the door seemed an impossibility. She might see David being loaded into a Penal wagon. *Then what? Scream? Cry?*

"Sit down, Mom." Rachel's hand guided her to the booth.

Kendra managed to reposition herself on the slick vinyl without turning into a puddle.

"Justine called me when she made the arrangements with Commander Steadfast: David had to come in on his own volition and be taken into custody to await trial without any unnecessary drama. He'll be evaluated for drug addiction and a medical response team will work out a primary healthcare plan." Rachel leaned in and stared hard into her mother's eyes. "Justine had to practically beg to be allowed to bring David here first. He wanted to see you one last time. Justine knew that it would nearly kill you if you didn't see him before he went in."

The words "one last time" rang in Kendra's ears like alarm bells. "Last time? I'll see him at the trial. I'll testify on his behalf!"

Rachel reached out and squeezed her mom's hand. "No, that's not how it works. David broke very serious Inter-Alien Alliance laws. There's no doubt about it. His fingerprints are all over everything. Between the treason charges and his heavy addiction to Blandish, an illegal substance abuse charge, he won't be allowed to have contact with anyone from his past life for the next two years at least."

All breath gone; Kendra was certain she could collapse. "What? That's ridiculous. He needs me now more than ever! He needs his family."

Rachel leaned back with a long sigh. "We didn't see this coming. I was busy at work. Everyone was busy. Too busy, maybe. Variant filled a need and so did the drug."

Rage lashed out, and Kendra slapped the table. "I am not to blame! I loved that boy with every fiber of my being. I love all my kids. So does your father. Don't lay this on us, as if we failed to satisfy some fundamental urge, and he was driven to reckless behavior."

Blinking back tears, Rachel stared at her mother. "I don't know what to say. I can't fix this or make it easier. The head of my department understands, so he might allow me some latitude in following David's case. At least we'd know what is going on with him, though privacy laws are strict." She pulled her datapad from a jacket pocket. "I'm calling Dad. He needs to know what's going on. Maybe he can swing by here and pick you up. I have to head back to work."

Wobbly, Kendra rose to her feet. She half wondered if she had been covertly zapped with a stun gun. "Don't bother. He's with Cerulean in Aram County, trying to figure out what Relevance has done to the animal population up there." Forcing her feet toward the door, she refused to acknowledge the sympathetic glances around her. "I'll explain everything when he comes home tonight."

Rachel slid out of the booth and stood aside as her mom opened the door. “Then what?”

“We’ll cry ourselves to sleep.”

Chapter Four

No Body Is Perfect

—Aram County, Relevance's House—

May, Year 74, Newearth Reckoning

Relevance swatted a carpenter bee aside as he leaned against his porch railing; Variant stood to the left, in a patch of shade, with an OldEarth D Z Strad violin cradled in her arms. He refused to reach for the precious instrument, knowing perfectly well that she was using it as ransom for the information she wanted. Still, his body tensed with heightened awareness that she might not like what he said, and the violin would pay the price of her wrath.

"Why do you want me to go? I don't like school. Never did. Even the Ingot tutors were a bore. I learned what I needed and got free. Why make me go back?"

Forcing himself to keep his eyes on Variant and not flicker toward the instrument, Relevance kept his voice calm. Even a hint of cajoling could send her into a rage. "It's not like the schools you went to as a child. This is an art academy." He leveled his gaze and tried to penetrate her demanding stare. "You have talent, Variant. Hidden under your confusion and obstinate fury, a spark of something glorious shines. I want you to discover what that is and how to best utilize it."

"Utilize something glorious?" She shook her head, closed the distance between them, and then lifted the violin in a disinterested offering. "You may be smart, tribrid, but you're not very clear."

Relief flowing over him, Relevance accepted the violin.

With a smile, Variant seemed to perceive his anxiety. "Don't worry. I wouldn't have smashed it or anything. I like listening to you play."

Compelled to check the strings, Relevance tried to maintain interest on the conversation. "That's why you should go to the art school. It's run by Bhuaci artists and if there is anyone in the universe who could help you discover your inner nature it would be them. The fact that you can appreciate music suggests that there is more to you than the eye can see."

A sniff and Variant retreated to the steep porch steps. "Not just a snake-skinned girl with only one good eye?"

Startled, Relevance looked up. "They may be mismatched but—"

"But nothing. I never did understand depth perception. It was David who realized the truth. He had me cover one eye at a time, and—lo and behold—one eye works, the other doesn't."

Torn by the desire to play his violin in peace and the shattering need to grab the poor creature before him and offer a comforting embrace, he simply stared at her, unblinking, as if some mysterious force would tell him what to do next.

She waved him off. "I honestly never noticed, and no one else cared. Only David. He talked about an Ingot implant, but I don't want one."

His gaze shifting between the brown and the blue eye, Relevance couldn't discern which one was blind. It should be obvious. But it wasn't. "Your strength of will could make you a powerful artist even with a disability." He shrugged and dropped his gaze, embarrassed by his inept probing. "Besides, you might learn more than you realize. There's a connection between art and something greater in the universe, a mystery beyond comprehension. I think Zara and her parents discovered it. That's how they bonded, even though they were so…"

"Unhuman?"

For a split second, Relevance pictured the DNA sequences buried within the two androids and the combined Human-Luxonian natures that defined Zara's physical being, and he suddenly realized that their connection went well beyond a mere human thread. His heart began to pound with the same excitement he had felt when he first imagined his animal-human experiments. "You must grow up, Variant, and decide what and who you want to be. Exploring your deep nature, despite an imperfect physical body, means that you might go beyond every barrier that has thus far held you down."

With a look of disgust, Variant slapped the railing. "Just because some people don't like me hardly means that I have been held down! David loves me."

Blind fury almost made Relevance want to smash something. Only the long-standing habit of restraint and sincere regard for his violin held him back. In protectiveness, he pressed his instrument to his chest. "David is incapable of love."

"How would you know?"

Wishing to dismiss the entire conversation, Relevance lifted his violin and tucked it under his chin. Then he realized that he didn't have his bow. He glared at Variant.

With a child's teasing smile, she sashayed back into the living room and reappeared a moment later. She swept the bow through the air as if painting an invisible picture. "Truth is, I can already draw. But only someone who loves me can see it."

The violin back in position, Relevance held out his hand, waiting.

Her smile gone; Variant slapped the bow onto his waiting palm. "David won't do well in prison. It'll kill his spirit."

Relevance placed Pachelbel's Canon in D score before his mind's eye. Distracted, his words formed without being properly processed. "Why do you care?"

Her eyes widening, Variant stepped backwards and almost fell down the steps.

Once again, torn between desires, Relevance focused on the girl. "What's wrong with you?"

Variant swallowed, then exhaled her words like a woman gasping for breath, "I'm a mutant with only one good eye, and yet you, with all your advantages, can't see what's right in front of you."

Stunned, Relevance watched Variant turn and pound down the steps. He stood silent, unable to make the strings sing, the hurt in her voice resonated too deeply in his uncertain soul.

—Waukee, Clare's Home—

June, Year 74, Newearth Reckoning

Clare tied the last colorful balloon in place and turned at the sound of the front door opening. Her heart lurched at the sight of her son. Herson T. Clare was home. He looked so good! Bigger, more filled out, his face clean shaven, his eyes clear, wearing stylish shorts and a smart collared shirt, his muscled body appeared every inch the commanding figure of a Human Services cadet. Pride swelled her heart till it might burst. *How could I have ever believed he was a brat?* Shocked by her own thought, she brushed it away and held out her arms.

Herson, looking distinctly embarrassed, lifted his hands helplessly.

Unmindful, Clare hobbled forward and wrapped her arms around him, offering the best hug her frail body had to offer. "It's so good to have you home again!"

An awkward pat on the back and Herson returned the enthusiastic greeting. "Yeah, I'm glad I got home before the storm hit. Lots of rain for the next few days, they say." He pulled away and stood back; his hands slid into his wide pockets.

Mindful of their strained history, Clare led the way to the kitchen, eager to show off the magnificent dinner she had prepared. Never a great cook, she had taken lessons from the Uanyi Breakfastnook proprietor, Riko, just for this visit, describing Herson's favorite meals, and after much practice, assembled a variety of side dishes to go with each entrée for the week that he'd be home. The words *storm* and *rain* had barely penetrated her mind, she was so eager for him to see what she had done.

Once in the kitchen, Herson halted, his face blank. He looked at his mother, puzzlement furrowing his brow. "Where did all this come from? I thought I was just coming for a visit. Looks like you could feel the entire Waukee force for a month."

Clare's "Surprise!" sounded weak in her ears. She forged on. "I know how academy food is. Been there, remember? So, I figured you'd need something healthy and delicious to make up for the paltry rations they dole out."

His head cocked to one side, Herson's puzzled expression deepened. "On the contrary, I love their food." He shrugged. "Maybe someone from your era complained, and they improved by the time I came along." He grinned. "There are some cadets who skip home visits just so they can relax and enjoy the food and entertainment when there aren't so many people around."

This was as close to heresy as Clare could imagine. The academy served *good* food? And what *entertainment* could he be talking about? She grabbed a couple of padded mitts and opened the oven door; a spicy scent filled the air. "I bet it was Bala. He always said that it was criminal to feed Human Services employees slop, as if we deserved nothing better." She blew a strand of hair out of her eyes, shuffled around the counter, and placed the deep dish on the well-appointed table. "Not that Bala would turn up his nose at free food. That man would eat an actual cow if he were hungry enough!" She tossed the mitts aside and, smiling, waved to the chair across from her. “Let’s eat.”

Obviously unopposed to the idea, Herson slid into his seat just as a bolt of lightning lit up the evening sky.

Clare ignored the flash and scooped a heaping spoonful of the hot curried rice with vegetables onto Herson’s plate.

An ear-slitting crack and rumbling thunder shook the roof overhead.

Herson jumped.

Exhaustion making her legs weak, Clare dropped down onto a chair and waved at the other offerings—flatbread with sliced almonds embedded in the crust, Swiss-cheddar cheese dip, a mixed greens salad laced with feta cheese, and ginger ale with cranberry juice. Blocking the storm from her mind, she dove into the rice again and ladled it onto her plate. “Eat up and enjoy. I picked out three of your favorite action thrillers to watch. We can make a night of it.”

With the rain splattering against the window sill, Herson shook his head and then copied his mother’s example and plowed into the offerings.

Only when she was feeling sick from overindulgence did Clare shove her empty plate forward and lean back on her chair. “I made a dessert, but that’ll have to wait.” She eyed her son. The satisfied expression on his face sent a shiver of happiness down her spine. “So, was it better than the academy slop?”

A teasing grin and Herson rose with a groan. “I’d say it was just as good, and more of it. I don’t usually get to eat my fill, unless I—” Flustered, he cleared his throat and headed for the living room. “Leave the dishes. You can do them in the morning. We need to talk about something.”

Alarm spread through Clare. *Leave the dishes? Talk about what?* Reluctantly she braced her hands on the table and forced her unwilling legs to stand. Then she hobbled around the central fireplace and into the living room. She flopped down on a recliner next to the couch.

Herson took the couch and, bracing his back against the wide arm, stretched his legs. He smiled at his mom.

Giddiness swept over Clare. The soft pattering of rain on the bay window created a rhythmic backdrop to this intimate family scene. *This is what I've always wanted. I was never good with kids. I just needed him to grow up to form a real relationship.*

"Mother?"

Clare pulled her eyes away from the mesmerizing droplets smashing themselves against the glass. She met her son's direct gaze.

"I contacted Relevance some months ago, and he never responded. Do you know why?"

Clare's mind went blank for a moment. Then she forced herself to respond with a calmness she did not feel. "Why should he respond?" The reasons for his refusal were too numerous to count.

With a heavy sigh, a martyr's patience being tried to the utmost, Herson enunciated each word with determined clarity. "It was a very nice letter. Quite conciliatory. After everything that happened, I would think he'd be willing to meet me halfway. He's the one who tried to kill me, after all."

Still sluggish from the meal and her body weary from the extra exertion she had put into all the preparations, Clare wasn't sure she could handle this conversation. For the first time in ages, she wished she had a strong drink at hand. "He didn't actually try to kill you." She leveled her gaze at Herson, an edge of anger making her more forthright than she intended. "If Relevance had wanted to kill you, he would have. The Taser was set low, for a small animal, and it could only stun, not kill."

Unfazed by her revelation, Herson nailed her back. "That's not what you said at the time. Your claim that he tried to kill me is what got him sent off-world."

As if he had slapped her, unbidden tears and mind-numbing nausea rose in protest. “I was angry and confused. I tried to apologize to him—and to you—for my behavior.” She dropped her gaze onto her hands clasped on her lap, defeat grabbing her soul, dragging her into utter abyss. “I guess it was never accepted.”

Herson threw his legs onto the floor and sat upright. “It took me a while, but I think I finally understand. We weren’t the sons you intended.” He smirked. “I suppose that’s pretty much always the case. Parents conceive, children deceive.”

Bitterness filled Clare’s mouth. “Except I never conceived you, not exactly.”

“In your mind and heart, you did.”

Uncertain if the comment was intended to comfort or condemn, Clare trudged through the murky conversation, praying she’d find her way. “What do you want to do? Relevance hasn’t been in touch with me or anyone I know.”

“Not strictly true. He was working with Bala’s son, David. Word has it that David helped to spread Relevance’s experimental reports all over the universe. That kid is going to be put away for a long time—the fool.”

Clare pictured Kendra’s anguished face and a pang of sorrow pierced her heart. She wasn’t about to explain Cerulean’s plan to use David as a spy and how awry that went. She sighed at the need to compartmentalize her relationships. The less said, the better. “He made a mistake and is probably very sorry about it.” A new sensation wriggled into her mind. “Relevance wasn’t working alone. A man named Dr. Anzi put the experiments into effect. Smart as he is, Relevance couldn’t have done everything himself. He may think he is doing something good in the service of science, kind of how Taug thought he was helping the Ingots when he created Relevance as a tribrid.”

Herson’s head reared back. “You think that Relevance is innocent?”

“I think it’s possible that he has been misled.”

Herson rose and paced across the room. He stopped at the bay window and peered into the darkness.

Clare waited, her breath stilled, her heart unwilling to beat.

Finally, he turned and smiled. "I'd like to see Relevance again. Or at least get in contact with him. Maybe you're right, and he's been deceived. It's my duty as a Human Services detective and as his brother to assist him in his time of peril."

Clare brushed the inaccuracies aside since Herson wasn't technically a detective yet and only a half-brother, certainly never that in spirit. "In his time of peril?"

"You know what happened to David. Who knows what the Inter-Alien Alliance will do to Relevance once they get their hands on him? He'll be lucky if he's given a life sentence on Bothmal."

Stricken, Clare's heart jumped back into action. "No! He's not that bad. What happened to him, getting shipped off when he was just a boy, that wasn't fair. He hardly understood himself much less the people around him. Is it any wonder that he's trying to create hybrids? In a way, it makes perfect sense. He's trying to understand his own existence, figure out his identity."

"I believe that you're getting soft in your old age, Mother." Taking the sting out of his words with a beguiling smile, Herson chuckled. "I want to save Relevance as much as you do. Perhaps even more." He stretched and yawned. "I'm really tired after that extravagant meal. But don't worry about your wayward son. I'll track him down and find out everything I need to know. I may even have a word with his ridiculous doctor. The guy is ancient, I hear, and can't last much longer. I suspect that this was his last mad attempt at personal glory before he shuffles off his mortal coil."

"You're going to meet up with Relevance?" Clare winced at her anxious tone; all trace of irritation had vanished. "He might not recognize you." She shrugged. "Without our holopad visits, I might not have."

"No worries, Mother. When Relevance and I meet again, I am quite certain he will know who I am." With that pronouncement, Herson nodded his goodnight and headed toward his bedroom.

Uneasy in mind and body, Clare knew that she wouldn't sleep any time soon, so, with only ragged drops streaming down the window to mark the passing storm, she headed to the kitchen. The dishes might as well be washed.

—Aram County, Cerulean's Cabin—

Cerulean knelt in the soft, warm soil of his garden, dug a small hole, and placed the young tomato plant gently in its new bed. After patting the loose dirt in place around the roots, he surveyed his morning's work with pride—three tomato plants, one mild pepper and one hot pepper plant, two cucumber vines, two zucchini plants, a raised box with lines of lettuce and spinach, two barrels packed with strawberry plants, and one barrel of new asparagus roots.

The sound of voices, yanked his attention away. He straightened and looked toward the path leading from his porch.

Walking Flower stepped daintily across the yard with Song at her side, while Taug plodded along behind, his tentacles swirling as if to keep his balance over the uneven ground.

Cerulean rose to his feet, undefined fear filling him. *What brings them all the way out here so early?* The fact that Bala wasn't with them added to his unease. But then he remembered David's fate and imagined Bala and Kendra clinging to each other in mutual misery.

Though Taug was definitely the senior authority among the small group, it was Walking Flower who took the lead.

She lifted her long arms in greeting and then folded them across her thorax with a slight bow.

In formal respect, Cerulean tilted his head and bowed in return.

At Walking Flower's side, Song nodded while Taug came to a stumbling halt.

Suppressing any hint of anxiety, Cerulean spoke with hearty cheerfulness. It was a beautiful spring day after all. "What an unexpected surprise! Have you come to bless my garden with useful advice?" He braced himself. "I'm sure I could use some."

With a shake of her head, Walking Flower's expression turned from pleasant to somber. "I'm afraid not, though I doubt you need any help from us. No, on the contrary, we have come to consult with you about a serious concern."

His nervousness increasing, Cerulean rubbed dirt from his hands and stepped out of the garden bed. He would gather his tools later. Imagining a bracing cup of tea, the invitation to go inside stood on the edge of his lips.

Before he could speak, Song hurried forward. "There's an outbreak! Everyone is getting sick."

Horror filling him, Cerulean froze. Images of dying masses on OldEarth after the last catastrophic war squeezed his heart. He glanced from Song to Taug. "What is she talking about?"

His head hung low, Taug nodded. "Though it might not be as bad as she makes it sound, it's very bad, indeed. A virus has appeared on three worlds—Newearth, Ingilium, and Sectine. Though Helm appears unaffected, as of yet, it may take longer for the symptoms to show themselves there." He shrugged. "The Crestonian High Tribunal says that there have been no reported cases, but they hardly ever reveal the truth. Someone else usually does that for them."

All thought of a comforting cup of tea obliterated, Cerulean pointed and started walking toward his newly renovated gazebo.

The small assembly followed his footsteps in ponderous silence.

Once there, Cerulean waved to the plush chairs and perched himself on the railing by the single step.

In her typical stately manner, Walking Flower managed to bend herself into the widest chair while Song plopped down on a rocking chair. Taug hunkered down on a sturdy bench.

Crossing his arms over his chest, Cerulean tried not to let the ruin of his perfect morning bother him. "So, explain what's going on." He looked from Song to Walking Flower and finally to Taug.

Walking Flower spoke first. "It appears that the dissemination of the hybrid animal-human experiments has already had an effect. The drug used for the suppression of native biological systems, called Dumplix, has made its way onto the drug market. Though it is supposed to be taken under strictly controlled direction, those who buy and sell it have few scruples about following through with its uses."

Her head in her hands, Song moaned. "Though we haven't had any reports of adverse Bhuaci reactions, it's only a matter of time. Many of my people are children in spirit. Being shape shifters, they have a natural immunity to many biological diseases, but this drug crosses all boundaries. It manages to suppress the natural system, allowing foreign elements to take root within." She met Cerulean's gaze with pleading eyes. "Can you imagine what would happen to my people if our unique abilities become compromised? We might lose control. Instead of a mouse, I might find myself a mammoth!"

Taug shook his head. "It's worse than that, really."

Cerulean's throat tightened as his chest constricted. "How could it be worse than that?"

"When Dumplix inhibits the natural system, it blocks the higher functions. Base emotions and primal instincts rise while intelligent reasoning fails. It's what allows the animal system to infiltrate the human system. Foreign systems only work together if the higher order gives way to the lower, otherwise, rational questions might halt the process. Survival instinct must take over." He glanced over at his friend. "You'd become a mammoth with a dangerous attitude."

Scandalized, Cerulean shot forward and paced across the gazebo. He faced the tranquil lake, though he could only see glimmers of it through the leafy woods. "But that's not how it worked with Squire and the others. It was the exact opposite. Base animal instinct was lifted to human reasoning."

Taug nodded. "In a controlled environment with carefully prescribed doses. Yes, that is one effect. But without other supportive measures, including environmental changes, training and education, and a series of other altering drugs, Dumplix, by itself, simply inhibits the natural order."

Song jumped to her feet, wringing her hands. "And that's what is out there! Dumplix has been disseminated with some prescriptive directions but not all of them. And even if the whole thing had been sent out with due care, do you honestly believe that everyone would follow the directions?" She spat her words. "Of course not!"

Walking Flower nodded. "I'm afraid she is right. Experimental procedures are hard to duplicate even under the strictest protocol. In this case, there hasn't been the slightest effort to determine who is doing what with the drug."

His mind flooding with horrifying possibilities, Cerulean needed clarification as soon as possible. *Roux and the Luxonian Council must hear about this and form a plan quickly. Not their natural manner.* He glared at Taug. "So, you are telling me that a drug that reduces people to their most base nature is spreading unchecked throughout Newearth?"

His tentacles lifted as if in supplication, Taug shrugged. "If it is any comfort, it will probably kill its hosts before too long."

Cerulean pictured Squire's gentle eyes. "What about Relevance's animals? What's going to happen to them?"

With a harrumph, Taug shifted uneasily on the bench. "Likely, they won't survive beyond the initial stages. From what I can determine, Dr. Anzi—not a true scientist in my estimation—never planned on creating a new race of beings. Rather, he intended to prove a personal point. He couldn't have any lasting expectations. The experiments were too rushed and attempted too much. No biology can take such a high level of change in such a short time. It takes generations for evolution to take place naturally. And sometimes those changes are not what we expect. Not all adaptions are for the better, remember." Taug shook his head. "No, Dr. Anzi had no long-term, high-ideal plans."

Closing his eyes, Cerulean tried to get a grip on his emotions. He wanted to scream at the world and sob in private at the same time. This was not what humanity was for—to send a curse into the greater universe. Then fury sparked. Behind the image of the unknown Dr. Anzi arose the shadowed forms of the marketers who were making money from the drug. Did they care? He rubbed his face with his hands and sent a prayer upwards. *Please, help!*

Walking Flower's voice rose with quiet dignity. "You are Newearth's premier representative in the Inter-Alien Alliance. What do you think we should do?"

Cerulean opened his eyes as bitter gall burned his throat. "Find out who is getting rich off this drug and cut their supply." His jaw hardened. "Leave Dr. Anzi to me."

—Aram County, LEAP Laboratory—

Herson never felt comfortable in medical situations. In fact, his aversion to his scheduled check-ups became legendary. He had found so many inventive ways to bypass the recommended reviews that other cadets came to him for excuses to miss their own doctor visits. He rarely assisted. As far as he was concerned, other people probably needed to be checked out, and if there was a way of eliminating the unfit from the organization, he was all for it. But as for himself, he didn't need to be evaluated. He'd had enough of that as a child. Never again.

Using Geo-Tracking, rampant media rumors, and his own instincts, he was surprised at how easy it was to locate the LEAP Laboratory. That being the case, why had Relevance been left to carry on dubious experiments without Inter-Alien Alliance interference? Usually, bureaucrats got their fingers into everything. All appeared still and quiet as he approached the main doors facing south. Though a part of the structure was likely underground, the surface building didn't appear very large. He had expected something on a much grander scale to fit the imaginative aspirations of its creators.

A cold chill ran over his arms as he pressed the bell announcing his presence. A beautiful day, he should be soaking up the sun at home while Clare busied herself with mundane Human Services duties and preparing his next big dinner. He set his chin, imagining his glorious future as a leader in Newearth with a seat on the Inter-Alien Alliance Commission. His plan to rise higher than his history would never come to fruition if he turned away from challenging situations.

The door slid open, and a man in a dirty lab coat stood before him. Disgust filled Herson. With stringy matted hair, slumped shoulders, and a dull cast in his eyes, the man hardly appeared professional. *This couldn't be the renowned Dr. Anzi?*

"Yeah? What do you want?"

Bypassing formal introductions, Herson immediately realized that this was merely some minor attendant, maybe a lowly lab assistant. With his cheap boots and rough work pants, the man didn't appear well paid. Mud splatters on the hem of his lab coat and what looked very much like dried blood on the sleeves suggested a lack of care. Squaring his shoulders, Herson stood as tall as he could manage, threw his chest out, and made his tone authoritative. “I’m here to see my brother, Relevance. Lead me to him.”

The assistant’s scowl expressed doubt, followed hard by reluctance to do as he was asked. “Relevance never mentioned family. Certainly not a brother.”

Using his most devastating stop-acting-like-an-idiot expression, Herson clipped his words. “He has no need to tell a servant anything beyond basic instructions. Now let me pass. I can find him myself.”

Bluster had its usual effect, and the assistant stepped aside, merely mumbling, “You don’t look anything alike but you act much the same.”

It didn’t take long for Herson to traverse the corridor to find the central lift where he took a short elevator ride to the top floor. Using the scant information from the assistant, Herson soon made his way to Relevance’s office. Surprisingly, the door stood open.

Herson grinned. *How opportune. I don’t even have to ask for admittance.* He walked right in.

With his broad shoulders and large build, Relevance made an imposing figure in any space, but with only childhood memories to go by, Herson was duly taken aback. His brother was a formidable physical specimen. Then he reminded himself, *Well, so am I!* But the claim ran hollow in his mind. Annoyance sparked. He dropped his voice to the most commanding tone he could manage. “Relevance, I’ve come to see you.”

Slowly, almost as if Relevance had expected him—though how that could be Herson could not imagine—his brother turned and faced him. There was no look of surprise or smile of polite greeting.

“Hello, Herson. Good of you to come all this way. I’ve been waiting for you.”

His annoyance flaring into anger, which he had to force under control, Herson played along with what he assumed must be the usual lie to gain the upper hand in their intellectual sparring match. He grinned disarmingly. "It's been a long time, Brother. I wanted to see how you are doing." Waving one arm, he motioned as if to include the entire complex. "You've been busy, I see."

His gaze fixed on Herson; Relevance kept his voice even. "Yes. I felt driven, you might say, to accomplish something that would benefit the world at large."

Herson could not help smirking. He chuckled softly. "Oh, you always were one with grand schemes." He shrugged and pretended a humility he did not feel. "I'm almost finished with the academy. One more term and I'll graduate. Nothing as grand as what you are doing, of course, but, like you, I feel called to do my part for humanity. Must be something we inherited from our mother; don't you think?"

A light knock on the door turned their attention.

Relevance looked over Herson's shoulder.

Herson turned around, curious, but also protective of his back.

The assistant stood there, his arms hanging limp at his sides, his eyes dull and a frown of confusion on his brow. "Dr. Anzi called for you, sir, and said that he wants to release the puppies today. You should drop them off at the Amens' place. They'll take them in without any questions."

Relevance chewed his bottom lip. "You put the kittens over there just a few days ago. That'll be a lot of releases in one place. Might cause trouble."

Another shrug, apparently the assistant couldn't argue the point.

A long pause and Relevance seemed to be evaluating the man. "You don't look well, Jeremy."

In mute misery, Jeremy turned and shuffled away.

Herson refocused on his brother. "If you need any help, I'd be glad to assist."

It took only a moment and Relevance accepted the offer. He strode around his desk and headed for the door. "I'm worried about that man. He was never smart, but he's been moronic of late. Almost as if…" He cut off his words and stopped in front of his brother. He pressed his shoulder. "I know we've had our differences, Herson, but perhaps we can start again—to our mutual benefit."

A tickle in his mind amused Herson. Yes, that was his idea, too.

They paced together along the corridor and, with Relevance leading the way, soon found themselves on the lower level and in the central laboratory.

Once inside the large, brightly lit room, Herson came to a dead halt. His mouth dropped open; he had to clamp it shut and swallow hard. Never had he seen anything like this. Even Taug's laboratory, spectacular as it seemed while growing up, paled in comparison. Only some of the better-equipped Ingot labs were on this level. He shook his head, disbelief warring with what his eyes were telling him.

Relevance stopped at an enclosure with four large puppies frolicking about. One tan, one black, another marbled white and brown, while the last pup was as golden as autumn foliage. He hefted the tan one out of the pen.

Herson strode over fully expecting the usual puppy antics. A cadet friend had once brought him to his countryside farm and showed off their hound dog's litter, so Herson figured that he knew all there was to know about puppies.

The exuberant bundle of energy squirmed in Relevance's grip.

Without thought, Herson reached out and took the animal into his arms. "Where do you want to put it for transport?"

His gaze steady, Relevance stared at the puppy.

It took a moment, but the animal finally lifted his head and gazed back.

Relevance cupped the dog's chin in his hand and enunciated his words carefully. "You are going home today."

A cross between yips and words issued forth. "Me, home? Home, home, home!"

Herson nearly dropped the puppy. "It can talk!"

Relevance chuckled. "Not really. It only repeats what we've taught it. But he understands more than he can say."

Though Herson had read the reports and heard the rumors, there had been a part of him that thought the whole idea of animal-humans ludicrous. He was only interested in the drug, Dumplix, since it was a very hot item on the market these days and would go a long way toward padding his meager Human services income. But this? This went well beyond all expectations. A talking dog! Possibilities exploded in Herson's mind like a flock of birds released from a cage. *What the Ingots would give to have one of these to experiment on! And the Cresta Ingal? They'd do whatever I asked. My position on the Iner-Alien Alliance Commission would be assured.*

Relevance stared at him, his eyes narrowing.

Immediately, Herson hugged the puppy and nearly kissed it. Aware that he appeared to love the adorable animal; his heart pounded in excitement. There was no end to life's ironies.

—Aram County, Woodlands—

July, Year 74, Newearth Reckoning

Relevance, wearing shorts, a sleeveless shirt, and sandals, tramped through the thick woods, trying mightily to shut his brother's words—*perhaps we can start again*—from his mind. He swatted aside saplings sprouting from the rich soil below and vines dangling from the canopy above. Ferns and long grass tickled his feet. Shots of sunlight illuminated intricate spider webs woven with expert care. He grunted in irritation as an overreaching blackberry branch scratched his arm.

Weeks had passed and not another word from Herson, who had insisted that his family meant everything to him. "I won't forget you, Relevance. Once my cadet days are behind me, I'll come back, and we'll forge a new understanding between us."

Though Herson had been smiling when he spoke, there was a hidden meaning just beyond Relevance's understanding. A veiled warning, perhaps. But nothing happened to fulfill either a promise or a threat, so Relevance focused on the job at hand. He needed to check on his first releases. Dr. Anzi insisted that they were beyond his care now, but Relevance didn't believe that. As far as he was concerned, the experiment's true worth would only be revealed in how it affected the lives they have changed so irrevocably.

A scuffling up ahead and Relevance stopped to get his bearings. He knew these woods better than his childhood home, though the summer growth had added layers of texture. He frowned. Squire's tree should be just about here, but there was no sign of the workbench or the hutch. Scanning the area, he ignored the rising fear that he had come the wrong way. His detailed memory never led him astray. Yet—

Another scuffle with squawks, grunts, and even a large mammal's bugle call startled him. Leaves rustled in the branches ahead.

Jogging forward, Relevance tried to ascertain the situation. Was there a fight—on the ground or in the trees? Anxiety squirmed in his gut.

Suddenly, Elch raced around a large tree trunk and nearly barreled into Relevance. The emaciated animal stopped short, heaving gasping breaths, then snorted and pawed the ground.

Shocked by the Elk's ragged appearance, Relevance lifted his hands in command. "What's going on?"

Huffing, the formidable animal, spoke in guttural nonsense. "Birds be damned. Attack always. Claw and peck!"

His mind swirling, Relevance tried to sort out the situation. "Branoc and Tuto? Are they bothering you?"

"Doomed we are!" With that, he reared back and then, his eyes red and flaring, he dashed deeper into the woodlands.

"Come back here! I want answers, Elch."

The fading sound of hooves pounding away left a strange ache in Relevance's chest. *He didn't look well.* A vivid memory of his assistant's disheveled appearance flashed in his mind. *That can't be. Elch was given the full treatment; Jeremy was never—* Images of his assistant, with his usual lack of protocol, filling medical syringes with ungloved hands, rippled through his mind. *But a man wouldn't be—*

A flash of blurry black and the force of flapping wings pulsed just over Relevance's head. Instinctively, he crouched with his arms lifted in defense.

A dark figure landed on the ground a few yards away.

Branoc.

At first sight of the bird with piercing black eyes—much larger than they should be and with hatred pouring from their depths—filled Relevance with horror. The crow had grown to enormous size, bloated even, with its sleek black feathers glowing iridescent in the light. It marched forward, its gaze unblinking.

Without thought, Relevance stepped back, his mind trying to grasp the unnatural pace of the creature. *Birds hop and leap; they do not march.*

Indomitable, Branoc halted a few paces before Relevance. "You, man, be guilty. Amends we never see!"

Though stupefied, Relevance still had wits enough to know that he was being accused of something by a bird. His own creation no less. "What are you talking about, Branoc?"

"Chiara broken. Tyto old. No Urchin anywhere."

Too many questions crowded into Relevance's mind. One jumped out before he could stop it. "Where is Squire?"

"Family need." A squawk, and Branoc flew into the trees. He alighted on a sturdy branch and glared down. "Elch rampaged in woods, looking for doe. Your fault. Wrong woods for elk."

"So, you attacked him?"

"No stopping angry elk, save death."

Furious, Relevance shook his fist at the bird. "That's not your decision."

"No, it be yours." With that, Branoc shot from the branch and flew deep into the dark woodland interior.

His heart pounding, Relevance paced into the shadowed depths. Where was Squire? And what happened to Urchin? *Bothmal! Why didn't Dr. Anzi keep the electronic surveillance activated?* Then it hit him like a gut punch. *Because he never cared what happened after the initial stages. The Animans were never important to him.*

Of all the animals they had released so far, these two tugged the hardest on his heart. Why he should care so much, he could not fathom. There were countless creatures in the wild woods, and he had released dozens of animal-humans by now. Yet Squire's wise eyes and Urchin's beseeching face added speed to his pace. He called out, "Squire! Answer me!"

No response beyond the scurrying of small animals hiding from his scuffling footsteps. He wandered forward uneasy and uncertain until the sun peeked in the sky and a recognizable scream met his ears.

Chiara alighted awkwardly on a fallen tree trunk. Her feathers so disheveled, it was a wonder she could still fly. Even her head seemed off-center with a large lump growing on one side. She screamed, "Pity's sake, follow me!"

Unlike the usual complaints, the bird's command galvanized Relevance's flagging spirits. "Chiara, do you know where Squire is?"

"Tuto cares. Mate gone, young helpless."

The image of a young female squirrel hovering in the background—on a leafy tree branch or peering over the edge of a well-padded nest—rose in his mind. He sucked in a deep breath and braced himself as he addressed the annoying bird. "I can't fly well, so perch on my arm and tell me where to go."

Dutifully, Chiara flapped to Relevance's outstretched arm and landed softly. "Straight ahead. Old oak, newfangled nest."

While stomping through the tangled woods, Relevance tried to imagine how he would climb an oak tree wearing sandals. He spared a glance for the deformed bird on his arm, and a surge of pity welled inside. He wanted to ask what had happened but her squawk, though weaker, still broke the silence with ripping force.

"Here they be!"

An old oak, all right, a huge dead tree with the top half fallen over, leaving only a wide, hollowed trunk still rooted in the rich, brown soil. The top part, which naturally would have been left open to the elements, had been covered with a peaked roof of saplings bundled tightly with vines. A cleared path wound to a wooden door facing west. Two small windows carved on each side allowed the light of day to filter into the interior, offering a view of a simple room with a large bed and a square table on opposite walls. A braided rug of long grasses covered the dirt floor.

Relevance's heart swelled at the charming scene. Then, as his eyes adjusted, he discerned the occupants on the bed. One grown squirrel with bright, inquisitive eyes sat up against a bundle of feathers and two smaller shapes were enclosed in the circle of his forearms.

An angry hoot, and Tuto flapped down from a tall pine tree. "You bring medicine?"

Crouching by the window, Relevance lifted Chiara off his arm and faced the ruffled Owl. "I didn't bring anything but my friendship."

Chiara cawed and flapped her wings. "Small good that be!"

Looking much older, with tufts of feathers out of place, Tuto's large, golden eyes locked onto Relevance. "Medicine bring us alive. Medicine keep us alive."

Understanding smashed into Relevance like a body blow. Why had he not considered it before? Swallowing down sudden bitterness, he searched his mind for answers. "Dr. Anzi said that once you'd become sufficiently humanized, your bodies would continue the process unaided." Max and Justine's android bodies rose before his eyes.

His feathers ruffling, making his body appear much larger, Tyto snorted. "Bodies not produce what they not know!"

Damned by the truth of the statement, Relevance could think of no good response.

Movement on his right caught Relevance's eye.

Hunched over, Squire hobbled from the doorway, two baby squirrels cradled in his arms.

Relevance dropped to his knees, shuffled closer, and resisted the impulse to gather the small creature in his arms. "Squire! Are you all right?"

Though there were no tears, the grief that shone in Squire's eyes made Relevance's throat tighten with an awful ache. "My mate was wild-born and bred; she could not live in a house. Our young are weak, and I fear they will not live to gather nuts."

His chest squeezed by a vice that must crush the very fibers of his being, Relevance reached out and caressed each infant on the head. One tiny face turned, and its pinprick black eyes opened and stared back at Relevance. Then it smiled such a sweet smile that it broke what was left of Relevance's heart.

—Newearth Docking Bay—

Herson stepped into the brightly lit Universal-Foods Buffet and considered the bustling scene. He scanned the banquet hall for the Ingot and Cresta connection that would make this risk to his reputation worthwhile.

At least a hundred people shuffled by ornate food stations, showcasing a variety of culinary adventures. Signs in fancy scripts announced Cresta Sea Sensations, OldEarth Comforts, Bhuaci Vegan Dishes, Ingot Energy Options, and even, Sectine Assortments. Curious, Herson started forward, keeping a look out for the Cresta and Ingot pair. He had only seen the Ingot once on screen, and, though all Ingots tend to look alike, he figured this one would find a way to make himself known when he was ready.

The flow of the crowd carried Herson toward the Cresta station where a large tank stood by. Flashes of color darted about the sea-green interior. He stood on his tip-toes and tried to see over the edge. Sudden pressure on his back lifted him off his feet, and he found himself leaning directly over the murky water.

A pulpy pink Cresta face grinned at him from the side. "You want to pick out your meal? I suggest the Alpha Eel. So slimy, they slide right down any throat."

His heart pounding with the shock of being caught off guard, Herson snapped without thought. "Put me down, Cresta-Bag, or I'll put something down your throat that won't slide so easy!"

Duly dropped to the floor, Herson stumbled and then righted himself. He glared at the enormous potbellied, bio-suited Cresta in front of him. The rank stink of fish and the flaccid, pale pink face nearly made him nauseous. He wanted to strike out at the interfering joker, but a firm grip on his arm held him in place.

A huge Ingot, nearly two-hundred centimeters, towered next to him, one spike-gloved hand demanding his attention. "You lack courtesy, human. My friend here simply made a polite offer. You should be grateful he didn't drop you in as one of the menu selections."

The Cresta grinned through gleaming eyes. "I wouldn't really. Not until after we'd had a chat, anyway." His grin disappeared. "Perhaps you'll convince me that you are worth keeping around."

Looking from one to the other, Herson realized his mistake. *How did I lose control of this meeting?* He cursed under his breath as he smoothed down his rumpled sleeve and squared his shoulders in an effort to regain his dignity and some semblance of an upper hand. After all, they needed him as much as he needed them.

An empty table stood in a quiet corner of the room. Herson jerked his chin in that direction. "Let's go where we can talk, and I'll see if you're worth *my* while."

A soft chuckle and the Cresta nudged the square-jawed Ingot forward.

Once at a tall, stand-as-you-eat station, Herson pulled a mini-datapad from a front pocket and held it out. "Eye-scan first."

Dutifully and in turn, the Ingot and then the Cresta placed one eye against the scan and handed it back to Herson, who then read the result and grunted in approval. "All right, let's get down to business."

The Cresta glanced back at the tank. "Aren't we going to eat first?"

The Ingot's deadpanned expression alerted Herson to the similarity of their thoughts on the matter.

"Well, drinks, anyway!" The Cresta waved a tentacle at a harassed looking Bhuaci in elven form, wearing yellow shorts and a matching top, who quickly hustled over. "Three Bohemians, please."

A nod and the server jogged away.

Resuming his business with as much professional dignity as he could muster, Herson tapped his datapad. "Very soon the Inter-Alien Alliance Commission will prohibit the sale of Dumplix, so I suggest we make this deal fast. I have a number of resources who are willing to export it off Newearth where they can dispose of it at their convenience." With practiced care, he glared at the two with all the authority of the Human

Services bureau at his back. "I'd hate to see what kind of trouble you two would be in if you had this stuff on your hands when the Commission outlaws it."

A look of concern wafted over the Cresta, but the Ingot didn't flicker a muscle.

With a flash, the server was back, and three tall drinks were set before them.

Aware that he was expected to tell Clare all about his day, which he would fashion to his needs, Herson ignored the offering and rushed ahead. "How much do you have? I'll need a quality report to go with the shipment so my buyers know what they are getting."

The Ingot slapped his fist on the table. "Let's talk price first."

The Cresta shook his head. "No, we must honor the establishment by tasting their products before anything else." He smacked a tentacle to his cheek in a scandalized manner. "It would hardly do to start our transaction by insulting one of Newearth's most promising businesses." He waved his tentacles as if embracing the hall. "I invested in this project when it was only a poor Bhuaci's bright idea. Look around and admire what invention, hard work, and monetary backing can achieve!"

Clenching his jaw in impatience, Herson dutifully took in the view. It was a significant accomplishment, though the thought of working as hard as the Bhuaci servers repelled him.

The Cresta lifted his glass, poured a significant amount of the goopy liquid into his breather helm, quaffed noisily, and then hummed in satisfaction.

His gaze fixed ahead, the Ingot took a swift gulp of the drink and swallowed it in one move.

Fighting his instinctual dislike of anything unusual, Herson resisted pinching his nose and took a small sip. Amazed, he tasted it again. Delicious hardly covered it! With a snort, he imitated the Ingot and downed the rest of the drink.

Sighing in satisfaction, the Cresta shoved his empty glass aside and leaned toward Herson, a silly smirk on his face. "I'd like to know what your buyers are planning to do with the stuff. I've heard that it can have detrimental effects if used incorrectly. I don't mind making a profit off my work, but I would rather not release a universal virus."

Herson stared at the Cresta. "Your work? I thought Relevance and Dr. Anzi created Dumplix."

This time, even the Ingot chuckled.

His belly jiggling, Cresta laughed out loud. "Don't be ridiculous! The tribrid hasn't any real skill. Just lots of fantastical ideas. Dr. Anzi is a notable geneticist, but Dumplix was my creation. It's been around for years. We just never knew what to do with it until Dr. Anzi came up with a new combination of drugs to inhibit natural animal instincts and encourage human-like development. Though it never lasts long. Not without the drugs."

Sirens going off in his head, Herson jerked back, his breath caught in his chest. "Human-like? You mean these creatures that Relevance experimented on aren't true hybrid human-animals?"

Apparently out of patience, the Ingot reached over and grabbed Herson by his collar. "Time to complete our transaction. How much are you willing to pay?"

Choked by the Ingot's tight grip, Herson spluttered. "Seventy-five per unit, up to five thousand units."

Just as unceremoniously, the Ingot released Herson. "That'll work." He yanked out his datapad embedded in his wrist and began tapping.

Shocked by the easy acceptance, a flicker of doubt rippled over Herson. "How do I know that your stuff is prime quality?"

The Cresta pulled his datapad from his bio-suit pocket and tapped away, ignoring the question.

A buzz from his datapad demanded Herson's attention. He glanced down. The order was set. All he had to do was transfer the funds and complete the transaction. Doubt still nagged his mind, but the thought of the contacts he had made as an understanding cadet, who was willing to work a side business and wink at private enterprises, shoved all other concerns aside. He looked at the numbers. With his percentage, he would make enough to build a very nice home on Helm as well as have a beach house on Crestar. He hit the transfer button and signed off.

The Ingot shoved his datapad back into place and started to pace away.

Startled by the unceremonious ending, Herson stared at the Cresta. "So, I can trust that my buyers will be pleased. The quality is good, right?"

With a hearty pat on the shoulder, the Cresta leaned in and grinned at Herson. "You'll know soon enough. I put a dose of it into your drink. You'll feel the effect soon enough, and all doubts will vanish!"

Herson watched the pulpy Cresta waddle away and knew without a shadow of a doubt that he should never have trusted him. Muttering under his breath, he fumed. "The liar, just trying to scare me." The savory flavor that had so pleased his palate earlier turned bitter. The only recompense was that he was now very rich, and he could honestly tell his mother that his brother was an absolute failure.

—Waukee Street—

Variant snuck around the quiet corner and pressed her body against the Artisan stone wall of the Grain & Feed store. She listened as footsteps approached, then dropped her gaze as Clare hobbled by pulling a wood-slatted wagon filled with overflowing grocery sacks.

Once Clare had moved on, Variant pushed off the wall and followed at a safe distance. What could Clare need with so much food? *She's only one person. Is she hosting a party?*

The image of Clare's grimace when she had bumped into her last autumn had haunted Variant's dreams all winter, through the spring, and even into full summer. When she had told Relevance about it, months ago, he had thrown her a birthday party to keep her mind from dwelling in dark places.

Only in her growing friendship with David had she found peace of mind. As childish as the guy could be at times, she reveled in her ability to monopolize his attention. That she might only be arousing his lust squirmed like a snake in the corner of her mind.

Clare stopped before her house and began tugging the wagon up a slight incline toward the door. A rock in the way, caught one wheel and stopped all progress. With a grunt, Clare tried to force it over the rock, but one foot slipped, and she fell with a yelp onto the wet grass.

Before Variant knew what she was doing, she dashed forward and snatched the rock out of the way. She halted with the rock still in her hand, suddenly aware that Clare was on the ground, staring at her, grimacing in pain.

With a grunt, Clare tried to stand, but she fell back, crying out.

Wordlessly, Variant dropped the rock and maneuvered herself directly behind Clare. She reached under Clare's arms and hefted the older woman to her feet, careful to keep ahold in case she started to slip again.

Wobblily, Clare gained her footing. She reached out and patted Variant on the arm. "Thank you."

A new sensation filled Variant unlike anything she had ever felt before. Those two simple words had more power than the rousing orations she had listened to in her Cross-Cultural Education class. She wanted to say something in return, but no words, nothing practiced or memorized, came to mind. She had never been thanked before and had no experience to draw upon. Instead, she did the only thing that made any sense. She strode over to the wagon, lifted two of the shopping bags in her arms, and waited for Clare to lead her inside the house.

In some unspoken understanding, Clare turned and hobbled to the door. She placed her hand on the key-code, and the door opened automatically.

Dutifully, Variant went back and forth, carrying all four bags into the kitchen; she set them on the counter in a perfect row.

With only a slight shake of her head and a perplexed expression on her face, Clare dropped her datapad on the kitchen table and flopped down on a sturdy wooden chair. She had watched in perfect silence as Variant placed each bag systematically on the counter.

Once her mission was accomplished, Variant stood in the middle of the room, her arms hanging limp at her side. She didn't know what to do next. Without premeditated thought, the question she had long wanted answered rose into the air before her. "When you saw me before, you acted repulsed. Why do I disgust you?"

Clare squeezed her eyes shut and dropped her head to her chest. The memory of first seeing Variant as a small child, being offered as Ingot sale item, and her instinctual reaction. She tasered the Ingot and refused to acknowledge the child.

For a terrified moment, Variant was sure the strange woman would start crying. The urge to run away nearly overwhelmed her. She swallowed hard and glanced at the door.

Then Clare lifted her head, tears in her eyes but not overflowing. "I am so sorry."

Once again, Variant felt her world shift. Four words, packing the power of an Ingoti Blaster. "You hate to look at me?"

Something between a groan and a cry of agony issued from Clare. A tear finally fell, and she patted the table, motioning to the seat next to her. "Please, sit. Let me explain."

Carefully, feeling very much like a wary rodent under the eyes of a hawk, Variant slid onto the chair; her eyes shifted from the older woman to a tear that had splattered on the table.

One hand rubbing her leg, Clare winced. "Sorry, but my leggings can only do so much. They certainly can't save me from slipping on wet grass." She locked on Variant. "I appreciate your coming to the rescue."

Variant nodded, waiting for more, uncertain of what.

Clare motioned to the bags on the counter. "There's a package of oatmeal cookies and a jug of cider in one of those. If you want to get them out, we can have a little snack. You deserve more, but I'm not sure what you'd like."

Oddly pleased with the offer, Variant rose and searched through the bags until she found the suggested items. Under Clare's direction, she found glasses and a serving platter in the cabinet. The simple snack soon in place, Variant retreated to her seat.

Clare sipped the golden cider and sighed in relief.

Variant followed her example. She also took a cookie and began to nibble the edges, still waiting.

Finally, Clare straightened and clasped her hands. "My parents died from a mysterious illness when I was young. I always thought they were poisoned by a alien who haunted my nights with searching questions. I grew up hating him, all aliens, really." She lifted her glass, took a calming sip, then caressed the edge with her thumb. "I was wrong. That alien, the Eternal known as Omega, was just curious about me and wanted to comprehend my suffering. He created Justine and Max and Zara. But he did not understand humanity, not until he was caught by the Crestas and learned the meaning of suffering for himself."

Intrigued and perplexed, Variant felt like a child listening to the stories the teachers told of OldEarth, the mysterious world of a bygone era. She shifted on her chair, letting one hand rest comfortably on the table, the other on her lap. "But how could an Eternal be caught and suffer? They are powerful beyond measure."

Clare waved languidly. "Don't ask me. The abilities of aliens have never been fully charted." She shrugged. "In any case, I realized my misjudgment—eventually. But it was very hard for me to accept." She took a deep breath and exhaled a long sigh. "Please, understand. Hating Omega shielded me from the pain of losing my family. It gave me a focus. As a Human Services Detective, I could right wrongs and protect humanity from villainous aliens infecting the planet."

In the most comforting sensation Variant had ever experienced, she felt as if her world was coming together, like shattered parts forming a clear picture. "So, you don't hate me for me? You hate me for being alien to you?"

A stifled gasp and Clare reached out, struggling to clasp Variant's hand. 'I never hated you!" Once again squeezing her eyes shut, Clare's lips quivered.

Variant watched, amazed and uncomfortable, but unwilling to move away.

Sucking in a deep breath, Clare opened her eyes, and like a fighter entering the ring once more, she focused on Variant. "When I met with Saran, the Ingot dealer, I had no idea what I was doing. I thought that my good intentions were all that mattered. When he tried to sell me the little girl—you—I was horrified. That's why I tasered him. But I shoved you out of my mind."

"When you saw me last autumn, you grimaced because you hated me."

"No, because I identified with you. I couldn't stand the idea that you had been at the mercy of that cruel, heartless alien, reminding me of my experience with Omega."

A long, silent moment and Variant tried to process what she was hearing. Finally, she frowned at Clare. "But you said that Omega wasn't bad." A lump she could not swallow down rose in her throat. "Saran was very bad."

Clare clasped Variant's hand between her own. "Can you ever forgive me?"

"You didn't actually *do* anything."

Clare nodded. "Exactly."

In the most shocking reversal, Variant felt a tear slip down her face. "You hurt too much to care."

Wordless pleading in Clare's eyes spoke for her.

The strangest sense of wholeness filled Variant, and she felt a smile spread over her face. "Yes, I forgive you."

The afternoon waned as the two women unpacked the grocery bags and put everything neatly away. Then Clare led Variant to the living room and showed off pictures in her photo album. Her cat, Jillian, wandered in and leaped onto the couch, startling Variant. Clare laughed and made proper introductions. The feline just stared impassively.

Variant had seen plenty of cats from a distance, but she had never petted one before. She found the sensation strangely comforting, especially when it began to purr.

As the sun set, spreading pink and purple hues across the horizon, Clare struggled to her feet and hobbled back into the kitchen. She murmured as she went, "I suppose you'll be wanting your supper." She pointed at the cat shadowing her steps. "I mean her, not you, though I'd be happy to fix something for the both of us." She grabbed her datapad off the table and tapped it to life. "What do you like to eat?"

Unsettled by the question, Variant shrugged. "Anything."

Clare glanced over. "No, I mean it. I've got thousands of recipes and a variety of ingredients; I can make a whole slew of different dishes. Herson is supposed to visit again soon, so I wanted to be ready." She eyed Variant, a smile hovering on her lips. "I'd be happy to have you stay. I enjoy your company."

Flummoxed by this unexpected turn of events, Variant struggled to answer the simple question. "I don't know what I like. Only David ever asked."

Clare paused, her datapad gripped tight, her eyes narrowing. "David? You mean Bala's son, David?"

Sadness plunged her spirits and Variant nodded.

Abruptly changing direction, Clare yanked a cutting board from behind a stack of pans. "Here, you cut vegetables, and I'll get the pasta and tomato sauce ready. I make a wonderful spaghetti with mushroom veggie balls. Kendra taught me. Lots of cumin and turmeric, works wonders on inflammation."

Figuring that healthy food was always beneficial, Variant accepted the cutting board, retrieved tomatoes, red and green peppers, mushroom paste, onions, garlic, and enough seasonings to spice up a Bhuaci festival. Inclined to follow directions exactly, she listened with care as Clare told her what to do.

Clare hummed a spirited tune as she arranged a pot of water on the stove. Then she glanced over as Variant cut a red pepper into thin slices. "So how do you know David?"

The image of David's face flashed in Variant's mind, and she put the knife down. "He was working at the Docking Bay. Relevance asked me to compile a list of scientists who might be interested in his hybrid work, but I didn't know how to do that. I saw David at the com station, so I asked him. He helped me. We became friends."

Clare cleared her throat as she set the pot to boil. "You know what's happened to him, right?"

"Yeah. He's at Louie Medium Facility. Poor man."

"You know why, too, right?"

"Because he broke the rules."

Using the counter for balance, Clare stepped closer.

Variant met Clare's gaze, waiting.

"Justine and Max trusted him. He broke that trust. Relevance had no business asking you to compile such a list, and David should never have used his Docking Bay clearance to get you that information."

"It was just a list of scientists. There were no secrets passed."

Clare frowned. "But there were. Relevance used David to pass along his findings to God knows who. Anyone can now create animal-hybrids and do even worse horrors, using that experimental data."

Thoroughly confused, Variant shook her head. "Scientists have been using each other's data from the beginning of recorded history. It's how science builds on itself."

"But there are laws in place to protect the innocent." Clare's face darkened. "Look at what happened to you. Some knowledge-hungry scientist, probably an Ingot, blended genetics just to see what might happen, and look what he did!"

"I *am* bad, then?"

Clare slapped the counter. "No! That's not what I mean."

Anger warring with a need to understand made Variant bold. "Taug experimented with genetics and created Relevance. Is he bad?"

Swaying, Clare nearly fell over.

Variant grabbed her arm, keeping her upright. "Sit down. Tell me how to finish, and then we can eat." She pointed at the pile of cookies on the serving plate. "Eat something to keep up your strength."

With a snort, Clare allowed herself to be led to the kitchen chair, where she sat down and dutifully snatched up a cookie. She bit down hard and chewed thoughtfully.

Variant picked up the datapad with the spaghetti recipe and scrolled through. It had a lot of steps, but they were simple enough. She scooped the peppers into a waiting pan, added the onions and other ingredients, and then started on the mushroom balls.

After brushing crumbs off her shirt, Clare straightened. "Variant, you must understand. I love Relevance. I never thought he was bad. But in the same way I reacted to you, I treated him poorly because I didn't know how to manage my own feelings."

Her hands deep in a bowl of mushroom paste, Variant looked over. "So how I was created does not make me bad?"

Blinking, Clare seemed to be trying to catch her breath. "It makes you a victim. You should never have been used as an experiment. Your parents should have known and loved you."

"Many people don't know their parents."

"That doesn't make it right. Our parents are part of our natural heritage."

"So just my body is bad, not me?"

A huff and Clare forged ahead. "A body is just a body. It can't be good or bad. Either it works well or it doesn't. No body is perfect, though some people have more attractive bodies than others."

"I wish I had Kendra's body. Everyone loves her."

A slight gasp and Clare leaned forward. "Is that why you helped David?"

For a moment, Variant could not move. The thought had never entered her head, but then she had to consider it. She had watched Kendra for years, from a safe distance, admiring her extraordinary beauty and unique charm. But then, when David's face flashed back into her mind, she knew the truth. "David loved me right away. No one else ever did that."

"What about Relevance?"

A hot flush working over her body, Variant felt distinctly uncomfortable. She held up the bowl of mushroom paste. "What do I do with this?"

Clare rose, hobbled over, added oil to a frying pan, then turned the heat on low. "Roll them into small balls with the vegetables and add them to the hot oil. Turn them as they cook, and then we'll add them to the tomato sauce. We'll pour it over the pasta when it's cooked through." She patted Variant on the shoulder. "You're a natural cook."

Warmed by the compliment, Variant followed the directions and then blurted out her deepest agony. "I love Relevance. He is always kind and compassionate. He even promised to give me a piano. I learned to play the Moonlight Sonata perfectly because of him. But he asks for nothing in return."

Clare leaned against the counter; her hands pressed together as if she were praying. Finally, she spoke in a soft tone, "You have given me the greatest gift anyone could give a mother."

Honestly perplexed and strangely uplifted, Variant smiled. "How?"

"You told me that my son can show love."

Variant needed more. She waited.

"Maybe he will love me some day."

With a nod, Variant savored the smell of the good food and felt her heart fall into place. *Maybe we will love each other.*

Chapter Five

Only Hope

—Louie Medium Facility—

August, Year 74, Newearth Reckoning

David sat on the edge of his hard metal-framed bed, facing away from the transparent, high-voltage prison door and gripped a tiny cloth bag in his hands. Though drugs were not officially allowed inside the facility, there were always ways to get what you wanted. Using his code name, Goliath, he had paid a high price for this small amount, but it would have to do.

Blandish was not as addictive as some prescription drugs on the open market, but his need felt just as desperate. Without Variant's enticing figure to encourage him, he had no future to look forward to. His life was a hopeless mess. During all the time he had been locked up, she had not come by or sent an encouraging word his way. His counselor said she was not allowed contact, but he figured they said that to everyone to hold off the grief of abandonment.

He swung the purple bag by its little loop. She was the one who had introduced him to the pleasures of the drug, saying that it was just a relaxant to help him sleep at night. Perhaps that's how it worked for her. For him, it had a much stronger effect. His whole outlook on life improved under the influence. Without it, the world appeared as dry and lifeless as an Ingoti desert.

An approaching shadow and shuffling steps drew near.

David shoved the bag under his seat.

A large guard stopped a safe distance from the door frame and spoke with business-like authority. "Hey, Sullen, get yourself ready. The medic wants to get his reviews over before lunch." He pointed to a pair of thin sandals in the corner. "Get those on and be ready to hop to it in fifteen."

David waited as the figure plodded away. Slowly, he pulled the bag out and let it dangle from his fingers. His mother would be horrified and his dad would be disappointed if they knew he had even touched this stuff. But like Variant, they hadn't come to see him. Rules, the counselor said, to clear the body and the mind of all past influences. He snorted. *Can't clear out the past unless you take my mind out of my head.*

He bit his lip. Blandish was supposed to have special abilities if taken in the right dose. Maybe he would understand his family better if he could rise to a higher plane. He was too depressed to shrug. *Probably just another story, like the ones Mom and Dad believe in—religion, spirituality, higher powers—all that stuff.*

His fingers trembling, David opened the bag and, crouching carefully to obstruct any spying eyes, he drew the vial forth. He had no future and nothing to hope for. Relief—that's all he wanted.

The vial with its built-in injector twinkled like a ruby in the light streaming through the translucent door from the bright corridor. He looked around. There were cameras everywhere. He had to work fast. He tugged one arm out of his orange prison one-piece, slapped the injector against his skin, and ejected every ounce of a month's supply into his system. An icy cold sensation washed over him. Sighing in relief, he let the bottle fall to the floor.

As the drug infiltrated his bloodstream, weightlessness filled him. His body flopped backwards onto the bed.

Childhood memories flashed before his wide-awake eyes.

His mom was dishing up supper at the kitchen table and his dad was rushing in at the last moment, pretending that he wasn't late; everyone giggling and playing along…

The whole family huddled together, sobbing, after the Uanyi invaders had trashed their house; Clare's fists clenched as she promised to protect them…

Time shifted.

As an adolescent boy, he was traipsing after Seth, literally following in the man's oversized footsteps, on a tour of Aram County woodlands…his older brother's muscled arm pointed out a nesting pair of eagles…

Then, just a couple of years later, Barni leaned over his shoulder as he applied for his big job at the Docking Bay…

Suddenly, it was Justine's cold stare, though he also felt her pat him on the back approvingly as he turned in his first official report.

One stormy evening after work, Max, with his bland face, sat across from him in the Docking Bay Diner, attempting to make a joke. The hostess stopped and Max paid the bill. *Did Max usually pay? Someone must…*

Memories began to swirl like a kaleidoscope at high speed.

Variant's glowing smile.

The cute little talking squirrel… *What was his name…*

His last conversation with his dad, sitting on the couch, his head in his hands…his dad's grieved face…

Don't be sad, Dad.

Mom? What's wrong? I love you. Really.

I didn't mean…

A sick sensation twisted his gut, and his mind whirled chaotically. Unable to form words, he tried to scream, *Dad!*

He knew no more.

—LEAP Laboratory—

Relevance sat before his desk and ran his fingers through his disheveled hair, dragging long, unwashed strands from his eyes. Irritating bug bites on his feet and legs barely rose to the conscious level. He rubbed a day-old mud splatter on the edge of his shirt with nervous fingers. Though his stomach didn't rumble in complaint, he felt the light-headedness of serious hunger and shoved the fact that he hadn't eaten a decent meal in much too long from his mind. Obsessed to the point of near insanity, he stared at the last of one-hundred twenty-three files that he and Dr. Anzi had created. The same question he had started with weeks ago still plagued his mind. What had gone wrong? Why were his animals deformed and suffering?

Repeated visits to the woodlands only confirmed his worst fears. All of his original releases were dying. They still hadn't found Urchin. He feared that the hedgehog had been snatched by a predator. He leaned back in his chair, closed his eyes, and slapped his hands over his face. *I won't even be able to give the little guy a decent burial.* His throat tightened.

Before despair took him entirely, he dragged his hands down his face and rubbed his eyes, directing his mind in a more positive direction. At least Squire had not yet succumbed. Though the first baby squirrel had failed to thrive, they were able to respectfully bury his tiny body beneath the roots of the tree where Squire had met his mate, which was some comfort. The second kit lived on and had lively facial expressions that warmed Relevance's heart. The image of Squire caring for his offspring with all that paternal affection could offer made Relevance smile. He sat up and forced himself to focus.

This is all Dr. Anzi's fault! He said that they would continue to advance without further treatments. The absurdity of that assumption now struck Relevance as ludicrous. He should have known better. But he had trusted the experience and wisdom of the good doctor. He snorted and slapped his desktop, muttering under his breath, "Good? Hardly!"

Fear and doubt mixed with rising anger. Since he could not find the cause for their failure, he could discover no remedy. There was only one thing left to do. He would write up a concise summary and present the doctor with the facts. All experimentation must stop. With that plan set in place, Relevance snapped on the intercom and directed Jeremy to bring him some food. His mood equalizing with the hope of physical and mental balance, Relevance returned to his computer screen and opened a blank page.

After a well-rounded meal of mixed greens and cheese salad, three fruit pockets, and a large bowl of tomato soup with crackers, Relevance felt like a new man. His summary had been completed and sent. He stretched his arms over his head as he waited in the quiet laboratory for Dr. Anzi to arrive for their appointed meeting.

All the cages were empty, and the tables had been scrubbed clean. Sun rays slanted through the tall windows, cascading over him like a radiant waterfall.

Swishing movement in a wall-sized water tank at the back of the room caught Relevance's eye. He blinked. *What is that?*

He paced over, sweat breaking over his skin. A variety of fish and sea creatures swam about in the murky water. *I thought we cleared everything out...* Since he had never seriously considered bringing sea creatures to sentience, he was surprised when Dr. Anzi had added the enormous tank. But when he had asked Jeremy about it, the man had merely shrugged. "Just something to entertain the other critters, I guess."

Relevance leaned forward, placing his hands on the tank, and stared into the dim interior. His heart began to race. With great care, he tried to catch the eye of any creature that swam by. None looked his way. All appeared normal. Rocks, coral, a sandy bottom, a crab, a couple of starfish, at least one lobster, though he could just make out the tail of another near a big rock. Sea horses bobbed and a stunning array of angelfish and clownfish swished around. His chest relaxed, and his heart rate returned to normal. *They were just—*

Slowly, a sea turtle paddled forward, his neck stretched out, his eyes, heavy-lidded, staring directly at Relevance. Their gazes locked.

Relevance's chest heaved, and his stomach churned.

To the right, the lift doors slid open, and Dr. Anzi stepped into the laboratory.

Cold fury filled Relevance. He pounded forward; his gaze fixed on the man he once called his partner. "What in Bothmal are you doing?"

With a satisfied smirk, Dr. Anzi stepped around Relevance. He halted before the tank and waved at the turtle.

The turtle waved a flipper back.

Horror engulfed Relevance. "We were supposed to stop! I told Jeremy to clear out the last of the animals. It's over! We failed."

His head tilted, Dr. Anzi seemed to be appraising the younger man. A slow smile replaced the smirk. "There is no failure in experimentation. Even when things don't work out as planned, we learn something. Perhaps more than if everything went as expected." He placed one hand on the tank's clear surface and tapped, drawing the turtle closer. "I named him Saint. Get it? The initials for sea turtle are s and t, which on OldEarth was an abbreviation for a remarkable person who showed extraordinary qualities."

Relevance darted a glance at the sea turtle who had fixated on the doctor, an expression of devotion pouring from his eyes. A similar look of devotion Squire had once poured upon him. Suddenly, Squire's pathetic expression as his dead kit was lowered to the grave replaced all else. Relevance's body tensed even as adrenaline poured through his system. He reached over and grabbed Dr. Anzi by the throat. He shoved him against the tank and began to squeeze.

Instantly agitated, the turtle began to thrash about, its eyes wide and its mouth gulping convulsively.

Dr. Anzi slapped with his arms and tried to kick with his legs, but his short, flabby body could do little against Relevance's tribrid strength.

The side door swished open and Jeremy loped into the room, his head down. When the doctor gasped, the man lifted his gaze. He stopped dead in his tracks.

In the shocked gaze of his assistant, Relevance realized what he was doing. He relaxed his grip, though he kept the doctor pinned to the tank.

His large hands hanging limp at his side, Jeremy padded closer. His voice rasped, "Hey, now. None of that. We do what we like with animals, but there are laws for men."

Relevance released the doctor and fought the urge to kick the man as he fell to his knees. He glared at Jeremy. "Are there? Laws for some people, sometimes. But how about the innocent who fall between the cracks or are crushed under injustice?"

Heaving and gasping, Dr. Anzi struggled to his feet. His indignant glare landed on Relevance. "I have a legitimate license to practice medicine and run experiments out of *my* laboratory. You are little more than an apprentice with the intelligence of a Cresta hatchling and the courage of a human baby." He rubbed his throat. "You have no medical degree, no connections, no authority. Get out of my laboratory! *I* have work to do."

Caught off guard by this reversal—he had always considered himself the creator of LEAP laboratories—Relevance stood frozen, his mind tearing over the landscape of their association. Dr. Anzi had arranged the funding details and directed much of the building… He swallowed. *Did I only help in preparation and design?*

The fullness of his folly slammed upon Relevance like a boulder shattering a glass image. He ground his teeth, then spat out his words, "You used me! Because I'm a tribrid, you used my nature as part of the attraction, the reason why elite scientists would want to invest in a speculative field, in something that had never been tried before, because I'm living proof that the impossible is possible!"

Dr. Anzi's smug smile was back, and Relevance wanted to smash it.

Jeremy, apparently perceiving the situation clearly, stepped between the two men. "By all accounts, it was the two of you who made this place run so well." He shook his head at Relevance. "It hasn't gone as you hoped, and I'm not doing too great myself, but there's no reason to end on a bitter note."

His hands shaking, Relevance balled them into fists and shouted, "Stop the experiments, or I will go before the Inter-Alien Alliance Commission and report everything you have done."

As if he was tired of dealing with an annoying child, Dr. Anzi waved Relevance away. His head high, shoulders relaxed, and his hands in his pockets, he ambled across the room toward the door. "Who do you think helped to pay for this whole thing? Several prominent members of the IAACC helped to advance my work. They have deep pockets which they hope to make deeper still."

Relevance could barely process the doctor's words.

Not bothering to turn around, the doctor spoke over his shoulder. "Touch me again, tribrid, and you'll find yourself doing a life sentence on Bothmal." The door opened automatically, and the doctor strode out of view.

Jeremy laid a hand on Relevance's shoulder. "It's hard after everything, but you'd better go. I'll clear out your office and send your stuff wherever you want."

Relevance focused on the man in front of him, acutely aware of another travesty. "You are not well, Jeremy."

Jeremy nodded. "Dying, I fear. But I've never had much to live for, so it doesn't much matter. The doctor will find someone to replace me soon enough."

Swirling thoughts crashing against each other, Relevance tried to pull one logical idea from the mess. "Don't you care? About living, I mean."

With his lips pursed, Jeremy tugged Relevance toward the lift. "I never did, really. But, you know, my heart went out to that little hedgehog. Can't say why, him so small and helpless and all. But he changed me." He shook his head and stood aside as the lift door opened, waiting. "Time to go, sir."

With the bitterness of regret and the taste of gall in his mouth, Relevance admitted that Jeremy was right. *Long past, really.*

—Louie General Hospital—

Kendra sat hunch shouldered next to the low hospital bed where David lay unconscious, her hands clasped steeple style against her face, and stared at nothing. She couldn't see or hear or think. The only prayer she could offer was, "Oh, God, oh, God, oh, mighty God," repeated over and over again. She wasn't sure it counted as a prayer. She wasn't sure she was breathing.

Bala had held her through the night while she rocked in mute misery, but as there was no change and none expected, he went with Rachel to deal with the formalities involved in a prison suicide attempt.

Closing her eyes, she drew in a long breath and managed to sit up. She studied her boy, his deathly pale face and still form under the white sheet, his arms at his side, his feet relaxed, pointing away from each other. *No. He didn't try to kill himself. That's not David. He wanted relief. He always wanted to feel good, no matter the damn consequences. The kid would've eaten a container of ice cream in one sitting if I'd have let him!*

A gentle knock at the door caught her attention. She glanced over, barely interested.

Most of the other children had stopped by throughout the night, though Seth had been delayed by a problem in the woodlands and would be along sometime later in the day. After racing over from the docking bay, Barni had offered a shoulder to cry on. Rachel, who had been working at Vandi Hospital, managed to arrive at the same time, but rather than offering comfort, she gained access to detailed information from the on-duty nurses. She had reported events with concise professionalism.

David had been unconscious when the Louie Facility guard arrived to take him for his medical review, which was later than expected because the prison doctor had received an emergency call from his wife and left abruptly. It had taken the better part of the afternoon to find a replacement. By that time, David had been overdosed for several hours and serious brain damage had occurred. Though he was expected to live, his mind would never function at full capacity again.

Rachel had managed to remain steady throughout the recitation, until the last sentence when her voice cracked, and then she broke down crying.

Shortly after Rachel returned to her duties, Kendra's three youngest children, Veronica, Martha, and Alexa arrived, hugged their mom and dad repeatedly, cried copiously, and then left. There was nothing more they could do. They had work and lives to manage. David had always been beyond their control, and they had no illusions about him now. Though Veronica, who worked as a special education teacher on Teal Islands, had offered to "keep" David at one of their facilities, and Martha, who ran a daycare, had offered to watch him at night, Kendra knew better than to saddle their young lives with such a burden. Poor Alexa had simply watched in tear-filled grief. She was just starting her IAACC Law Program and had only her prayers to offer.

Probably the only good we can really do…

As the sun crested the horizon, Kendra hugged each of her children goodbye. They would eventually inherit the fallout of this tragedy but not yet. First, she had to figure out what David needed and how she was going to meet his needs herself.

At the repeated knock, she glanced over, half expecting to see Rachel with another update, but a strange woman stepped into the room. Immediately repelled by her physical oddities, Kendra stood up and braced herself. As her gaze traveled over the mottled skin, the mismatched eyes, the long flaxen hair, Kendra realized who she was staring at. She tried to speak, but no words formed on her lips.

Instead, the woman lifted her hands in surrender, her gaze darting beseechingly to the bed. "My name's Variant, a friend of David's. I just came to see if he's all right."

Kendra's voice sounded dead to her own ears. "He's not and never will be again."

That damning pronouncement didn't stop Variant. The young woman, seemingly pulled by an invisible cord, didn't halt at the railing and stare at the comatose body. She leaned over and kissed David's pallid cheek; one hand reached out and began to stroke the disheveled hair from his forehead, crooning a gentle song under her breath all the while.

Kendra stood back, dumbfounded. Then a question rose in her mind. *What is she?* Snapped words were out of her mouth before she could stop them. "Who is your mother?"

Clasping David's hand in her own, Variant leaned against the bed, relaxed and calm. The question didn't seem to startle her in the least. "I don't know my antecedents. I was conceived in a lab."

Finally able to follow a train of thought, Kendra pursued it with a vengeance. "Surely, the donors, your parents, left some kind of contact information—for medical reasons." She frowned in reflection of Variant's puzzled expression. "So, you'd know your family history, your genetic makeup. Full disclosure and all that, right?"

A slow shake of the head and Variant dismissed such responsible procedures. "My DNA antecedents were either paid for their service or bred for harvesting." She reached for

David's limp hand and then caressed it with a disconcertingly soft smile. "Not like him. He knows how to love."

A jolt of horror sizzled through Kendra. *Had they? Were they...?* She scraped her voice clear and tried to keep it from trembling. "How close were you two?"

Keeping her gaze fixed on David's face, Variant hardly moved, though her body conformed itself to the bedside like a comforting blanket. "Not intimates, if that's what you mean. We were friends. He loved me. I liked him." A pause and Variant sighed as she laid his hand back on the bed. "A lot."

Kendra felt herself pulled by the same invisible cord that had drawn Variant to the bed. She stopped at the woman's side, and they stood shoulder to shoulder gazing down at the pale face that should have been caramel colored with a hint of pink in the cheeks. She wanted to ask how Variant knew that David loved her, but it would have been cruel to inquire. *We're suffering enough, no need to add to it.*

In some odd way, Variant must have read her mind. She glanced up and met Kendra's gaze. "David was always kind to me. Once, when we were out having fun, my autoskimmer broke down. I knew how to fix them usually, so I got off and started to examine the machine. It was a hot day, and I was sweating. David pulled off his shirt." A smile flittered over her lips. "He held it up to block the sun from my face while I worked."

Kendra blinked back fresh tears. "He turned himself in because he thought it would please you. Did it?"

Variant shrugged. "I didn't want him to go to Bothmal. He always tried to please me. Like I always tried to please Relevance. David probably thought I had abandoned him. Relevance probably thinks I failed him." She frowned through a deep sigh. "What we intend and what happens are so very different."

Kendra wanted to say, "Not always," but the words stuck in her throat.

"I should be sent to Bothmal for bringing David into this mess."

In the first measure of decency in this hopeless situation; Kendra placed her hand gently on Variant's shoulder. "I'm glad you're here, instead."

—Louie General Hospital Café—

Seth stared at his brother sitting opposite him at the small, white table in the spacious hospital cafeteria and wished he could read minds. He fiddled with the coffee cup in his hands, his stomach too unsettled to tolerate anything stronger than water. Letting his gaze wander the room, he wasn't honestly sure he could keep water down at the moment.

Images of Squire, holding his small son, both cradled in Jeremy's arms, Branoc, Chiara, and Tuto, all perched on Elk's sunken back, and their grief-stricken faces when he buried Urchin's body would haunt him for the rest of his life. For once, Chiara didn't scream. Seth had wanted to, though.

When he had come across the scanty remains, he figured it was simply another animal killed by the manifest laws of nature. Then he saw the carved leather belt that Squire had given to Urchin, fashioned from material Jeremy had given him. It was a marvel how the animals communicated the sad news to the woodlands at large and gathered around in mutual support. Strangely enough, they even informed the LEAP laboratory. Apparently, illness could do a man a great deal of good. It sure had changed Relevance's assistant. Jeremy had cried when Seth lowered Urchin's remains into the ground.

Seth muttered under his breath. "Didn't think it was possible."

Barni set his cup aside and stared intently at his brother. "What? That David would end up in prison or that he'd take drugs?"

Seth shook off the brutal memories and met his brother's gaze. He couldn't read his brother's mind and, clearly, his brother could not read his. Before he could explain, a woman stepped up and pulled out a chair with calm authority.

Seth acknowledged his sister, Rachel, with a nod.

Barni sat up straighter, all thoughts of the woodlands and its suffering creatures shoved aside. "How is he?"

Rachel shrugged noncommittally. "No different." She set a cup of black coffee on the table and cupped her fingers around it as if she were cold. She glanced from brother to brother. "You have to understand, from what the scans show, David's brain was seriously damaged. Likely, there will never be any real change."

Barni's jaw clenched as his hands strangled each other on the tabletop. "You mean, he'll be a vegetable for the rest of his life?"

Seth's chest constricted even as his blood pressure spiked.

Her eyes narrowing, Rachel zeroed in on Barni and blasted him. "Don't you ever call him a vegetable!" After glancing around at the turned heads, Rachel lowered her voice to hard steel. "David's brain is damaged but he is still David—our brother. If his legs and arms had been blown away, you would still know him. Just because another part of his body is damaged hardly means he isn't human anymore."

Duly chastened, Barni scraped his voice clear. "Sorry. You're right. I didn't mean that. It's just an expression." He stared at Seth and then at his sister. "But you do understand what I mean? He's incapacitated for life. What will happen to him? Mom and Dad can't take care of him forever."

Seth exhaled a long breath. "They shouldn't have to. He is our brother, after all. Everyone needs to help."

Barni nodded, his shoulders drooping. "I have a full-time job, and you're away most of the time." He eyed his sister. "At least you work in a hospital and you can check in on him. Could David be moved to Vandi Hospital?"

Nodding, Rachel leaned forward. "I've already spoken with the doctor in charge and explained the situation. He understands that Vandi is the best setting for him. Once he is sure that David is stable, he will arrange transportation to Vandi Hospital, where we have a long-term care unit. Dad and Mom can visit as often as they like. Even Veronica, Martha, and Alexa can take turns. If we all do our part, then David will be well cared for." She gazed across the room, her brow furrowed. "I just wish everyone in his condition were loved as much."

The image of Urchin's tattered body rose before Seth's eyes. His stomach lurched.

Barni swigged the last of his coffee, keeping hold of his cup as if he meant to leave soon. "Are there many people in David's situation?"

Rachel nodded. "Too many." Her face hardened. "Those blasted drug pushers don't care what they're selling." She sucked in a deep breath and then expelled a dirty truth. "David probably just figured that more was better, would give him a stronger high. But the vial was laced with impurities. That's what did the most damage." She shrugged. "It was bound to happen. A person who plays with fire won't stop till he gets burned. But I'm convinced that this wasn't a suicide attempt, just a desperate act of an immature mind."

Seth squeezed his eyes shut as words eked from his mouth. "I should've done better by him." A hand pressed his shoulder and he opened his eyes.

His face etched with sympathy, Barni stared at him. "It's not your fault. Hey, I'm the counselor, and I didn't see this coming." His voice cracked. "Or rather, I did, sort of, but I figured that David was protected somehow. Mom and Dad tried to do everything right and…I don't know…I never imagined something this bad could happen to us."

With both hands, Rachel reached out and clasped her brothers' hands. "We have to help each other get through this. I know it'll be hard, but we'll do whatever it takes, not only for David but for Mom and Dad, too. They'll need our support." She glanced aside and back and then dropped her voice to a conspiratorial whisper. "I've even contacted someone at the IAACC, a drug investigator that Alexa heard about, to find out more about Blandish traffic on Newearth. Perhaps we can get funding to help other prisoners with the affliction so this doesn't happen to more people." She pushed back her chair, ready to get back to business.

Barni smiled as he stood up. "You're an inspiration, little sister."

Seth had to agree. As he climbed to his feet, he pictured Squire and the other suffering animals and, with a new plan in mind, his heart rose just a bit.

—Planet Lux—

Cerulean could no longer travel as he once had. His days of pure Luxonian light were long past. Though Omega had intended his hybrid human nature as an addition to his native Luxonian identity, like so many of Omega's good ideas, it didn't work out as planned. Progress always costs something. In this case, his human body weakened his Luxonian ability to move as a light being. He was surprised that the loss of his long-range transmutation abilities didn't depress him. He shrugged as he swung a bag of carefully packed herbal teas, baked goods, and a few new plants over his shoulder. *The human body offers more than quick travel.*

Stepping from the Ingoti trader ship onto the landing platform under the brilliant Luxonian sun, Cerulean waved goodbye to the disarmingly garrulous captain. He shook his head, amused at the incongruous nature of the huge, dour-faced cyborg who carried within him a carefully crafted sense of humor. *The guy must get lonely. Never knew an Ingot who could chitchat so fluently.*

As he turned away, Cerulean lifted his hand to block the brilliant rays of light and scanned the waiting crowd.

Roux, dressed in a shimmering white tunic over loose pants that fit snugly at the ankles, stepped forward, his arms extended. "Welcome home, native son!"

Glancing around at the varied assembly, Luxonians and aliens alike, meeting travelers from distant planets, Cerulean pursed his lips. *Look who's making jokes now.* He knew perfectly well that Roux struggled between dismay that Cerulean wasn't pure Luxonian anymore and envy that he, himself, had never experienced the joys and travails of a human body. With a surge of bitter-sweet gratitude, Cerulean dropped his bag, lifted his arms, and then clasped his friend in a very un-Luxonian hug. "It's good to see you, Roux."

Clearly taken aback, perhaps with the conscious knowledge that they had become a spectacle with gazes darting their way, Roux broke off and waved toward a luxury autoskimmer with an open trunk. He grinned to cover any hint of embarrassment. "I have procured transportation for you and your goods to my humble abode for the evening. Tomorrow, we'll convene a meeting with the other Supreme Judges to discuss recent events on Newearth. But tonight, we will celebrate the prodigal son's return with a welcome home party and a feast."

Covering a deep sigh as well as he could manage, Cerulean carefully laid his precious goods into the trunk and then climbed onto the autoskimmer. He never liked these modes of transportation and would have preferred to simply walk. Cerulean glanced aside as his friend blinked away. But then, Roux probably knew that.

—Roux's High-Rise Apartment—

Cerulean leaned over the balcony and sucked in a lungful of rarified air. Amazingly, his human lungs didn't seem disturbed by the scarcity of oxygen. He turned around and considered Roux's apartment with an eye for details.

One translucent wall offered a breathtaking view of the city with its numerous shimmering towers pointing to the sky. Flowering walkways connected carefully designed parks, learning centers, care facilities, governing offices, and businesses of commerce, so that the entire city was a tribute to natural beauty and Luxonian ingenuity. He had to admit, Lux had changed since he was young. In no small part due to its near self-destruction not long ago…Images of his son, Viridian, pierced his heart. It had been ages ago, but Viridian's execution would forever haunt him. Never had a son been more loved. Never had love been more rejected.

Soft footfalls behind him recalled Cerulean to the moment. He turned and faced the newest and youngest Supreme Judge in Luxonian history. "You look well. Sterling would be proud of how well you managed." A snort escaped before he could stop it. "He would certainly admire your dexterity."

An analytical expression, and Roux, for a moment, appeared to be a complete stranger. Then a smile spread over his face. "You know as well as I that dancing is a part of the job." He motioned toward a huge curved couch before a highly polished table in the shape of OldEarth infinity sign with trees growing from each center and the flat top loaded with a variety of dishes. "I placed the desserts you brought along with standard OldEarth fair for the enjoyment of the other judges and a few elders who can hardly wait to catch up with you."

A slight twist in his gut alerted Cerulean to his mixed feelings on that score. Old friends were often strangers now.

To get his mind off social anxieties, he pointed to the array of weaponry adorning the south wall. "What's with the new collection?"

A variety of swords, guns, knives, cudgels, maces, blasters, lasers, evaporators, and other worldly weapons hung in artistic display upon the wall.

Roux chuckled. "I like to advise visitors that I'm an accomplished warrior skilled in the handling of various tools of self-defense." His gaze turned sharp and serious. "I don't need to say anything. Everyone knows what weapons do and where they lead. I just want to keep a reminder in pride of place."

A brief flash of Viridian almost knocked Cerulean off his feet, but the swish of an opening door saved him.

One of the oldest Supreme Judges, wearing the traditional white robes that Sterling had so loved, strode into the room, emanating both vigor and authority.

Roux edged closer to Cerulean and whispered low. "That's Alizarin. He's the one you must speak with. Once he understands, the others will follow."

Cerulean forced himself to unclench his jaw. "And tell him what? That once again humanity had let loose horrific evil into the universe?"

Roux reared back as if slapped. His expression of hurt quickly morphed into determination. "No. Tell him the truth: evil haunts us all, and we must work together to stop it."

Cerulean nodded as his eyes followed the procession of guests streaming into the large, airy room. If only it was that easy. The last image of his son as his particles were scattered into the universe was replaced by Squire's sensitive eyes, pleading for understanding. Cerulean sucked in a deep breath of thin air and focused on his only hope

Chapter Six

The Price of Sentience

—Aram County, Woodlands—

September, Year 74, Newearth Reckoning

Squire, dressed in a comfortable pair of blue overalls that Relevance had given him to protect bald patches on his skin, leaned over his son's nest of moss and dried leaves in the bedframe he had set up against the south wall of his home and sighed contentedly at the small, slumbering form.

With all of his innate squirrel senses alert, he glanced around his living room. Broken shells, cherry seeds, plant stems, and other mess from their evening supper lay scattered across the low table. No chairs were needed since his son didn't understand the concept. His back aching, he tread carefully across the room, drew a tattered cloth from his back pocket, and, with a few swift swipes, cleared the smooth surface of crumbs and scattered bits. Ignoring the throbbing in his paws, he then snatched up his homemade broom and began to methodically draw the bristles around the mess and drag it to the open door. He swept the litter out the doorway and away from the neat path to his home.

A glorious sunset spread wide rays of pink, orange, and gold across the green woodlands tinged with yellow leaves. Evening birds chittered and twittered their goodnight songs. A chorus of frogs rose from the creek in a nearby field, singing a gentle harmony and soothing to his overwrought nerves. Industrious spiders awoke and climbed into high branches and started work on their webs, undoubtedly hoping to catch a savory evening meal. The last of the cicadas hummed goodbye as their short lives came to a seasonal end.

Soft chattering in a distant pine caught his attention, and his heart lurched. He knew that sound! Searching frantically, he finally discovered her, his mate, high in the branches staring down at him, her gray tail swishing.

He wanted so much to call her down, to make her understand, but there was no way. His early attempts had only frightened her from the nest, leaving him to care for their offspring alone and uncertain. She had returned several times, drawn by maternal instinct or some innate attraction neither of them understood. Squire sighed as he considered her adorable twitching nose and sparkling black eyes. She refused to move beyond the third branch, and his heart sank. *We don't understand each other…or ourselves.*

Flapping wings broke the moment, and Tuto's bulky body landed on the path in front of Squire. The owl cleared his throat hastily. "Two approach. Be prepared."

His legs nearly buckling with a growing ache, Squire winced against the pain and braced himself with the broom. "Relevance? Jeremy?"

Tuto's head turned side to side in silent denial.

Confused, Squire couldn't imagine who else might be coming. Dr. Anzi never came into the woods anymore, and Bala had stopped by for a short visit only the day before.

He heard crunching footsteps before he saw the two forms. One, a tall man he recognized, the other, a woman he had never seen before. He murmured under his breath, half aware that Tuto might not know what he was talking about. "Bala didn't tell me that his son was coming."

Tuto's feathers rippled as he prepared himself for an announcement. "Bala friend. Others unknown!"

After a darted glance at the swishing tail of his mate as she scurried away, Squire waved off Tuto's comment. "I know Seth. At least, I met him once, and Branoc and Elch say he is strong in goodness."

Tuto's eyes widened alarmingly; Squire could not guess why.

Seth's long strides were tapered to match the younger woman's more careful steps as the two made their way along the brambly path. His brown eyes appeared golden in the evening light, and a sparkle of something akin to joy emanated from their depths as he came to a full stop before Squire and Tuto. He tipped his head in a formal salute. "Good evening, Squire." He moved his gaze to the owl and offered another nod. "Tuto. I have brought a friend to assist you in your difficulties." He took the woman's hand and led her a step closer. "This is Rachel, my sister. She's a doctor. She wants to examine you and see if she can get proper medicine to help."

Before Squire could respond, Chiara flopped out of a nearby hedge, her feathers disheveled and a lump on her head knocking her off balance, so that she practically crawled to Rachel before dropping limp on the ground. A meager squeak rose in a sad reflection of her lost voice. "Help…me."

Rachel fell to her knees and began examining the pitiful bird.

Tuto's feathers fluffed. "She be damaged bird, not human!"

Seth crouched before the ruffled, golden-eyed Owl. "Rachel knows that, but she wants to help. She's been reviewing the files that Dr. Anzi sent out and, though she can't offer a cure, she might ease your pain a bit."

"What good—all die in wilderness!"

Seth sighed. He glanced back at Rachel as she tenderly lifted the frail, broken Killdeer into her arms. "Can you do anything?"

The grief in Rachel's eyes spoke for her. She shook her head.

Squire closed his eyes, fresh grief welling in his chest, setting his heart pattering at an alarming rate. A gentle pat on his shoulder opened his eyes. He met Seth's steady gaze.

"I'm fixing up a place at my house for all of you. It's not fancy, but it'll be comfortable and safe." He blinked as tears welled in his eyes. "None of you will die alone; what happened to Urchin will not be your fate. Not on my watch."

Limp in Rachel's arms, Chiara's head flopped to the side, her tiny black eyes, half lidded, seemed to speak with the old demanding strength as she glanced from Tuto to Squire. "Come, too!" she croaked.

Stiff-legged, Tuto strode forward and glared at Seth. "I go where she goes!"

With an accepting smile, Seth held out his arm.

Tuto hopped on, then peered over at Squire. "Take care of little one. We come back and bring you home."

Squire watched the foursome make their way through the dusky evening down the path to he knew not where. A spark of hope flickered in his chest as he gave one last swipe to a stray branch that had fallen on the path. The sun had set, and night was moving in. He must check on his son and snuggle in for the night, locking the door against intruders with vicious intent. But perhaps tomorrow or the day after, he would lead his son to a new home, a welcoming place where, when he passed on, as he soon must, his son would not be alone.

—Vandi Hospital Long-Term Care Unit—

Bala battled twin horrors—guilt and grief—as he made his way to his son's new accommodations in Vandi Hospital's Long-Term Care Unit. The broad, white corridor with windows facing south allowed a full stream of morning sunlight to brighten the distance from the nursing station to a line of rooms facing north.

He stopped at the half-open door with David Jha written in bold black letters on the ID plate. His hands shaking, he clasped them together and halted a moment to gather his strength. *Dear God, help me.*

Marshaling his courage, he stepped inside and then froze in place. There at his son's bedside sat the strangest woman he had ever seen. He knew about Variant since both Kendra and Clare had described their personal encounters, but he hadn't really understood. Their descriptions had fallen short of the physical reality. Perhaps they had not wanted to focus too heavily on her weirdness and prejudice him against her. *Don't they see how repulsive she is?*

Variant turned her head and seemed to study him as thoughtfully as he was studying her, perhaps with just as harsh an opinion. Unexpectedly, she lifted her hand and beckoned him closer.

Initially annoyed that a strange woman was beckoning him to his own son's bedside, Bala forced the grimace from his face and padded over. He stopped when he came to the railing. Ridiculous to put up a safeguard for a man who can't move. He focused on David's pale face, his closed eyes, and unmoving body under the white sheet. A slim oxygen tube entered one nostril. Another thin tube extended from his right arm to a humming unit hanging by the bed—fluids and nutrients undoubtedly.

"His eyelids flickered."

Jolted by Variant's oddly melodious voice, Bala jerked his head in her direction. "What?"

"He's coming up from the depths. I can feel it."

Attempting to transcribe her words left Bala breathless, submerged beneath fathoms of water, paddling for his life, desperate to reach the surface. He clutched the railing for support. He bent low and spoke softly into his son's ear, "David, can you hear me? It's Dad. Wake up and talk to me."

Variant leaned forward, her shoulder rubbing Bala's arm, sending the image of a snake wriggling through his mind. He glanced over.

Her whole face glowed with watchful care; she seemed unaware of his presence much less his reaction to her presence. *She doesn't care about me...she only cares about*

David. This thought so unsettled his mind that he barely registered her gasp. He returned to his son's face and shivered when he realized that David's eyes were fluttering. The man inside was still there, trying to wake up.

A strangled scream demanded release as he ran to the doorway and then raced down the hall, calling for a nurse, a doctor, a medic! Anyone to come rouse his son to consciousness.

Before he was halfway to the station, a male Bhuaci nurse in tall elven form with snapping gray eyes hustled up and gripped his arm, turning him back toward his son's room. "I just got the alarm. Let's go."

Dutifully, Variant stood back as the nurse and then a stout woman doctor arranged themselves at David's bedside. They ran through standard checks, their motions precise and well-rehearsed, like dancers who knew each step perfectly.

A soft moan drew Bala closer, his throat tightening and an ache rising behind his eyes. He should message Kendra…the kids…but he couldn't take his eyes off the scene. He had to fight every nerve in his trembling body to keep from jumping to his son's side and cradling him like a baby.

A soft hand slid into his own.

Shocked, Bala looked down. Variant's brown hand, strangely similar to his own, had clasped on gently. He glanced over. Her eyes stayed fixed on the bed and the bent backs of the administrating angels of mercy.

The moaning stopped, and all was still.

Bala's heart sank into a bog of despondency. David was gone again.

Variant's hand offered a tight squeeze and then let go. She stepped to the side as if getting off a bright stage and returning into the shadows.

The doctor turned around. He met Bala's gaze and stepped forward. "You must be Bala, David's dad."

Bala nodded dumbly, his gaze shifting to the white coated nurse who was busy replacing the fluids bag.

"I'm Doctor Nagy. Your son has done very well and is progressing better than expected. You should be proud of him. He has a strong spirit."

Stupefied, Bala began to babble. "I thought his brain was destroyed…he was dead…I mean, his mind dead…"

The doctor's gaze softened. "No, he's not dead. Though he will never be the man you knew, he will likely regain consciousness, open his eyes, see the world, hear sounds, and feel sensations. How well he will understand what he sees and hears and feels is unknown. How much motor control he will gain is also a mystery at this point."

His world spinning, Bala tried to grasp new possibilities, hope he had dashed against the hard rocks of reality. "He could wake up and know us…maybe talk to us?"

The doctor's hand rose and rested on his shoulder, her gaze strong and profoundly deep. "Do you remember the first time your baby boy looked into your eyes, and you knew him?"

A vivid image rose in Bala's mind—the evening shortly after David's birth, when Kendra had burned eggs on the stove and needed a time out, so he had taken charge. David had been asleep in his crib when he awoke with a wail. Crooning in his own unique style, Bala had hurried over and, just as he reached for the newborn, David looked up and met his gaze; their eyes locked onto each other. The screaming stopped suddenly, and David smiled. Bala could hardly believe it, but they knew each other instantly.

In understanding, the doctor nodded and spoke with measured care. "He may never do anything more than speak through pleading eyes, but he is your son, nonetheless."

Bala bowed his head.

The nurse finished his work and followed the doctor out the door.

Variant stayed back, apparently waiting for Bala to go first. Bala stepped up to David's bedside and considered the boy he had known. He reached out and caressed the side of his son's face. Words fell like raindrops. "I love you, David. Always have. Always will."

Variant was at his side, her hands resting on the railing in calm acceptance, her gaze peaceful.

Bala straightened and considered her more carefully. "Why do you still come? He's got nothing to offer you."

A blink and Variant met his gaze. "No. I have something to offer him."

Bala waited, uncertain if he wanted to hear her explain.

She sucked in a deep breath and plopped down on the chair she had been sitting in when he arrived. "He was a friend to me when few others would be. I want to be his friend when few others can be."

Sudden rage surged through Bala. "I want to kill whoever gave him these drugs."

Variant shifted aside. "That would include me." She sighed. "David was always sad. I thought he was high strung, like a taut wire that could never relax. He took everything personally, as if everyone who didn't think as he thought was challenging him."

True words that Bala hated to admit. But then he understood and his fury started to flow again. "You started him on Blandish? Then you're as guilty as anyone. That's why you come here!"

Her shoulders slumped, Variant's head dropped onto her chest, a distressed girl who couldn't face her accusers. "Blandish never affected me much. Sometimes it helped me sleep, but that's all. I didn't know it had a stronger effect on other body types." She ran her hands along her legs as if rubbing out the mismatched colorations. "He started using it without me, and I warned him to be careful. But then he just stopped talking about it. I guess he figured that it was his business."

Another truth. David never liked to discuss his misdemeanors. He always pleaded ignorance. Still, the fact remained. “You started him on the drug that nearly killed him.”

A convulsive swallow and Variant’s shoulders shook as she sobbed out her words. “I did. I am so sorry.”

His rage still hot in his blood, Bala hardly knew what to do with himself. He wanted to smash something, to yell and curse and kick the universe. He pounded across the room three times before his eyes caught a new expression on his son’s face—anguish. He hurried over and cupped David’s face in his hands, nearly bumping Variant off her chair. “What is it? What’s wrong? Are you in pain?”

Variant sniffled, and Bala glanced over. When he turned back to his son, the realization that he had just shouted at the woman his son loved slammed him in the gut. *David doesn’t blame her. Even Kendra pities the child.* Clare’s last words on the matter echoed in his head. *I see why David loved her.*

Bala backed off and straightened, calmness filling him as his words fell soft and true. “It was a mistake, Variant. We all make mistakes. It’s time to stop making such big ones.” With a gentle stroke, he swept a thick lock of hair off his boy’s forehead. “Love you forever, David.” Then he pressed Variant’s shoulder as he turned and crossed the room. “Sometimes it takes a tragedy.”

Chair legs scraped over the hard floor, and Bala peered over his shoulder as he passed through the doorway.

Variant held David’s hand, and the boy’s anguish was gone.

—Taug’s Laboratory—

Faye, dressed in her autumn-colored one-piece pantsuit, strolled around the perimeter of Taug’s laboratory, her arm linked with Walking Flower’s and pointed out various pieces of equipment and medical tools, explaining their uses to the best of her spotty knowledge. She glanced at Taug who stood like an island between the two dissecting tables while the noon sun poured over him from the skylight above. *Why doesn't he say something? He used to be so proud of his lab; he wouldn't stop jabbering on about it.*

Finally, Walking Flower had seen enough and halted next to the procedure chair—a cushioned sectional armature that maneuvered into multiple positions, allowing Taug to work on any number of body parts with relative ease. Keeping her thorax well clear of the chair, she glanced pointedly at the enclave with a wide couch and soft chairs set before a fish tank in the back.

Faye took the hint and started forward.

Taug seemed stuck in the middle of the room.

What is wrong with him? After assisting Walking Flower to the couch where she could sit with ease, Faye bolted to Taug's side, grabbed a tentacle, and, standing on her tip-toes, hissed in his ear hole. "What's come over you? I brought Walking Flower here to impress her with Newearth's advanced technology, so she doesn't think that we're all a bunch of mad scientists bent on—" Taug's stiff, unmoving form suddenly shivered in understanding, and a flash of anxiety ran through Faye. "Are you all right?"

Even through his breathing helm, his lips pursed noticeably. With a far-away expression in his eyes, Taug stared into an unseen distance.

Faye's anxiety increased, and she squeezed his tentacle with as much force as her lithe elven form allowed. "Get a hold of yourself, Taug. I need you!"

As if coming out of a trance, Taug shook himself and regarded Faye with slow care. "I've always been a fool, haven't I?"

Stumped, Faye couldn't think of a thing to say.

With typical Mantis dignity, Walking Flower rose and beckoned Taug closer.

Faye tugged twice before he plodded along at her side and finally plopped down on the wide chair at Walking Flower's left. Faye perched on the edge of the table between them.

Taug appeared beat, as if he had lost his final fight and could not enter the ring again. If he had bruises on his pulpy, white flesh, it would not have been clearer. He was a defeated Cresta.

Her heart wrung by the sight, Faye clutched her hands together and prayed for strength. *I wish Song were here. She'd know what to say...what to do.*

Though not considered a font of wisdom by her people, Walking Flower was a leader, and she took the lead in the most dignified manner possible. After retaking her seat, she leaned forward and laid a soft hand on one of Taug's limp tentacles. "We are all fools at one time or another. My people were deluded enough to believe that mere appearance would halt the travesty of hate. That if we just looked more attractive, we would fit into the larger universe." She shook her head in slow acceptance of a grievous truth. She glanced at Faye. "Do you remember what I asked you nearly a year ago when we met on Helm, after I arrived on my ship?"

Squinting, Faye pulled up the memory of strolling the beach with Walking Flower last December, her anxious fears, and Walking Flower's good-hearted decency. "You wanted to know if we could prove our worth by being our honest selves?"

Walking Flower nodded, then her gaze slid to Taug. You have been your honest self, Taug. A scientist with insatiable curiosity, always searching for ways to broaden the scope of knowledge."

Taug's head hung low on his chest. "You are too understanding. I doubt the IAACC will think the same. I breached all sense of propriety when I created Relevance, and we all know the high price of my excessive curiosity."

Wincing at the bald truth which she had struggled with numerous times, Faye tried to force down the rising memories of her own duplicitous motives when she first came to Newearth. She bit her lip in apprehension, uncertain what to say without being guilty of hypocrisy and personal betrayal.

Either ignorant of their dismal personal histories or leaping over them to a better future, Walking Flower extended a long finger and pointed it directly at Taug. "You have amends to make, certainly. But the truth is that Dr. Anzi and even Relevance could not have done so much in such a short time without a great deal of support, of which my people are not blameless." She cast a sympathetic eye at Faye. "Your people have always been caught in the middle. Shapeshifters seem to have the best of all worlds but rarely do they experience the benefits. Hounded and experimented on, hunted as a dangerous threat, the Bhuac's very passive nature, allowing them to mold themselves into the likeness of other beings, is their greatest curse. You never fought for your identity because you hardly own one."

Faye had to clench her jaws hard to keep from choking.

Taug wriggled in his seat uncomfortably. His deeply sympathetic feelings for Faye showed in his eyes as he glanced her way.

Walking Flower pressed her hands together. "We all have guilt to bear in this matter of unchecked experimentation. Perhaps not intentionally or even personally, but certainly, as part of the larger universe, we have a part to play in the forming or deforming of our collective worlds. So, if I may make a suggestion? Let us expose Dr. Anzi's real aim, proving beyond a shadow of a doubt that his work is fraudulent and wrought with mistakes. Exposing the damage done to sentient beings and how such behavior will haunt the future of us all should awaken slumbering consciences."

Taug's eyes widened, a gleam of excitement rising from their depths.

Faye's chest swelled with the first real hope she'd felt in ages beyond count. "I know just the person to see! Lang from Universal Reports would love to do a story on this." She met

Taug's steady gaze, and they reached an unspoken agreement. Her gaze slid to Walking flower, gratitude harmonizing with the essence of her being. *Thank Goodness.*

—Aram County, Seth's Harbor—

October, Year 74, Newearth Reckoning

Relevance thrashed his way through dense woodlands, ignoring the leaden sky, the crisp chill in the air, and gloriously swirling autumn foliage.

It had been two months since he had left LEAP Laboratories and, for the most part, he had spent that time hiding at home on the west end of Aram County, watching enormous harvesters bringing in bountiful crops. He had hardly left his porch, merely sat on the built-in bench, and observed the sun rise and set with seasonal regularity. There had been a blessed peace in doing nothing, having no grand scheme to carry out, a complete lack of purpose. His mind had wandered over his childhood and then through his various youthful travels. He considered everyone he had ever known from various angles and realized how unfit he was to judge them. He was seventeen now and felt like he had lost years rather than gained one since his last birthday.

It wasn't until he received a message from Bala's son, Seth—passed along from Variant—that his heart rate quickened. It was an invitation, strangely enough, to a grand opening of "Seth's Harbor." Relevance was inclined to think it was a joke, but the tone in Variant's attached note reflected an earnest plea. She even added that Squire had asked him to come.

Rousing himself, Relevance took a much-needed shower and donned fresh clothes—a plaid shirt and thick work pants that would handle the rough terrain to what he assumed must be a primitive shack in the woods.

According to his datapad and the directions Seth had sent, Relevance had to make his way across the densest part of the woodlands to the southeast corner of Aram County on the edge of the Great Lake. He squinted at the map. Apparently, the renowned Luxonian, Cerulean, lived directly north of Seth.

I wonder how well they know each other. Of course, Clare and Cerulean were always buddies, though the light being certainly didn't take much part in my upbringing.

A vague rumor of Cerulean having been altered somehow tickled the edge of Relevance's brain. He dismissed it. He tapped his datapad against his hand as he set out. Seth, being Bala's son, another inner circle member of his mother's cohort, never seemed eager to spend much time with Clare's dubious offspring, though for some unidentifiable reason, Relevance had always liked Bala and wished he had known him better. Probably just as well. An image of David's anguished face as he slammed him to the floor filled his mind. Shame heated his face, and Relevance hurried his steps, thrashing aside the brambly bushes and saplings that stood in his way. *I hope Seth is different from his brother.*

Near noon, he broke free of the last stand of trees and came into the clearing around the house, Relevance's mouth dropped open. Before him stood a structure unlike anything he had ever seen before, except in OldEarth European images. The rectangular base was built of huge, craggy stones expertly fit together. Enormous double doors, crafted from dark wood and studded with golden fasteners and ivory hinges, opened to a shadowy entryway. Large, wood-framed windows punctuated the first and second stories, while a tower with a finely crafted turret capped the whole. Three huge chimneys spread across the peaked roof, and a weather vane, outlining the form of an eagle in flight, pointed west.

What on Newearth is this?

Before he could process what he was seeing, an elk tottered forward.

Elch?

Appearing much older than his years and with a wobbly gait, the shrunken elk limped closer. “Been waiting for you.”

Though there was no ominous tone or shadowed threat, Relevance felt his body stiffen, alert and watchful. He slipped his datapad into his pocket and followed along behind the pitifully emaciated creature.

Seth waited just inside the doorway, his hands clasped, and his shoulders back. He didn’t look like a man about to attack. But then, it was hard to tell what a person might do. Relevance could still see Dr. Anzi’s smug smile, and the word “Bothmal” rang in his ears.

Relevance faced Bala’s son, a man he had never formally met but felt that he should know. Words rose before he had a chance to censor them. “Your father and my mother were always good friends.”

Stoic in his stance, Seth’s gaze remained steady. “Still are.” He shrugged like a guy who was about to go off a rehearsed speech. “I met you once, though you probably don’t remember. When you were a baby, my mom brought you home to help Clare learn to manage the whole motherhood thing. I don’t remember if it was bottle feeding or diapering that she was struggling with, but I recall Mom getting so mad she had to chant a litany of prayers to keep from losing her temper.” A chuckle broke forth. “Clare tried hard, but she didn’t have a clue. As a kid, I thought it was funny.” His grin faded. “But it couldn’t have been easy for you.”

His jaw tightening against an ache he could not explain, Relevance regained his emotional footing by focusing on the elk who leaned precariously at Seth’s side. “Hello, Elch. Thanks for waiting for me. How are you?”

The trembling elk didn’t seem to know how to respond. His head hung low and his eyes appeared unfocused. If an elk could shrug, he probably would have.

Seth patted Elch on the flank. “He’s growing old fast, and his hearing isn’t so good. But he’s mellowed a lot since I found him. The poor guy kept running in circles muttering under his breath, but I couldn’t understand a word he said. Surprising that he spoke to you at all.”

Relevance chewed on this observation a moment. “Perhaps seeing me brought back some of his original training?”

Seth nodded and then waved toward the large hall before them.

Stepping into the grand room felt like walking into a painting from OldEarth archives. Streams of light poured in from two arched windows on either side of a large built-in fireplace. More light fell from a high, curved window above a staircase leading to an upper landing. A large table flanked by wide wooden benches dominated the west wall. Two sturdy bookcases packed with what seemed like OldEarth relics stood between the stairs and another set of windows. The open space in the center had been redesigned from its typical purpose as a community gathering space to a hospital of sorts, though it appeared much more comfortable and homier than any hospital Relevance had ever seen before.

A curved bed made of soft material and lined with straw formed a perfect place for Elch, while a living tree had been planted in an enormous base near the south wall with the three main branches terminating in perfect little nests filled with natural materials, one for each of the birds—Chiara, Branoc, and Tyto. Their heads were just visible over the edges of their beds, though none appeared able to rise. Relevance’s heart constricted when he thought of the shabby accommodations they had fashioned in the lab. Nothing this charming. He forced his gaze to keep moving. A large circular bed rested on the ground before what appeared to be a feed box with a side table packed with IV bags and medical monitors. Within the ground nest, Squire lay huddled with a quilt tucked over his small body up to his chin. His son scampered about outside the nest, chasing acorns as they rolled over the hardwood floor.

A woman came down the steps and took a position next to Seth. She patted Elch's wavering back and nudged him in the direction of the largest bed on the other side of the table. Hobbling slowly, the quivering animal worked his way across the smooth floor.

Relevance watched in fascination, his throat dry and his heart parched. He had no idea what to say, but words rose scratchy and thin anyway. "Seth's Harbor, I see."

The woman lifted her hand in greeting. "I'm Rachel, Seth's sister."

Relevance nodded. He had heard what happened to David and that his sister, a nurse, had been able to get him transferred to the Vandi Long-Term Care unit. But his mind was still stuck on processing what was before his eyes.

Seth sucked in a deep breath and pointed to the table. "I know you hiked a good distance today, so I prepared a little something to keep you going while we discuss the future."

Amazed, Relevance could hardly move. He glanced aside at Squire, who managed to tip his head toward the table and mouthed the words, "Eat. We'll talk later."

The simple repast of crusty brown biscuits with pear jam, slices of orange cheese, and a terrine of steaming potato soup created a pretty scene. Seth ladled the thick, creamy liquid into three mugs and passed them along, while Rachel piled three muffins on her plate with healthy dollops of jam next to each.

Not to seem unsocial, Relevance took a muffin and a slice of cheese. He slid onto the smooth bench and cradled the warm cup in his hands, trying to order his thoughts. Too many images crowded his mind. Finally, after a sip of the deliciously spicy soup, he glanced between Seth and Rachel. "You must have thought I was an odd little kid."

In the first unguarded expression Seth had shown, he snorted through an abrupt laugh. "We were just kids, too, and truth be told, we were a little odd ourselves." He nudged

Rachel's shoulder. "Remember the games where Dad would chase us all over the backyard, pretending to be a space monster ready to devour us?"

A slow smile crept over Rachel's face as her gaze turned inward. "You were our great defender. He usually ate you first!"

For the life of him, Relevance couldn't understand what they were laughing about. He frowned, trying to recall historic events. "Years ago, there was a space monster that nearly devoured Newearth, right?"

Rachel shook her head; an expression of understanding softened the glow in her eyes as she met Relevance's gaze. "It was dark humor, the way we coped with fear and tragedy."

Seth cleared his throat as he sat up straighter. "Not so much to laugh about these days, though fear and tragedy follow us, nonetheless."

Rachel kept her focus steady. "You weren't the only weird person, Relevance. No stranger than everyone on Newearth, though I expect that you felt out of place. Clare wasn't exactly a comforting mother."

Seth hurried his sister's comment into oblivion. "Another time." He motioned toward the animals. "The question before us now—how can we ease the fear and pain of our friends here?"

A lump rose in Relevance's throat. "You've done better than I." He swallowed hard. "I hope you believe me, but I never intended to hurt anyone. I really thought we were bringing animals to higher sentience. It was a gift I wanted to bestow on others."

Rachel's jaw tightened. "It wasn't your gift to give."

Befuddled by everything that had gone so terribly wrong, Relevance shook his head. "I don't see why not."

With a deep sigh, Seth leaned back, resting his head against the plastered wall. "Look, you weren't raised with faith the way we were, but surely nature speaks louder than words." His gaze rising as if piercing the ceiling to the unseen universe above, Seth clasped his hands around his cup and spoke like a weary pedagogue. "I never understood my parent's beliefs—the prayers and rituals, history and all the rules. It all seemed out of touch with my actual life. But after a while, when I was tromping through the woods, I'd come across mysteries that my mind couldn't fathom—great and terrible mysteries. The glory of sunrises that would lift my spirit to unimaginable heights, and the next moment, I'd find the remains of a disgusting battle between critters where the victor ate the innocent while still alive…"

As if in pain, he winced and then shook it off before going on. "I needed something more than my rational mind could comprehend." Seth sat up and peered deeply into Relevance's soul. "Eventually, I understood. Not everything and not all at once, but slowly, day after day, season after season, it came to me that I am a part of a much greater whole, and I do not have the capacity to understand it all. I am not supposed to. I am not the Creator-God."

Unspeaking, Rachel seemed to be studying her hands, though there was acceptance in the nod she offered.

A comforting sensation filled Relevance, like a soft blanket on a chilly day, a drink of cool water under a hot sun, and he knew that he had ignored the whole idea of a Creator-God for too long. But what he would do with it, he could not fathom. He could only mutter, his gaze unseeing. "I don't understand."

With an honest laugh, Rachel slapped the table. "Join the club."

More befuddled than ever, Relevance looked over his shoulder at Squire. "How does this help with…"

While picking up his cup and plate, Seth scraped back his chair and stood. "We're all part of creation. That's what matters. Now, it's time for you to get reacquainted with a few old friends. I'm afraid they haven't much longer for this world."

It was the most exquisitely painful afternoon that Relevance had ever known, but by the time he headed back out the door into the evening twilight, he was the happiest he had ever been. An enormous weight had been lifted from his chest, and he felt more alive than at any point in his life.

Squire had been barely able to speak, but the wise-eyed squirrel nodded toward his young son repeatedly, and Seth had understood. He sat cross-legged on the floor while the kit scampered about, racing up and down furniture, and then stopping to snatch a nut that Relevance held out to him. After a bit, Relevance had returned to Squire's bed, carrying the tired little critter and set him in the crook of Squire's arm. "He's your son, all right. What an inheritance."

Squire's eyes lit up, and he nodded vigorously, his body trembling.

Seth came and stood close by. His smile radiated toward the two small creatures. "I think he wants you to name him that—Inheritance. After all, he's a gift passed down from generations, right?"

And so, it was done. Seth made a production of it to the joy and amusement of all. Even Rachel joined in the naming ceremony, creating a scroll with fancy writing in OldEarth style, bequeathing the title—Inheritance Squire—upon the small sleeping form.

Chiara flapped a weak wing and managed a thin squawk, "Well, done!" which had pleased Relevance more than all her irritating commentaries ever bothered him in the past. He wondered, as he had smoothed the ruffled feathers on her misshapen head, how he had missed the person inside the frail drama queen. But gratitude filled him at the knowledge that he had been there when she passed into her final sleep a few hours later, at peace for once in her anxious life.

Branoc maintained his defiant dignity after Chiara's passing. "She's better off." Relevance knew it was true, though he couldn't imagine what world she might be entering…though he felt strangely certain that she was still alive, somewhere.

A mix of stoic silence with a knowing look in his eyes, Tyto didn't need to say anything when Relevance had stood before him. A nod and silent understanding passed between them, soothing Relevance's burning guilt.

Unexpectedly, it was when Elch tried to rise from his bed and fell backwards that tears rose in Relevance's eyes. Choking sobs clawed their way up from his chest and would not stop even after he stumbled to the table and fell onto the bench, dropping his head onto his hands. He cried like a baby, completely unmanned, until his emotions were spent and a firm hand rested on his shoulder.

Seth's voice rumbled steadily but charged with emotion. "You gave them a glimpse of the life we all wonder about—the step just above our own. If you'd made me an angel or taught a slug to fly, you'd have lifted us up, offering a new view of our old world. That it could not last was never yours to say. You could not have done what you did, if it had not been allowed from above."

Though his mind could not process Seth's words, Relevance's heart skipped all rational wranglings and accepted the truth of them. Peace settled in where guilt and anguish had lived.

His goodbyes were not final when he shook Seth's hand and then Rachel reached out and gave him a parting hug. Relevance had no idea when he had ever been hugged before, and the sensation lingered like a cleansing summer bath.

He loped through the autumn-scented woodlands with golden leaves fluttering in a gentle breeze and knew he would be back. Squire and Inheritance, Tyto and Branoc, and gentle-eyed Elch were still alive in this world, and he would see them to the end.

That he had found kinship in Seth and his sister Rachel amazed him more than anything. Perhaps he'd stop by Vandi

Hospital and visit David, see if he could help. Variant would probably like that. Relevance felt a smile spread over his face.

Then the shadow of his brother, Herson, clouded his sunny mood. Shoving that dark reality away with an irritated snort, he strolled through the woods, savoring the taste of potato soup and the feel of a gentle hug.

—Breakfastnook Café—

Taug always enjoyed a tall Green-Nutrient drink at Riko's café, though it felt odd to be alone in the booth without Faye. Once she had set up the meeting with Lang, the Ingot Universal Reports reporter, she had insisted on retreating to Helm once again. She wanted to spend time with Song in prayer and meditation, considering their role in the universe. Her plaintive question rang through his mind like the wail of an injured child. "Are we to be seen as nothing more than helpless victims in a ruthless universe?" Taug hadn't known how to respond, so he waved goodbye at the Docking Bay with all the cheer of a friend who understands but doesn't know how to help.

Riko, wearing his trademark tight white uniform over his bulky exoskeleton, advanced with a towel draped over one arm and a scowl riding roughshod over his face. His goggle eyes were narrowed in a decidedly unpleasant manner.

Taken aback by the proprietor's expression, Taug sat up and leveled his gaze on the Uanyi. "What's wrong, Riko? You look like someone just poisoned your stew."

After slapping the towel on the table and removing a tiny smudge with a vicious swipe, Riko glowered at the nearly empty room and dropped his voice to a husky whisper. "Someone spiked one of my drinks last night, and a Uanyi thug is now in cold storage at the morgue." He wrung the towel within an inch of its life. "There's a new drug on the market—a mix between Blandish and something else. Makes some people super aware, while others get their minds turned to mush."

A cold shiver worked over Taug, and he had to clear his throat twice before he could get his words out. "Well, as it happens, I'm meeting Lang here today to discuss that very thing."

Riko leaned in, his eyes narrowing alarmingly. "This has something to do with that concoction Relevance and his doctor friend created, the one that brings animals to sentience, doesn't it?"

Taug nodded through a shaky smile, hoping that his connection to Relevance wouldn't be held against him.

The door chimes ringing merrily, a bulky Ingot figure swept into the diner.

Taug glanced over, relief calming his overwrought nerves. He wiggled a tentacle in Lang's direction to catch her attention.

Riko straightened, his eyes finally widening to their more natural state.

Surely the infatuation between the Uanyi and the Ingot was long over, though Taug kept his eyes peeled for any unexpected developments.

Jayla, Riko's wife, hurried into the room, cradling her latest offspring and motioned to Riko to her side.

Riko skedaddled.

Oh, blast, I didn't order my drink yet.

Lang strolled over as only an Ingot in techno-armor can. Lucious as usual in her glinting form-fitting outfit, she exuded a hint of dangerous power and mysterious knowledge. Of course, that was merely Lang's Universal News trademark.

Taug knew better than to believe it. "How are your fosterlings doing, Lang? I hear that you've got a better placement record than Human Services, and that's saying a lot."

A humble shrug and Lang dropped onto the red booth across from Taug. "Oh, you know how it goes. It's not about numbers, it's about getting good homes for kids who deserve them."

Abashed by the direct hit on the decency mark, Taug decided he would do his best in that arena as well. "Turns out that I have a story for you. Well, you probably already know most of it, but I think a comprehensive investigation by Universal Reports would do us all a great deal of good." He looked aside as Riko ushered his wife and baby into the well-appointed back kitchen. "Even Riko is having trouble. These new drugs on the market, you know, Blandish mixed with Dumplix, the drug that Dr. Anzi used to bring animals to sentience, are a powerful mix that could do unimaginable harm."

A world-weary expression filling her eyes, Lang's mouth drooped to subterranean gloominess. "It's the sellers. They open up markets before we even know what they're selling. Once word gets out that buyers have something new and an eager population wants a fresh experience, high or low, everyone gets in on it. Totally out of control."

His innards twisting, Taug roused himself to make another stab at hope. "But if we could warn the public, let everyone know that this is a dangerous drug, that it might destroy your mind or kill you outright, that'll help, right?"

A sad smile and Lang placed her blunt gloved hands on the table. "If a person thinks he or she can gain a new level of consciousness, they'll reach for it, blast the consequences."

"But it doesn't make any sense! What's the point of a moment of exuberant clarity when you could end up as dumb as a shattered rock a little later?"

Lang chuckled. "Who said that sentience means intelligence? And intelligence doesn't equal wisdom, as far as I can see. Look at…well, all of us."

Disheartened, Taug felt his body slump. Could he never make reparation for his part to play in this mess?

Lang reached across the table and patted his shoulder. "Don't get all despondent on me, Cresta. Cheer up; I'll do what I can. Everyone who listens will be one person who doesn't end up in Vandi Long-Term Care Unit or in the morgue, right? We do what we can, but free will still rules." She lifted her hand and beckoned to Riko. "I'll buy you a tall glass of Nutra-Green, and we'll celebrate."

Taug lifted his head and stared at the beautiful cyborg he would never understand. "Celebrate?"

"Innocent lives will be saved because you dared to care. Decency matters, don't forget."

Taug straightened and decided he would remember that.

—Universal News Reports—

November, Year 74, Newearth Reckoning

Lang reporting!

Talking squirrels, birds prophesying doom, elks with a grudge, puppies demanding bedtime stories, cats with social calendars, and a sea turtle building a sandcastle? Are you wondering what on Newearth is going on? Join the bewildered club. Some farmers and townsfolk are charmed, while others are terrorized and kill the newly sentient animals and anyone suspected of being part of Dr. Anzi's LEAP Laboratory experiment.

The Cresta High Council has ordered that unwanted specimens be sent to their laboratories for further studies, while Helm Leadership and the Luxonian Supreme Council insist that animal-humans—now known as Animans—have all the rights accorded Newearth Citizens.

What does "Sentient-Miracles," the laboratory that makes and distributes Dumplix, Blandish, and a host of other "Reach Your High" drugs make in universal sales? Bet my Ingot armor it is out of this world. Their last stock was sold to an unknown buyer at a premium price and sent to undisclosed locations. Who knows how these experimental drugs will haunt Newearth in the future?

Known side effects of these drugs involve brain damage, including loss of judgment and uncontrolled emotional reactions. In several cases, the medulla gets in a muddle, and that's never a good idea. Expect a miserable death to follow.

—Taug's Laboratory—

Relevance stopped before the large metal door in the surprisingly clean alleyway and braced himself. He tugged the sleeves of his cable knit sweater so they matched evenly and took a calming breath. Heavy work boots and thick pants protected him from the late-autumn frost that edged the building. His heart pounded as if he had run the whole way, and his mind raced with nagging doubts. *Why am I here?* Without coherent thought or even conscious direction, his hand rose, and he pounded on the door. "Taug, let me in, or I'll bust through!"

Anticlimactic silence followed. *I know he's in there. I saw him go into the Breakfastnook.* A disquieting thought followed. *What if he's still eating breakfast?*

To his relief, the door slid open.

No time for introductions or explanations, Relevance darted forward and pounded his way to the middle of the laboratory. He looked around, his hands clenched, ready for a fight.

Shockingly, the Cresta stood before a huge water tank nearly naked, water dripping off his body, with only a towel wrapped around his middle, his thin breathing helm askew.

Thrown off guard, Relevance stared. No words rose to his lips; his mind halted, stymied by the sight.

A humble shrug—as if he was caught au naturel every day of his life—hinted at Taug's lack of surprise. "I wondered when you'd return."

Forcing down a scream, Relevance advanced and then stopped before the dripping figure. "I never planned to."

Head bobbing, Taug seemed to understand more than Relevance had imagined possible.

Time to blast his target with the devastating truth; Relevance enunciated his words with precision. "It's—all—your—fault."

The towel started to slip and, with quick reflexes, Taug did two things at once. He readjusted the cloth, maintaining a modicum of modesty, and returned fire. "I agree."

The thrust of his accusation stalled so abruptly; Relevance struggled to recoup his argument. "When you started playing with hybrids and tribrids, when you created me, you set in motion this whole Animans travesty." He lifted a clenched fist and shook it at Taug. "I needed to understand myself! Blast you! I thought by creating other hybrids I could make a home for myself, a place where I would fit in. I would show you all, hybrids are just as good as you."

After readjusting his breathing helm and motioning toward the chairs in the sitting area by the tank, Taug moved the conversation to a new setting.

With nothing to lose, Relevance stepped over and plunked down on a plush seat. Memories rose and images of himself as a kid playing on this very same chair stirred. They were not unpleasant recollections. In fact, shockingly, a rosy glow accompanied an image of himself and his brother Herson playing hide and seek. He swallowed a lump rising in his throat.

A long sigh and Taug plopped onto the chair on Relevance's right. A smile brightened his pale face as his gaze lingered on the small pool before them. "Do you remember the first time I took you in the water? You were terrified."

Images rolled through Relevance's mind: him and Herson racing around the laboratory throwing medical instruments at each other, his climbing the pool ladder first because Herson insisted, and then freezing on the top step as he stared into the murky depths. One memory saved his dwindling pride. "Herson never went in."

Chuckling, Taug lifted his round chin and stared at the ceiling as if the past were running across it. "Nothing I could do would convince him that it was safe. Poor child, he was more Ingot than you. His body was never strong. Not like yours. I should have offered him enhancements, but Clare probably wouldn't have allowed it."

A deep craving, as if he was being offered a cool drink in the middle of a desert, burgeoned inside Relevance. A sudden hope for answers to questions he had never dared ask pounded against his brain. "You couldn't tell Clare what was best for us? You designed our bodies, surely, she'd have trusted your judgment."

The snort that erupted from Taug sent swirls of bubbles through his breathing helm. "Don't be ridiculous. Clare never trusted me. No one trusted me." His gaze turned inward and softened. "Except maybe Faye. But then"—he glanced aside—"no one ever trusted her, so she understood better than most."

This was getting into deeper territory than Relevance could handle, though the Bhuaci mindset had always intrigued him. Still, he needed to stay focused. "So, Clare just did what she wanted with us? No one advised her?"

Tapping his tentacles together in a thoughtful manner, Taug seemed to examine the questions from all angles before he responded. "I wouldn't say that. Plenty of people advised her. Bala and Kendra for one and two. Certainly, Cerulean offered his wisdom, such as it was. Though his relationship with his own son…" Taug shook that thought away. "But Clare always had her own mind. Unfortunately, she didn't know it very well."

Hot on the scent of enlightenment, Relevance leaned forward. "What do you mean?"

Taug stroked his chin and then met Relevance's gaze head on. "I suppose you don't know." He sat up straighter and cleared his throat. "Clare's parents died under mysterious circumstances when she was a child. The Eternal known as Omega visited her in his own quest to understand humanity better. Unfortunately, his questioning tormented Clare, and she grew up nursing a powerful grudge against aliens. It makes sense…this used to be their planet for many long ages."

"Then why did she come to you and ask for a hybrid baby?"

A wince ripped over Taug's face. "She didn't ask for a hybrid. She asked for a baby. She didn't think she'd ever have a family naturally and bemoaned her state in life when I offered to help." Taug's eyes glinted with sincerity. "I really meant to help."

His brain in overdrive, Relevance tried to piece his family history together. "So how did Herson and I come about? Why a hybrid? Why a tribrid?"

Taug scratched his chin in a meditative manner. "Clare wasn't the only one who needed assistance. You see, at the same time, the Ingots were suffering a debilitating loss of progeny. Their reproductive procedures failed, and their offspring were too weak to survive the necessary technological implants or they simply failed to develop. The Ingot race was on the verge of collapse."

With the satisfaction of snapping puzzle pieces together, Relevance spoke the next part out loud. "So, you decided to do two things at once—give Clare a baby and…" He stopped short. "But why Tabunite? Why not make Herson Human-Ingot?"

"We happened to have some Tabunite seed available. Don't ask me how it was acquired; it's too shameful to speak of but that wasn't my doing. Besides, we needed strong stock, and Tabunites had just been introduced to Newearth. I thought it was providential that we could unite two fractured races in such a productive manner."

"So, you created Herson first?"

Taug nodded as he glanced aside. "It's not that you were an afterthought. In fact, you were a brainchild of a remarkable opportunity. A chance to use one of the last strong Ingot DNA strains came my way, and I imagined that since all the races were rooted in human DNA, that a tribrid might be possible. As far as I knew at the time, it had never been tried."

"You wanted to be the first."

"I am a scientist after all. Knowledge is my life's blood, so to speak."

Relevance fell back against his chair and stared at the ceiling. "Clare had no say in our being hybrids?"

"She didn't know."

"How did she react when she found out?"

"You don't want..."

Relevance shook his head as if clearing water from his ears. "But I don't understand. Why did she accept Herson but not me?"

Taug hesitated and then he leaned forward and pressed a tentacle on Relevance's knee. "Herson looked the most like her."

An Ingot kick to the gut could not have hurt more. It made perfect sense, but his soul cringed at the brutal truth. *My mother rejected me.* His conclusion rose like a haunting specter that had finally become visible. "She wished I never existed."

With a last pat and a sigh, Taug fell back, his gaze rising. "She did not know what to do. Humans have limited capacities. Once they are overwhelmed, they begin to jettison anything that hinders survival."

"How did I threaten her survival?"

Taug's gaze locked onto Relevance. "She was a Human Services Detective who thrived on being a model human citizen. Once she engaged my services, she stepped over a line. Not only had she collaborated with an alien scientist in a personal matter with non-regulatory results, but she had no idea what motherhood really meant. She undoubtedly imagined herself as something between a kind benefactor and a fun aunt. You were far outside her limits. If it's any consolation, she didn't reject you, she simply reached her limit and didn't believe that things would work out all right."

A flashing glimpse of Squire's face and a mountain of grief descended upon Relevance. "It certainly didn't."

It took three tries, but Taug finally hefted himself out of the chair. "I wouldn't say that. You are a remarkable person, Relevance, and I am glad I've had a chance to know you better."

Tears unbidden rose in Relevance's eyes as he stayed in place. "I repeated your mistake and interfered. The Animans have suffered because of me."

Gripping his towel and his dignity with care, Taug beckoned Relevance to his feet. "We all make mistakes, dreadful ones, sometimes. It's one of the things that unites us." He chuckled. "Bala told me that repentance is the price of sentience."

A small well-spring of hope bubbled through the bleak ashes of despair. "Bala's son and daughter welcomed me at Seth's Harbor, and I was allowed to name Squire's son." He stood up and faced Taug. "They don't hate me."

Padding toward the pool, Taug continued to beckon Relevance forward. "Never saw much use for hate. Very unproductive." He pointed at the swirling pool. "You may not have any Cresta in your DNA, but humans have always loved the sea. Come swim with me and be refreshed."

His feet moving on their own accord, Relevance came alongside Taug. "I need to stop Dr. Anzi."

Wrapping a tentacle around Relevance's shoulder in a fatherly motion, Taug led Relevance to the ladder. "Your part in that business is done. Cerulean is good at that sort of thing. Let him manage it."

"I don't know the Luxonian. Not really."

Taug smiled as he blinked innocently. "No one does. We're all mysteries." He dropped his towel and started to climb the ladder. "No modesty in a pool. Follow me."

Amazing himself, Relevance did.

Chapter Seven

Releasing the Inner Animal

—Taug's Laboratory—

December, Year 74, Newearth Reckoning

Message from Taug to Faye

My dearest friend,

I miss you. I am sitting along in my quiet laboratory, on this cold, dark evening, reviewing my life. I find myself uncertain if I am an unsung hero or a selfish villain. Perhaps a bit player in a much larger drama.

Relevance has been a pleasure to get to know. He has visited three times now and has been fascinated by my personal history—even appeared surprised that I had one. I offered to show him the programs I used to arrange his tribrid nature, but he wants to hold off on that. He still feels the burn of unregulated experimentation.

I finally ventured to ask about his brother, but he had little to say. He mentioned a meeting with Herson last summer in which they had become quite friendly. Relevance had expected to hear from him again but figured that since he was in his last term at the academy, he was too busy to check in.

By the puzzled expression in Relevance's eyes, I suspect that Herson confused his brother as much as charmed him. Herson was always a better manipulator, if you remember.

Ironic that the tribrid with greater strength and mental acuity should prove the less dangerous. I know, you'll remind me of Relevance's experiments, and I quite agree, but it must be remembered that he was not working alone. Dr. Anzi was the real force behind the Animans creation.

In any case, I wish you'd return to Newearth soon. I am working on an antidote to offset the Blandish addiction and to soften the devastating effects of Dumplix on the brain. I could use your encouragement. I don't dare tell anyone else what I am doing for fear that I'd be sent to Bothmal. Not that I wouldn't want to assist those doomed to a prison colony, but I know too well that information in the wrong hands... Well, you know.

I do wish I knew what happened to Herson. I tried locating him, but the academy insists that he never returned last semester. I wonder if Clare knows.

Please come home soon so we can share a tall glass of Nurta-Green together and discuss the dramas of our days and how we can't help but get muddled up.

Benevolently yours,

Taug

—Waukee—

Herson knew he was lost, but since that had been the plan, he wasn't worried. *Am I lost?* He rallied his mind, swiping at the hazy fog that seemed to surround him. *Not lost, hidden.* Dressed in summer shorts and a sleeveless shirt, he appeared ready for a summer day on the beach rather than a visit with his mother at the tail end of autumn.

A cold wind swept down the alleyway, but Herson hardly felt it. A brief flicker in the corner of his mind wondered why. He looked up from the ground and his gaze fell on a white picket fence surrounding a picturesque backyard where a tiny Bhuaci girl in a thick, blue coveralls played with some sort of a creature. *A cat? No, too big, but it can't be a dog, what—*

A Bhuaci woman in a long dress of woven gold-brown material called from the doorway, "Samrta, come in now. Leave Lili in her nest."

Nest? Herson knew he was going to be late to his mom's house, but with all the intensity of an eager boy, he wanted to see the nest. Throwing one leg over the fence, he perched on the edge, his body relaxed and his mind darting, undirected. He scanned the yard. On the right a castle-like playhouse stood with two round windows and a tiny turret, a green swing hung limp from a high tree branch over a low gully, and a row of naked fruit trees reposed against a low embankment. To the far left, a huge oval nest made of stout sticks and thick branches was embedded in the dirt bank.

"By the Divide, that's no songbird nest! I'd love to see the eggs."

Her eyes widening with alarm, the child ran across the yard and flung herself into her mother's protective embrace.

From the middle of the yard, the creature rose, growing enormous, its feathers ruffled and huge golden eyes fastened on Herson.

In his baffled confusion, Herson stared back at the creature. *Those are feathers, right?*

A low hum vibrated from Lili's chest, rising in pitch as it advanced.

A dozen questions buzzing in his head, Herson wanted to call out to the woman who stood like a statue with scared eyes, but a sudden squawk startled him, knocking him backward off the fence.

Like a raptor, the angry face scowled down, its long neck easily reaching over the fence. Its pointed brown feathers fully fluffed, wings erect, and standing on decidedly sharp claws, fierce animosity hovered directly over Herson's head.

A dim light dawning through the cloud of his understanding, Herson scrambled to his feet, slapped dirt from his hands, and, with an abrupt turn, ambled down the alleyway, his heart pounding erratically.

Once at the end of the alleyway, he glanced around and then, surprised, he noticed his mother's house across the street. He couldn't understand how it had gotten over there. He had never seen it from this position before, and it looked like a scene out of a picture, snug between two white houses with massive maple trees standing guard beside each.

Oh, here I am. Herson shoved nagging confusion from his mind and jogged across the quiet lane. As soon as he clambered up the porch steps, the front door jerked open.

Dressed in black leggings and a long, white sweater tunic, Clare stood with one hand braced on the door frame, the other beckoning him inside. "There you are! I was getting worried." She followed him into the living room as he paced forward. "Why are you dressed for summer? It's cold out there!"

A quick reassuring smile, and Herson did a three-sixty, his mind absorbing vivid details of his mom's house he'd never noticed before. "What a great place."

Her frown deepening, Clare stared at him. "You were just here a couple of months ago. Nothing much has changed."

Herson wanted to shout, "I've changed!" but a new thought struck him. "That bird creature down the way is huge!"

A calm, almost professional expression tightened Clare's features. She clasped his arm and led him toward the kitchen. "You need to eat something."

Herson wondered about this. Yes, it could be true. He couldn't remember when he last ate.

Throughout the dinner at the large wooden table in the middle of the open kitchen-living room, Clare encouraged him to take another bite, to drink more clear liquid that hardly tasted like anything, to rest and relax.

Herson ate, drank, and relaxed until he nearly fell asleep. It wasn't until his mother led him to the bedroom and nudged him backwards onto his bed, the one he had slept in as a child, that he thought of what he needed to tell her. "Relevance is a fake."

Tugging his shoes off one by one, Clare sighed. Then she unfolded a blanket from the end of the bed and laid it over his prone body. "You told me that last time you were here, remember?"

Uncertainty bewildering his mind, Herson scrambled for the next important piece of information he needed to pass on. "Gavin messaged me. Wants to come visit. Be a dad."

The anxious expression in Clare's eyes made Herson want to sit up, but his body wouldn't budge. The blanket was too heavy and the bed too soft.

His mom leaned over, her eyes searching. "Why do you say that?"

"Fool thinks feelings matter."

Clare's face retreated but her voice still carried, even after Herson closed his eyes. "Is he really coming back, to Newearth?"

There was no point in shrugging. The darkness called, and Herson wanted to go.

Bright shafts of light awoke Herson, nearly blinding him. It took several tries before he could roll off the bed and find his feet. They weren't stable, but they would have to do. He muttered under his breath, "Blasted Ingots and Cresta! Gave me an unbalanced batch again. Bothmal to the lot of them." Shakily, he made his way to the cleansing room and managed to accomplish the necessities before he braced himself at the sink and stared into his bleary, pink-tinged eyes. "Oh, dunghilian! She'll know." With a retching in his stomach, he gripped the sink tighter and forced himself to breathe slowly. A veiled vision of his former euphoria wavered before him. *I'm not like them. I'm special. Suffering is a ladder.* Memories of the glories that had filled him just days before sent shivers over his body. He took a deep breath.

Once the nausea passed, he splashed cold water on his face, then ran the shower, stripped down, and jumped in. The raw power of cold water blasting his thin, pale skin reoriented his mind.

He rehearsed his speech as he lathered and rinsed. "I can explain everything. Out with some friends. They slipped me a little something, probably thought it was funny. A graduate, you know how everyone wants to take me down a peg. It's what they do. Not funny, I know, but nothing to get upset about…" Yeah, he knew what to say.

Once at the breakfast table, sitting before a stack of pancakes and a side dish of sliced fruit, he acted his role with humble precision. Clare's frown nearly turned upside down. But not quite. He wasn't sure why, but it didn't matter. He only needed one thing, and Clare could give it to him.

After pushing his empty dishes aside, Herson propped his hands together, a sage paying a kindness to his devotee, and offered a warm smile to the woman sitting at his right. "Hey, Mom, I want to thank you. You've always been so generous, paying my way through school, all the graduation expenses, and even that little party you threw for my class. Everyone appreciated your renting the Docking Bay Great Hall. Made for a great send off into the real world."

With her eyes shining, Clare reached over and pressed Herson's arm. "It's been an honor to be a part of your life."

His chest tight, Herson readied himself for his next precarious step.

But the sun disappeared behind a cloud, and Clare rose from the table. Her voice quivered as she gathered the breakfast dishes. "I'm glad you appreciate the chance you've been given. It's one I almost threw away." She lifted a cautious eye and made tremulous contact. "Never play with forces that could control you."

Stiff as an Ingoti spinal column, Herson snorted in irritation. *What? Hypocrite!* "You taught me well, Mom."

Pain filled Clare's eyes.

Direct hit.

Herson smiled, stood up, and reached out. Patting her arm, he leaned in as if for a hug. "You mean everything to me, Mom." He had her now.

Clare opened her mouth, but Herson preempted her words. An itch was beginning to crawl along his back and arms. He could still manage for days without another dose, but he had tried to quit three times and failed. The combination of Dumplix and Blandish had turned out to be more than profitable, it had lifted him to heights he had never imagined possible. He had seen God and become one with the Universe. Unfortunately, it cost more than it paid.

He softened his smile, a hint of a worried frown strategically placed between his eyes. "I just wish I could get a good position, you know, with people who will treat me right. I hate being suspicious, but there are some Human Services types who can make it tough on a person."

Letting Clare imagine what kinds of tough things he had already been through, Herson stepped aside from the table and started for the door as if he had someplace important to go.

With breakfast dishes in her hands, Clare stopped and turned to him. "Where are you going?"

Sad, duty-calls smile. "Well, there's a really good position on an island chain in Ishtar County, but my chances of getting it are nonexistent. Have to know the right people, which means going to the right events, which means having the units to pay the entry fee and associated costs. Out of my orbit, if you know what I mean. So, I'm going to see if I can find a spot in the Siren section and work my way up."

The dishes nearly collided as Clare jumped forward. "Not there! It's filthy and dangerous. The worst of Uanyi, Crestas, and Ingots rule that hole with ruthless efficiency. Even the Inter-Alien Alliance Commission turns a blind eye."

Herson lifted his empty hands and shrugged. He kept his smile tucked away for later.

—LEAP Laboratory—

Cerulean crashed through Aram woodland underbrush, unmindful of thorns and brambles catching his cotton sweater or latching onto his heavy work pants. His hands clenched and unclenched of their own accord. He knew he should have brought back up, but after what he had just witnessed at Seth's Harbor, he could not wait another day to confront the man who had caused so much misery. Besides, plans were in place, and he didn't want anything to mess them up.

While visiting David in the hospital the day before, Bala had regaled Cerulean with all that Seth had done to create a safe retreat for suffering creatures. Impressed, and upon hearing that even his neighbors in the Amens community had dropped off even more disfigured, dying Animans, he felt it was about time he stopped by to see what conditions were like. Arrangements were soon made and early that morning, he had entered Seth's Harbor uncertain of what to expect.

Despite the pleasing setting and quality care, horror had filled him at the sight of so many pitiful creatures—Squire, Branoc, Tuto, Elch, two Labradors, a hound dog, five cats, a woodchuck, three raccoons, one rabbit— four other rabbits had died already, and nearly thirty more innocents, not all of them Animans. The sound of their squeals, moans, and intermittent pleas, twisted his gut till he felt nauseous. He didn't know how Seth and Rachel maintained their composure.

Seth arranged bedding and food and kept up his usual woodland management, bringing in injured patients—sentient or wild—acting as a determined yet calm force of nature himself. In a similar manner, a strength of will ran through Rachel, an undercurrent in a gently flowing river.

Cerulean had stood by and watched in silent amazement. *Does it take the worst in humans to bring out the best in humanity?*

Despite everything Seth and Rachel did to alleviate pain, there was no hope of recovery. Even Squire held on by a thread, his body all but emaciated. Only his deep love for his son tied his body and spirit together.

Cerulean's last conversation with Roux and the other Guardians on Lux had not left him confident that the Inter-Alien Alliance Commission were of one mind on the Animans issue. They merely agreed that Dr. Anzi should leave Newearth as soon as possible.

What's wrong with them? This is the very thing that Luxonians have worried about for ages—the creation of new life forms without any respect for the larger universe.

His heart pounded as he thrashed his way through the woodlands, rehearsing the formal directive escribed on his datapad: "Dr. Anzi is hereby ordered to take the next available flight off Newearth or face charges of crimes against sentient life…"

Finally, he broke into a cleared space and surveyed the octagonal structure known as LEAP Laboratories. He took a long slow breath. Then he pulled out his datapad and messaged the only person who could help him now.

Once he made it to the sixth branch of the building, he slowed his pace, glancing at the identification plates on each door as he passed. Finally, he came to the end of the hallway and the largest, most ornate door stood before him. He pressed the bell.

A carven image of a serpent eating a round piece of fruit slid by as the door opened, and a short, stout man with a full head of black hair and wearing a long white lab coat over black pants and a sweater stood before him. With a flicker of a grin the man returned to the interior of the room. “Jeremy sent word that you were coming. Said you looked fierce.”

Cerulean stepped into the large well-appointed room. He had never seen anything like it, except perhaps in an OldEarth museum. Sturdy shelves lined two walls with an assortment of bones, skulls, stuffed animals, charts, graphs, plant and mineral samples, and even a large fish tank. Lifesized human, Ingot, Cresta, and Uanyi manikins stood against one wall. He looked around for a Bhuaci representative but didn’t see one. A holopad took a central position on the floor before a gleaming metal desk.

“They don’t hold their shape, so I couldn’t stuff one.”

Cerulean refocused on the strangely diminutive man standing behind his desk. *I thought he’d be taller.* “Excuse me?”

Dr. Anzi waved his hand at the manikins. “They’re real. For some reason, most visitors assume that they are merely well-crafted copies.” He shook his head, a weary pedagogue exhausted by stupidities.

Holding back a gasp, Cerulean stared hard and realized that the doctor was telling the truth. All the horror and fury that had propelled him across the woodlands, into the complex building, right to this specific office evaporated in icy determination.

“I have a warrant for your arrest.”

Doctor Anzi shook his head again as he flopped down on his padded leather chair. “No, you don’t.” He seemed to study Cerulean as he tapped his fingers together meditatively. “I know the same people you know. In fact, I support many of the people you know. They don’t want to arrest me. They believe in my work.”

Standing in front of the desk like an errant child before his teacher, Cerulean made certain that his boots didn’t touch the holopad. This wasn’t going to be as straightforward as he had hoped. "Your work, Dr. Anzi, has caused great suffering. It will stop. This laboratory will be reutilized as a hospital for those suffering from addictions."

"Ha, ha!" The abrupt laugh hardly sounded sincere, but the twinkle in the doctor's eyes challenged Cerulean to doubt him. "My creatures aren't suffering because they are addicted. They are suffering because they don't work right. I haven't solved the cross-species dilemma. It's all a delicate balance and way over your head, Luxonian." Suddenly, his eyes lit up. "But then, you are a crossbreed yourself, aren't you? A hybrid Luxonian-Human created by an Eternal who had a bit of a head start. Can't blame me for that. Besides, it doesn't really matter. My point has been proven abundantly; don't you think?"

Cerulean itched to check his datapad, but he was fairly interested in what the doctor might say, so he was content to keep the conversation going. "Point?"

"Humanity destroyed itself ages ago, when it first left OldEarth. Only a remnant survived, and when I die, humanity dies with me. Talking dogs are all you have to look forward to now. It's all you've really had since the conception of Newearth, you just didn't realize it."

His voice steady, Cerulean forced himself to answer reasonably. "The OldEarth remnant lived on Lux. They were faithful to their origins and recommitted themselves to this planet. Why do you believe that the remnant is dead when there are hundreds of thousands of humans living here today?"

His face nearly purple with rage, Dr. Anzi slammed his fist on the table. "They aren't the remnant. They ran away! Cowards. Living on Lux changed them into alien slaves. When they returned, they submitted to alien rule. No true human would have accepted that. My people didn't accept it. We held on, faithfully!" His voice rising to a scream, his last words barely had enough breath to carry them. "I am the last!"

Interrupting the tirade, a flash and two forms materialized on the holopad— Squire rested on a pillow cradled in Jeremy's arms.

For the first time, Dr. Anzi halted, his face bewildered as he stared at the man. "Where in Bothmal are you? And what are you doing holding a creature like that? Sentiment, Jeremy! You know what I told you about getting attached."

His head bobbing, as if to accept the criticism in honest fair play but insisting on having his point taken, Jeremy's thin voice wavered as it rose. "I'm at Seth's Harbor. Have been for weeks." With a tilt of his head, he gestured at Squire. "This is one of your first projects, remember? Squire's his name."

Puckering his lips, it appeared that the doctor might spit. Instead, he circled around his desk, stopped before the holopad, and shook his finger accusingly. "By the Divide, what do you think you are doing? I didn't give you permission to leave your station. Who's been taking my messages and…"

Cerulean stepped aside and allowed the situation to play out. After all, a confrontation between these two was long overdue.

Clearly too exhausted to get emotional, Jeremy's voice remained placid. "I arranged everything so you'd get your meals on time, and your messages would be passed along. At least, after they had gone through proper channels."

Stock still, Dr. Anzi's face drained of all color, his voice turned husky. "Where are my animals?"

"Here."

The doctor blinked. "Where is that?"

"Doesn't matter, really. It's a safe place for us. You see, sir, you may not have given me permission to leave, but you didn't give me permission to die either, and I'm doing both."

"Craven animal!"

Squire lifted his head, and his voice rose squeaky but remarkably clear. "We all die, Doctor. How we face life, and death in its turn, well, that's what really defines us, don't you think?"

"Defines? You're a creature. I'm a human being."

Jeremy locked his gaze on the doctor. "You lost your humanity when you lost faith in the human race, sir."

Cerulean couldn't have said it better. He watched Dr. Anzi closely for the slightest sign of remorse but saw none.

With a furious grimace, Dr. Anzi slapped his console. The holopad went dark. He glared at Cerulean. "Get out of here before I have Interventionists escort you to Bothmal."

Slowly, Cerulean pulled his datapad from a deep pocket and tapped the surface. "Where do you want it? Personal or business address?"

Frozen, Dr. Anzi remained silent.

"Both, then." Cerulean tapped in directions and heard the double pling of received messages on Dr. Anzi's console. "You're right about the people we both know. They don't want you to go to Bothmal, not a great place to send a mad scientist, but they do want you off Newearth. It's something we all agree on."

A smirk lifted one side of the doctor's face. "So, there's no arrest warrant."

Solid as a mountain that would outlast the ages, Cerulean stood his ground. "There is. Dated for tomorrow."

—Ingot Sails Commercial Ship—

Dr. Anzi stared out the main viewing window on the dining deck and rubbed his shoulder where he had bruised it getting on board the clumsy transportation ship. What personal belongings he could pack in a hurry were stowed in his compartment while his professional materials had been boxed and loaded on the Docking Bay harbor. *They better have stowed everything properly, blasted fools.*

Since Jeremy was no better than a traitor and he had no friends to speak of, he had related his difficulties to a few key managers, and they had ordered new assistants to help him arrange transportation of himself and his goods to a hospitable setting on Crestar. It was hardly his first choice, but the Cresta Ingal had always shown quiet support. *Want to get their tentacles on my research, undoubtedly. Probably think I'm hoarding all sorts of secrets.* He chuckled. *Won't they be surprised when they find out that I don't have anything new to add to the reports I sent out earlier?*

An Ingot steward stepped up and offered an array of colorful drinks. Wanting very much to snub the mechanical man, Dr. Anzi sneered at him, but his stomach was as empty as the void he faced. *Might as well keep my strength up.* He chose the pink one, tossed it back, and enjoyed the pleasant burn as it slid down his throat.

A Cresta wearing the slimmest bio-suit Dr. Anzi had ever seen moseyed forward and stopped on his left side. If he had been taller, they would have stood shoulder to shoulder. As it was, the Cresta towered over him.

Uncomfortable at the nearness of anyone to his physical being, Dr. Anzi looked around for the server and beckoned for another drink.

The Cresta lifted a tentacle in salute. "You like to stay well lubricated; I see. A smart man."

Dr. Anzi resisted the urge to snort. He maintained a passive demeanor, as if strange Crestas chatted with him every day.

With the tentacle still outstretched, the Cresta grinned as he smiled down. "I'm here to see you safely settled at your new home."

Pleased, Dr. Anzi finally turned and faced his newest acquaintance. "Very good. I expect that arrangements have already been made for proper accommodations for myself and a laboratory made available for my continued research?"

A slow nod and the Cresta kept his gaze watchful, as if keeping an eye out for something. "We are especially interested in your recent successes. Much of your early work has been attempted before. We were the originators of Dumplix, if you remember?"

The server appeared at his elbow just in time, and Dr. Anzi chose the bright blue drink. *Might as well sample a variety!* He suddenly laughed out loud, giddiness bubbling like a fountain from within. Was this success? Revenge tasted sweet, they said. His plans might have been too narrow, merely encompassing the poverty-stricken human population. Now that he was unleashed from the planet, home-world as they liked to call it, he could…

"Have you ever tried it?"

Jolted from his pleasant thoughts, Dr. Anzi scowled up at the blanched face with its large brain sack hidden behind a pink spiral shell. "What?"

The Cresta motioned to the drink in his hand. "Drink up first."

With nothing better to do, Dr. Anzi gulped the contents swiftly, enjoying the second burn as much as the first.

"I was just curious if you have ever tried Dumplix."

Irritated and wondering if he was talking to an idiot, Dr. Anzi scowled to show his disapproval of personal questions. "Of course not. It's for animals, not people."

A soft laugh and the Cresta seemed distantly amused. "Aren't you an animal?"

Heat flushed Dr. Anzi's face. "What gave you such a ridiculous idea?"

"Humans say it all the time. They based their lineage on being descended from animals."

Must be a Cresta dimwit. He cleared his throat and used his pedagogue voice. "Descended is the keyword. Humans evolved well beyond animals eons ago."

"When was that, exactly?"

Thrusting back his shoulders, Dr. Anzi wondered if he could smack the Cresta and get away with it. "There are records! OldEarth data shows when humans gained complex abilities, true sentience, a conscience, the ability to think beyond the present, and interact on more than physical and emotional levels."

"I thought you claimed that you are the last true human, yet others on Newearth appear to have such abilities."

His voice rose in vitriolic fury. "I am pure blood! We never left the planet!"

The Cresta gestured to the viewscreen. "Until now. Are you sure you're still human, doctor?"

Alarmed by hot tears burning his eyes and foggy confusion blurring his mind, Dr. Anzi raised his fist and shot a punch at the soft, plump figure before him. "You're the animal! You and all aliens who desecrated our planet! We should have killed you, no compromises, no treaties. Damn you to—"

His knees buckling, Dr. Anzi felt himself falling to the floor. Hitting it didn't hurt a bit. His eyes still open, he could see the Cresta's boots near his face and he wasn't surprised to hear a distant chuckle.

"Dumplix has many qualities. Releasing the inner animal is one."

Amazed at the bitter taste in his mouth and befuddled by the greatest surprise of his life, Dr. Anzi started to cry. Tears burned his face. Relevance's face rose in his mind and, as he was lifted onto a stretcher, darkness swirling through a limitless void, he wondered what had become of the young man.

Chapter Eight

Beyond Our Care

—Breakfastnook Café—

January, Year 75, Newearth Reckoning

Herson smashed through the café door, sending the chimes into a frenzy. He screamed at the room full of diners who immediately froze in place, startled expressions uniting them. "Where is he!"

From the throng of confused patrons, Taug rose from a back booth and padded forward. With a soothing tone, he called out, "Herson, I'm here. Come with me."

Herson would have none of it. No more orders from anyone. He'd had enough of that from his mother and cadet school. Standing his ground, he crossed his arms over his heaving chest. "No! You sent Dr. Anzi away. The only person who could help me. Now you better live up to your reputation, Cresta, and figure out how to make things right."

With a surreptitious signal to a Uanyi dressed in white, Taug advanced, his tentacles floating before him like flags blowing in a soft breeze. "Riko is going to get you something to eat, and we'll go to my lab and—"

"That den of horrors? Never, you-you monster!"

Leaving their breakfasts half finished, patrons began to slip out of their seats and dart for the door. Mothers grabbed their children and held them close, fear filling their eyes.

As if someone had pricked him, leaking power from his limbs, Taug's tentacles flapped to his sides and his gaze fell flat.

Fury churned Herson's gut while his blurry mind tried to sort out the situation. He quickly reached an obvious conclusion. *Too many people watching.* He pointed to a booth near the back wall.

Taug stepped aside and let Herson lead the way. When they sat across from each other, Taug clasped two tentacles on the table, and waited—like a good Cresta—for further instruction.

Attempting to subdue rising panic, Herson glanced every which way. *Probably spies all over this place, monitoring me. Think I don't know, but I know.* Dizzy with fractured sights and sounds overloading his mind, Herson had to clap his hands over his face to concentrate. Finally, with a calming breath, he opened his hands and zeroed in on Taug. "I need some clean Hash. Dr. Anzi was going to get some. He knew the best places, but he's gone now, thanks to you."

Taug's silent stare either proved he was behind the times or trying to think up a good lie. Finally, he leaned in, lowered his voice and assumed a friendly intimacy between them. "What's Hash? And how does one make it clean?"

Herson's knee bounced as his heart rate spiked. He hissed, "A blend of Dumplix and Blandish! Don't play stupid; you know what I'm talking about, Cresta."

Unexpectedly, Taug's expression hardened, his eyes narrowed. "You know my name, Herson. Use it. Or I will have an Interventionist escort you to the nearest rehabilitation center."

Flabbergasted by this sudden show of strength from a pulpy weakling, Herson slapped the table. "Stop the games, Taug!"

The door chime, which had been tinkling in a subdued manner every few moments as patrons slipped out, suddenly clanged loud and clear. A collective intake of breath caught the edge of Herson's attention. That patrons had left as soon as he entered barely scratched his consciousness but aware now that someone padded *toward* him sent prickles down his arms. He glanced aside and disbelief nearly choked his brain.

Relevance?

Taller than he remembered but as handsome as always, his half-brother stopped beside the table, nodded at Taug, and then met Herson's gaze.

"May I join you?"

His throat parched, Herson jiggled his arm at a Uanyi dressed in white standing in the background. "Drinks! Bring us something cold. It's too hot in here."

Gazing up, Taug scooched over and patted the red plastic seat at his side.

Relevance slid into place.

Herson laughed as he considered the Cresta and the tribrid in front of him, both so large that they barely fit on the same booth. "What? No one wants to sit by me?"

Taug murmured something to Relevance as an aside.

Fury blotted out all other considerations. "Stop whispering! No more secrets, understand?" He leaned forward and laced his words with salty irony. "Where's *Mother*? Isn't she going to join our *family* reunion?"

A formal throat clearing, and Taug straightened. "Relevance and I have come to a better understanding. We've been meeting here regularly for the last couple of months. It's you who dropped by unexpectedly."

Molten hatred filling him, Herson wished he had a dustbuster. He dropped his voice to silky sweetness. "How nice. So gratified that my closest relations have bonded. Could not be happier." He offered an exaggerated grin. "If only we could get Gavin and Mother to join us." His fingers itched for a trigger.

Relevance didn't appear unduly disturbed. He leaned back and threw one arm over the back of the booth, relaxed and casual. "Gavin is coming."

"I know that, brother! I already contacted him. He's coming to my gradu—" Herson shuddered. Something wasn't right. Did he graduate already? He had a party at the Docking Bay. His friends had come. He ate and drank…plenty of Blandish…

In his ever-superior tone, Relevance pounded his point home. "You never graduated, Herson."

Shaking his head to clear his muffled ears, he forced himself to focus on the brown-haired man across from him. *Are those muscles? No, Ingot enhancements, surely. Such a fake!* He snorted and dismissed his brother with a wave. "You're so stupid!"

A vision of himself standing before his lead officer hovered before his wide-awake eyes, an authoritative man intoning judgment—*not enough points…reports of suspicious connections…illegal commerce…behavior unbecoming a Human Services…*

A roaring wave washed over Herson, sending him to his feet. He had to grab the edge of the table to keep his balance. "I had a party! Clare paid for it." He glared at Taug. "Bet you killed Dr. Anzi, didn't you? But I have my rights. You better get me a new supplier, Cresta."

Taug extended a tentacle and attempted to clasp Herson's hand. "We can help you. Addiction is a serious—"

Herson jerked away, standing back. "Liars! Always judging me with your snide looks; I know what you think—just a stupid hybrid, how boring!" The image of Gavin popped into his mind. Instantly, former dreams blossomed. *He'll help me.*

Riko hovered on the periphery, a tray of drinks in his hands.

Relevance nodded at the proprietor. "Thanks, Riko. We could use some refreshment." He directed his gaze at his brother. "Sit down and drink something, Herson. Let's discuss options. Maybe a little time in Vandi Rehab—"

Exploding with laughter, Herson almost felt free, as if a fresh jolt of Hash had flooded his system. His future spread before him like an unrolling tapestry. *Gavin always welcomed me. It'll be perfect! I can make a fortune, build a house, let them see what success looks like.*

Taug reached out, but Herson twirled away like the wind. He practically danced to the door.

As the door chimes rang out once again, Relevance's words carried across the distance, "Let him go, Taug. It's no use."

You'll see! Just wait; everyone will want to be my friend.

Under the bright morning sun, Herson grabbed an idling autoskimmer from a Bhuaci girl who stood to the side, chatting with friends. As he revved the vehicle into high gear and then directed it to the Docking Bay, he could hardly stop a grin from splitting his face. *Time for a new life!*

—Newearth Docking Bay—

Herson knew his way around the Docking Bay. Departures were listed on flashing boards on every level. But none were currently scheduled to Tabun. That left only one option.

He made his way to the top level, where small, nearly obsolete vessels were left for quick trips to nearby planets. Tabun wasn't *that* far away. Any ship would do.

Managing security measures was ironically one of the few classes he passed with high scores. Rerouting the system was so simple, he giggled as he worked at the console in the central Communications room. Strange that no one seemed to be around. Not his concern. He just needed a few minutes.

Ship seven was ready to go, its tiny hull stashed with Ingot wares.

Voices bubbled down the corridor.

Herson's fingers flashed as he unlocked the portal and altered the ship's destination. All set, he darted from his chair, sprinted down the opposite corridor, smacked in the key code, waited with heaving breaths for the door to slide open, then crashed into the tiny cockpit and landed hard on the pilot seat. Hands trembling, he raced over the coordinates and gave the thrusters full power. A siren blared. Oh, damn, he'd forgotten to unlock the portal arm. A few taps and that annoyance was managed.

Slowly, clumsily, the ship eased itself from the dock.

Alarms, louder and more insistent, blared from the bay. Faces appeared in the viewing window, staring at him across the blackness. Hands waved frantically.

Herson laughed, a giddy sensation rising from his toes to the top of his head. "Ha! Fools can't stop me now."

Grinning, he smacked the thruster button.

A flash of light.

Herson knew no more.

—Clare's House—

Clare sat on her couch before the big bay window as night descended and could hear her voice screaming, "No!" The sound repeated itself endlessly in her mind, like a Bhuaci hymn cycle but without meaning or beauty. A harsh, unrelenting No! allowed not a particle of discussion. Justine and Max had merely stared at her as she turned, marched out of her office, and then made her way home alone.

She had been surprised when the two Docking Bay managers showed up at the Human Services office. She had assumed they were looking for Bala, something about the ongoing Animans investigation. She had winced at the thought of anyone asking Bala about David. Bala's son might be sitting up with his eyes open, but he didn't appear to really see anything, and he hadn't said a word. Neither Justine nor Max were going to get much help from the guy. And how they expected Bala to help, she couldn't imagine. She was just about to intercept them when they turned and headed in her direction.

Standing at her office door, she welcomed them with a patient smile. She had steered clear of the Animans case because of Bala and Relevance's part to play, but if it would save her partner grief, she would talk to them now.

Justine, with her superior abilities and chill demeanor, had always irritated Clare. But as painful life events had mounted up, Clare began to appreciate Justine's quiet integrity. She had to hand it to Justine, even when her daughter, Zara, had died, the android woman never fell apart. Took some time off, but then, who wouldn't? A couple of weeks later, she was back at work. But now, seeing her in front of her office door, it was as if Zara had died all over again.

Unnerved, Clare looked to Max and waited for the situation to play out. Had something new happened? Some villain vandalized the Docking Bay perhaps?

Never exactly smooth, Max spoke with short, simple words, as if his preciseness would make his meaning irrefutable. "Herson died on Docking Bay Seven this morning. He misjudged his launch and thrust his ship into an oncoming one. Three people died, including him.

It took a moment for Max's words to process through her brain, but once they did, that's when Clare screamed, "No!" She repeated it three times. Then turned around as if she needed something, couldn't remember what, and finally, she stalked past Max, brushed by Justine, ignored the startled expressions from people milling around the central meeting space, and made her way home. Had she walked? Unlikely, but she couldn't remember getting an autoskimmer. She couldn't remember anything except entering her living room and knowing, with profound certainty, that Herson would never come home again.

The agony in her chest practically tore her body apart. She rocked in misery on the couch, curled up into a ball, and sobbed uncontrollably until the sun fell from the sky and night rose.

Now nothing. She stared across her living room and saw only darkness.

A knock sounded. Not the chime. Not a text bling warning her that someone was coming over. Exhausted, her whole body ached. *No.*

With a sigh, Clare dismissed all care. Might be Bala. Might be Cerulean. Could be God Himself for all she knew. It wouldn't be Herson, that's all that mattered.

The door opened, and footsteps padded across the hardwood floor. Unfamiliar footsteps.

Part of her brain woke up and sent a spike of fear through her. She tensed, though, in so much pain, she couldn't hold it stiff and went limp again almost immediately. If it was a thief, let them steal. If it was a killer, let them kill. She could not care.

"Mom?"

The voice was deep and strong. A man's voice. An almost familiar voice.

Her head lifted, though she refused real interest.

A man silhouetted in black stood before her. Large build, bulky almost.

She dropped her gaze. She would not care.

Footsteps paced closer and stopped. "Mom, it's me, Relevance. I just heard." A choke and then a heaved breath. "I'm sorry."

Spiking pain flourished and new tears flowed. Clare couldn't stop them. She couldn't hold back the primal scream that should have sent any sane person out the door.

But Relevance, this bulky man-child she did not know, did not run. He sat down and gently wrapped his arms around her.

He cried, groaning with her, their tears mingling in a thousand injuries that cut so deep, neither could explain why they hurt so bad.

Clare buried herself in the only comfort she had left, pain and darkness.

The next morning, Clare woke to snowfall. She blinked at the brightness of a world covered in white, snowflakes swirling from a gray sky. Amazed that she had slept so long and deeply, remorse engulfed her. *I should not have slept. I should have prayed, or made arrangements, or done something useful.*

Memories crashed against her skull. Relevance's appearance, their crying together for what seemed hours, confused her. *Did he say he was sorry?*

She knew why she had cried.

Do I?

She thrust back the covers and staggered out of bed.

Why did Relevance cry?

Barely able to manage her trembling fingers, Clare pulled off her night dress and tugged on a heavy sweater, enhanced leggings, and slip-on shoes. After a quick brush through her hair, she hobbled out the bedroom door as fast as her legs allowed.

All quiet and still. The kitchen and living room were unchanged. If they witnessed a scene of agony last night, they weren't breathing a word of it.

Hesitantly, she made her way forward and called out, "Relevance?"

No answer. Not a sound.

A sinking sensation dragged her spirits back to a dark pit. Had it been a dream? An illusion born of extreme grief?

Her stomach, empty for too long, clenched in a painful knot. She needed to eat though she didn't want to.

But her legs moved and her feet plodded along dutifully. She halted at the kitchen counter and wondered if she could ever swallow again. Perhaps she would turn to dust and blow away. A fitting end.

Her datapad, forgotten on the counter, pinged. A notice popped up. From Relevance.

Hello, Mother,

Thank you for your understanding last night. I shouldn't have come over unannounced, but the shock of Herson's death... Well, you know.

I have a lot to think about. You, too, I suppose.

The Inter-Alien Alliance Commission subpoenaed me to appear at a formal Hearing at Vandi Courthouse next month concerning the creation of Animans. There is a full investigation underway, and data is being collected as I write this. My part to play is a big one, and I do not expect to go unpunished. I should be.

I just want you to know that I am sorry. All my life, I have judged you harshly without knowing the full situation. Can a child ever see his parent in a clear light?

Herson contacted me months ago, and I hoped we would have a chance to start over, but I did not know about his addiction then. By the time I found out, it was too late. Or so I thought at the time. Now it really is too late.

I do not know what the future holds, but I wish to make amends for my past. If that is possible.

Your son,

Relevance

Clare collapsed on the kitchen chair and allowed her heart to break anew. Herson was gone beyond her reach, but Relevance still lived. Could grief give passage to hope? She didn't know. But suddenly, to her amazement, she realized that she did care. That would be her first step.

—Vandi Hospital Long-Term Care Unit—

Relevance stood just outside the doorway and watched Variant wash David's naked upper body with all the expertise of a trained nurse. The young man sat up in his hospital bed, the rails down, his eyes open but glazed, as if he could only see an interior world. A white sheet covered the lower half of his body, which, from what Relevance could see, was as bare as the day the man was born. Neither David nor Variant seemed unduly concerned with modesty.

Uncertain whether he should knock and ask admittance or if he should simply leave and return another time, Relevance hesitated.

Suddenly, a hand tapped his shoulder, and Relevance turned to see Kendra standing beside him. The last time he had seen her was when he was a small child, before he had been sent off planet. A lot had happened since then. There were no words to cover the mountain range of experiences, so he just attempted a smile and hoped she'd accept that.

She smiled back. A soul weary smile, but still welcoming. "Come on in. You're here to see Variant, I suppose."

Variant looked up, though her hands continued to work, caressing David's golden skin with a wet cloth, working her way over his shoulders and down his arms. Her salutation seemed sincere but strangely detached. "Hi, Relevance."

With all the awkwardness of being the new kid in the room, Relevance hovered by the wall, afraid to come closer and too proud to run away. "Just came to see how you're doing. I heard that he's doing better…" He swallowed. The memory of thrashing David at LEAP Laboratory collided with his intentions to distract himself from recent misery. He glanced at Kendra who stood beside the bed.

Variant broke through his memories as she handed the wet cloth to Kendra. "I did his back already. Just the front and his legs are left."

Horrified at images rushing into his mind, Relevance couldn't stop his words. "Where's the nurse? It's her job; she's paid to do this."

A sharp glance and Kendra stared at Relevance. "He's my son."

Bewildered, Relevance tried to collect his thoughts. "I didn't mean—"

Variant slipped her arm around Relevance's and directed him to the door. "Let's get something to eat. The café has a great pastry selection. I could use a hot drink and something sweet. How about you?"

The role reversal baffled Relevance to the extreme, but he was willing to be led since he had no idea what else to do.

Once seated at an intimate table for two before a huge window, Relevance stared upon the glory of an ornate courtyard with sculptures and statues, a still fountain, and stone benches, resting comfortably under a soft blanket of snow.

Variant carried a tray to the table and carefully set cups of steaming coffee and a plate of pastries between them. She grinned as she took a sip of the strong brew and then a large bite of a cherry tart. She chewed meditatively and then wiped her lips and sat back, her gaze studying him.

Relevance didn't know what to make of the woman he had always considered childish and easily confused. Never in his wildest dreams had he ever imagined that she could appear so composed and…what? Peaceful? He wanted to ask what had changed her but there was no way to word the question without being insulting.

Variant seemed to read his mind. "I met Clare, and we talked."

Holding his breath, Relevance wasn't sure if he would ever be able to speak again.

"She's not so bad once you get to know her."

A desire to laugh suddenly rushed up and nearly overpowered Relevance. He managed to contain it to a snort.

Misunderstanding, Variant scowled. "No, I mean it. I've gotten to know her. She explained everything, and I understand now. It was never me she hated. It all had to do with stuff that happened to her when she was a little girl. She just reacted to me because she couldn't handle any reminders of her past."

Taug's recital of Clare's past and his own conception rose in his mind. *It was never about me either.* He tried to put this new reality into proper perspective. "So, what? You're friends now?"

Variant's scowl deepened as her gaze bored into Relevance. "Yes. We are. I hope that doesn't bother you."

Relevance had to clench his teeth to maintain control.

Her expression softening, Variant nudged the pastry dish closer to him. "Eat something. You look washed out."

Admitting the truth of the observation, Relevance took a large gulp of the hot coffee, scalded his throat, and then covered the burn with a large bite of a cinnamon bun. His mind returned to the image of David sitting blank-eyed in bed. "Tell me about David. And Kendra."

Nodding through a grin and another bite of her tart, Variant appeared happy to please. "Well, you probably know about how David took the overdose, and we weren't sure he'd live, but then he came around. He's able to sit up and can even respond to some things. He'll eat when we put food to his mouth and drink from a cup, though it took a while to get him to stop dribbling so much. It's like teaching a very slow child how to do the basics, if you know what I mean. He'll never be like he was, but he'll get better. So, it's worth it." She grinned and took another bite.

Relevance couldn't help asking, "Is it?"

Her eyes widening with a slap-down glare, Variant shot him with silent meaning. "I would think that you—of all people—would see the value of helping someone!"

He could not argue with the idea, though his rational mind couldn't help digging deeper. "But why you?" He held up his hand to keep her eye-darts from tearing him to pieces. "I mean, I don't understand why you ever liked him in the first place. David was always weak, easily led. Not very smart, to be honest."

"Your beating him up was smart, though?"

If slinking to the floor and melting into the tile was an option, Relevance would have seriously considered it. Shame heated his face. "I was wrong about that. But so was he!"

"Why? Because he cared about me? Because he helped me to help you?" Slapping her hands together in a serious need to get rid of pastry crumbs, Variant hammered her gaze on Relevance. "You always thought I was a stupid child, didn't you? Your grand ideas to make new hybrids, to show the universe that you were better than everyone—Taug would stand back in admiration, Ingots would be amazed, even Tabunites would hail you as a God! I was just some wild thing that you could soothe and use when needed. Did it never occur to you that though I was a mistake, never wanted by anyone, I still was just as worthy of respect as you?"

Relevance wasn't sure he could take any more. His gut heaved, and his mind whirled. He wanted to hate someone, but the only target in view was himself.

A woman, *Kendra?* hustled toward them, her face tight with pain and anxiety.

Variant shot to her feet.

Kendra held up her hand, stalling any sudden movement. "David's fine. I left the nurse with him." She reached over and clasped Relevance's shoulder, her eyes grave. "Bala just told me. Clare's all torn up. He's with her now."

Gratitude flowed through Relevance, and he wanted to hug this woman he did not know but suddenly wondered if he could love. “Thank you. I’m glad Bala is helping her. I couldn’t.”

Variant’s eyes flickered between the two. “What? Why is Clare all torn up?”

Kendra sighed and then met Variant’s perplexed gaze. “Herson was killed in an accident yesterday.” She seemed to swallow a choking lump. “He tried to steal a ship. High on Hash, he made a mistake and crashed into another ship. Killed himself and two Ingot traders.”

Variant’s hands trembled as she pressed them to her mouth, her eyes filling with tears. She dropped to her knees at Relevance’s side. “I’m so sorry. I didn’t know. I didn’t mean to be so harsh.”

Relevance shrugged. The truth in the hands of such decent people seemed to make it more bearable. “You were right. Every word.”

Her arm embracing him, Variant lifted her gaze to Kendra, who stood like a tower in a raging storm. “How did Herson get on Hash? He was a cadet, right?”

Relevance shook his head. “Never graduated. He was kicked out but lied to Clare. She even threw him a party with his friends.”

Kendra pulled out a chair and flopped down with a weary sigh. “Bala said that it looks like he was dealing Dumplix. How he got his hands on it…” She shrugged. “But Cresta and Ingot dealers are known to experiment, and they came up with Hash, a blend of Dumplix and Blandish. A unique high that comes and goes even weeks after it has been consumed.” She wiped her eyes. “Herson may not have planned to take it. Could have been slipped in his food or a drink. A useful way to keep a supplier compliant.”

Vivid images of Herson in the Breakfastnook Café rose in Relevance’s mind. Taug would have run after him. But he had stopped the Cresta. He muttered his haunting words, “It’s no use.”

Variant squeezed his arm. “Why do you say that?”

"That's what I said the last time I saw Herson. I didn't let Taug go after him. Maybe…maybe we could have gotten help. Saved him." His vision going blurry, Relevance felt his mom's wrenching sobs as they clung together in overwhelming grief.

Kendra crouched at his side and caressed his arm, her sad gaze fixed on the air in front of her. "We'll never know what might have been. He could have done more harm in the long run. It's a tragedy that shouldn't have happened but did."

Variant slipped back onto her chair. "It's terrible in a way, but my body doesn't react to drugs, not like most people. I'm immune, just watch from a distance. I should never have given David…"

With a sigh, Kendra regained her footing. "The dead are beyond our care. Let's do what we can for the living."

With a nod, Relevance thought of his mother. He knew he would visit her again soon. He stood and faced Variant. He had a lot of amends to make. He would start small, since he had no idea what else to do. "I have a new piano piece I'd like to teach you. If you'd be interested."

A weak ray of sunshine pierced the dark clouds, and Variant nodded as she started after Kendra. "That would be grand."

Relevance followed the two women, returning to the room of a man who could neither see nor hear, the word "grand" running through his head like the first chords of a song.

Chapter Nine

Forgive Me

—Seth's Harbor—

Justine didn't exactly hold Max's hand, as they stood shoulder-to-shoulder in the Great Hall of Seth's Harbor, but they had suffered so much together that even when they didn't touch, they were still intimately connected. The truth of their bond went beyond her rational comprehension but that didn't particularly matter.

Max's mouth hung open as he turned in a one-sixty and took in the startling array of OldEarth architecture and Newearth comforts. Light streamed through a stained-glass window and pooled on a holopad encircled with sparkling stones, creating a beautiful unity of old and new. Rays from two arched windows slanted across the clean stone floor while a flickering fire warmed the room despite a cold wind blowing snow in scuttling drifts outdoors. His heart leaped at the sight of an evergreen decorated with colorful lights set in a round container near the south wall.

Rachel smiled and pointed to the tree. "We replaced an old mulberry tree we used for nests with this evergreen in respect to ancient traditions. Besides, we no longer needed the nests." Her expression wavered, but she rallied and ran her hand along the soft, blue-green needles. "It's from an OldEarth ritual, a spiritual reminder of life even in the midst of death."

Max sighed, his hands pressing his chest as if he were trying to keep his nonexistent heart in place.

Justine understood his wonder but didn't want him to overdo his expression. She nudged him in the side and pointedly tapped her chin.

Max closed his mouth, and then made eye contact with his hostess.

Beams of happiness shot from Rachel as she refocused. "I grew up with stories of you two! Dad didn't let his profession intrude on our family life when he could help it, especially not after that horrible home invasion, but still, he couldn't keep his admiration out of his voice when he spoke of you."

Justine held her tongue. Compliments made her uncomfortable.

Not Max. He soaked them up like a Globeflower after a deluge. He stepped over to a bookcase stuffed with OldEarth volumes and dared to trace his fingers along the spines in a loving gesture. He spoke with his usual honesty. "You and Seth have achieved high renown yourselves. Lang wants to do a write up for Universal News."

Rachel's eyes practically doubled in size.

To keep the mutual admiration from inflating anymore, Justine tugged the two innocents back to reality. "We came to see how you manage your patients."

Professional demeanor back in place, Rachel nodded. "Yes, of course." She pointed to the steps between the two bookcases. "So many have passed on that we moved the last of the Animans into more comfortable quarters upstairs."

Justine followed the young woman up the circling flight of stairs to the second floor. "How many are left?"

"Not that many, sadly. Squire is our celebrity. He and his son, Inheritance, draw quite a crowd. Relevance comes frequently—" She stumbled and almost fell.

Justine reached up and kept the young woman from slipping backward.

A deep blush and Rachel scurried up the last of the steps and onto the landing.

Once Max joined them, Rachel hurried down the wide corridor to an open doorway at the end. "Only twelve patients are left, none of them very big. It seems that the larger

Animans suffered the worst. We had to keep Elch heavily medicated at the end, poor thing."

The sight of a hound dog propped on one paw staring at a comic book before a fireplace, a cat in a long dress nestled at his side pointing at the pictures and whispering, a raccoon sitting against a wall, his legs crossed, chomping on a sandwich, two chipmunks playing cards on the lower bunk, and several other creatures under blankets in different parts of the room, all with human expressions, froze her at the doorway. An image of David when she had last seen him, staring mindlessly into space, clouded her mind.

Max tugged her arm to get her to enter.

Rachel led the way to Squire's bed. The wise little face with inquiring eyes seemed to understand Justine's hesitation and forgave any natural revulsion.

Little Inheritance sat up, his black eyes flashing and his tail swishing.

Squire patted his back in a soothing manner. "Just friends come to visit, little one."

Rachel pointed to Max and Justine in turn. "These are the Docking Bay Managers, Max and Justine, that Cerulean always talks about."

A pained expression flitted over Squire's face. "He told us about the accident. Must be hard."

Justine's gaze drifted out the window. The sound of an explosion had jolted her from a quiet moment in her daughter's room. She had been reading one of Zara's favorite books, trying to see what her daughter had seen, feel what her daughter had felt. Live what her daughter had lived.

When she arrived at the scene of the accident, there was little anyone could do but contain the damage. It took just over an hour to review the video feeds and discover Herson's identity. Informing the Ingot High Command that two of their traders were dead was another matter. She should have caught the override in the system as soon as Herson did it, but she hadn't been at her post. She had been reading a child's book.

Slapping her forehead, Rachel stifled a gasp. "I forgot all about that. Clare must be devastated! So tragic to lose her son like that."

Max didn't appear to hear.

Justine pretended she hadn't.

For some reason that Justine could not fathom, Squire seemed intent on soothing her as well as his son. He could hardly get to his feet, but he managed to roll onto his side where he could meet her gaze straight on, even if there remained a significant distance between them. "Relevance once said, 'Our bodies do not define us.'" A grin flittered over Squire's face. "You know better than anyone." His smile faded. "But he was confused. What makes a person truly human? He asked me, his humble servant, to help him understand."

It was barely a whisper, but Justine heard Max's question loud and clear.

"Did you?"

His eyes twinkling, Squire nodded. "Yes, I think I did."

Justine's nerves, which she knew perfectly well she didn't have, were about to snap. "What then?"

Inheritance nudged his father in the side playfully. The little squirrel wanted to run around.

Squire ran his paw over the youngster's back, calming him. "Discover the best in others, even your enemy. Only true humanity can do that."

Max clasped Justine's hand and puffed out his chest like a man preparing to make a speech. "We're going to open a facility to assist addicts from all over the universe. It'll be called the Right from Wrong Center of Healing."

Rachel's eyes shone as she breathed her words. "So, Relevance was right."

Justine dragged her attention from Squire's wonderful little face to Bala's daughter. "How's that?"

"He said that you were two of the best humans on the planet."

Not that Justine needed confirmation of her inherent decency, but it had been a long time in coming. That it came from a man about to be tried for crimes against sentient life only made it rather ironic. She wondered what Zara would say.

Max held his hand out to the little squirrel. “May I?”

With a grin, Squire nodded.

A spirited leap, and Inheritance ran up Max’s arm. He soon settled on his shoulder, chattering excitedly the whole time.

Rachel burst out laughing.

Justine didn’t need matching DNA to laugh with her.

—Waukee Peaceful Repose Cemetery—

Cerulean stood before a mound of dirt encircled by mud and melted snow and bowed his head. *Too many graves.*

As a fresh cascade of flakes swirled gently from the white sky, images of those he had known flittered through his mind. Anne Smith’s voice resounded in his ears, and he could see her at the kitchen table kneading bread…in the garden, watering bountiful zucchini plants…sitting in her living room, murmuring ancient prayers.

“Where are you now?” The question hung in the frozen air, unable to answer itself. It could have been directed to a dozen others—his father and mother, his wife, son, Sterling, those humans he had observed through centuries untold, watching humanity grow up in a universe that could never fully understand their virtues amidst their sins.

A flash of red caught his eye, and he almost laughed at a redbird alighting on a sleeping oak tree. “Are you here to tell me something, my feathered friend?”

To his astonishment, the bird took flight and landed at his feet, looking up at him with an impish grin. Then it morphed, elongated, and took an elven shape, becoming the form he knew as Faye. She was dressed in a long red winter coat with fluffy white cuffs and dainty laced black boots. A tasseled hood was thrown back over her shoulders.

She quirked a smile at him. "I didn't want to intrude on a private moment, but when you spoke to me, I thought you realized who I was."

"Not at all. But I've learned to accept surprises without going into cardiac arrest."

As she stepped to the edge of the grave, Faye pulled a daffodil from her pocket. She then laid it on the top of the mound and bowed her head.

Respectfully, Cerulean followed her example and bowed his head, staring in uneasy silence at the mud on his shoes.

Finally, Faye lifted her gaze. Her lips trembled as she spoke. "I lost my family young, but I miss them still."

"They would be proud of you, Faye, for what you have achieved despite terrible difficulties."

"Do you think they know…see us now?"

Cerulean lifted his hands in acceptance or surrender; he wasn't sure which. "Perhaps. We both know that there is much we do not see with our eyes."

A sniff and Faye spoke to the mound. "That's what Walking Flower said before she headed home: that our bodies are like veils, allowing us only a glimpse of our spirits. There is so much we do not see."

Surprised, Cerulean thrust his cold hands into his coat pockets. "She was at peace with the closing of LEAP Laboratories, then?"

"Oh, yes. She never had any illusions that Dr. Anzi could help her people. She feared that, in their desire for greater acceptance, perhaps for greater power and wealth, some of her people would believe the lies he spread."

A shrug, and Cerulean couldn't stop himself from laying the bare truth before her. "The formula for creating Animans is loose in the universe."

"So are the voices of those suffering from its effects. Though some willingly believe a lie, not so many will be fooled. In time, the term Dumplix will be seen as a curse, not a cure."

A perplexing question tapped on Cerulean's mind. "Walking Flower wants her race to accept their fate? That Insectine people will always be looked down upon by other sentient beings because of their physical forms?"

Faye shook her head, her impish grin back in place. "Not at all. She said that—given time—the best of them would set a new trend and Insectine style will become all the fashion."

The laugh that bubbled up inside Cerulean dissolved when his gaze landed on the white snow mounting on the grave mound. "Herson won't have that chance."

Joining him in solemnity, Faye's voice revealed her strength of will. "Not here. Not now. But we do not know the limits of the Creator's imagination. World's unseen, remember?"

With that hope in his heart, Cerulean took Faye's hand and led her out of the graveyard.

Relevance ignored the muddy prints around his brother's grave, though the flower caught his attention. *Who left that?* The dull ache that had lodged in his chest at the news of Herson's death throbbed with the force of an impending disaster. *My brother's bad choices were not my fault!* He wondered if that were completely true. If he had treated Herson with more kindness, would he have chosen a different path? Nausea twisted his gut. *Like mine?*

In an emotional downpour, futility pounded his heart. Only the distant flickers of Clare's need, Variant's happiness, and the understanding expression in Kendra's and Rachel's eyes offered any light to steer by.

As snow fell in fat flakes, Relevance rubbed his cold hands together and argued with himself. *Clare doesn't need another disappointing son. For Bothmal's sake, I'm going before the IAAC to be punished for my crimes! I can't teach Variant a new piano piece or bring Rachel into my wretched future.* Self-loathing rose into a strangled scream. "What kind of a monster am I?"

Out of the corner of his eye, an odd scene demanded his attention. A man had stopped, hesitating, on the circular driveway. A black coat strained at his muscular frame while new hiking boots hinted at a Newearth recent arrival. The man lifted his boot, stepped on the snow bank, and his foot plunged into the depths. He jerked it free and stood back, considering the situation as if facing a ring of fire.

If any shred of humor still existed within Relevance, he would have laughed.

Clearly reconsidering his options, the man stepped back, took a deep breath, and then leaped, sailing neatly over the half-meter snowy mound and landing on the other side. If the landing had stuck, or the danger in any way real, it would have been an impressive show. But as the snowbank could have easily been forded and his landing turned into a wobbly skid where the man ended up on his back, the event appeared more pathetic than powerful.

Returning his attention to the mound, Relevance studied the flower again. *What does a daffodil symbolize?* For some reason he could not explain, his attention was lured back to the fallen figure. Against his rational will, he stepped carefully across the snowy expanse and then held out his hand. "You all right?"

The man clasped the offered support and was pulled to his feet; a deep chuckle emanated from his chest.

I know that sound!

Shock sped like fire over Relevance. He peered at the stranger. "Gavin?"

Slapping wet snow from his pants and coat, the Tabunite, a Neanderthal cousin to the contemporary human race, chuckled in fits and gasps. "Shouldn't have tried that. Didn't know what else to do." He met Relevance's gaze head on. "Little snow in the plains where I live." He waved his arms as if to encompass the snowy landscape. "Not like this."

As if he had been dropped into a frozen lake, Relevance could hardly process his crashing thoughts much less Gavin's words. Finally, he eked out his primary question. "What…are you…doing here?"

Gavin's surveyed the graveyard and halted on the snowy mound. His expression sobered, and his voice fell to a husky whisper. "I told you I would come."

His mind cracking into a thousand splinters, Relevance didn't filter his words. "Herson wanted you to see him graduate."

Clapping his hand on Relevance's shoulder, Gavin kept his gaze firm. "Yes, I know. Clare told me."

The mound called, as if Herson didn't want to be left out of the conversation, so Relevance retreated to where he had been standing, filling the mud-stained snow with his prints once again.

Silently, Gavin followed and took his position next to Relevance.

In a desire to make a clean start, Relevance hardly hesitated, offering no niceties to ease into the stark reality they faced. "So, you know he never graduated. He lied to Clare, sold Dumplix on the black market, got addicted to Hash, and killed two innocent people and himself in a moment of madness?"

Gavin nodded; his expression stricken as he stared at the wilting flower.

Out with it. Tell the whole truth, not just the sins of your brother. "You know that I joined with a doctor who brought animals to sentience with no redeeming expectations beyond proving the worthlessness of the human race? And I now face criminal charges?"

Another nod. Gavin's attention stayed fixed on the dead bloom.

Relevance's hands burned with cold. He stuffed them into his pockets. "I ask again—Why did you come?"

Gavin tilted his head, his gaze rising to the sky. The snow had stopped and brilliant blue peeked through the retreating clouds. "After false hopes die, real hope is born."

His breath caught; Relevance didn't dare breathe. He wanted to hold that thought and bring it alive inside himself. Finally, he exhaled. "I have followed after many lies."

Gavin's wan smile offered soothing comfort. "You're young. Illusions are a part of the journey."

Jabbing his finger at the frozen mound, Relevance couldn't deny the truth of his despair. "But Herson is dead. Buried deep in the ground. What was left of him anyway."

Gavin shook his head. "Herson is not here."

His head jerking so hard, it twitched painfully, Relevance wondered if he had cracked something. He stared at the man he had once called father.

Undisturbed, Gavin stared at the distant horizon, rosy with the setting sun. "His remains are here, yes. The clothing we call a body is here. What is left of it—as you say. But whether it drifts in space, burned to ashes, lays in a graveyard, makes no difference. The spirit of Herson, my spirit son, still lives."

Rational denial battling a yearning desire to believe rose in a mighty scream. "How can you believe that? You're a primitive people who know nothing about…everything!"

A pronouncement. "We are not technologically advanced." Gavin shifted, facing Relevance directly. "That is why you left? Because Tabunites are primitive?"

The disappointment in his eyes was enough to shrivel Relevance from head to foot.

"We have no eyes to see with, no ears to hear with, no minds to think with? I suppose, we have no feelings to feel?"

It wasn't the questions that flooded Relevance with shame, it was the sudden realization that his perceptions had been skewed, his pride blind, and his heart viciously hard.

Barely whispering, he could offer no excuse. “I didn’t mean...”

With self-contained dignity, Gavin gave Relevance a moment to gather his wits. He crouched by the mound, extended his hands, and closed his eyes. A rhythmic hum rose from his chest. The melody, like a Bhuaci prayer, traveled over distant lands and ancient times, undulated around tragic loss and forlorn love, hopes and ardent dreams, trailed after mystical scents long spent, and wavered to silence, its haunting rhythm still beckoning the spirit. As the chant ended, Gavin lifted the limp plant, held it to his face, and he breathed deeply. Then he offered a gentle kiss and laid the withered flower back on its cold bed. He climbed to his feet and studied Relevance for a quiet moment. He spoke with his usual firm resolve. “I will stand at your side during the coming trial, my son.”

Wanting to cry but refusing to allow himself the relief, Relevance stood as straight as he could and accepted his father’s compassionate gaze.

—Vandi Hospital Long-Term Care Unit—

February, Year 75, Newearth Reckoning

Clare didn’t have much time but the compulsion to see Bala’s son, David, and find out how he was doing could not be refused. Besides, she had told Variant she would stop by so they could go to the courthouse together. She knew perfectly well that she wasn’t doing Variant a favor but rather it was the other way around.

With images of David as a mindless zombie lying in bed, staring sightlessly at the ceiling, she tip-toed hesitantly into the room. She blinked in surprise at the sight that met her eyes.

Variant lay cozied up with David on the hospital bed. She held up an oversized datapad and pointed as she spoke. "That wood was full of rabbit holes; and in the neatest, sandiest hole of all lived—"

David began tapping Variant's arm.

Variant followed his gaze and met Clare's puzzled expression. "Oh, there you are." She set the datapad aside and jumped up from the bed.

Squinting, Clare could just make out the cover as it appeared to close over the printed words: *The Tale of Benjamin Bunny* by Beatrix Potter, lettered in bold print on a green background with a picture of a bunny rabbit wearing a fancy hat. The image drew Clare like a magnet, enchanted, she wanted to pick up the datapad and keep reading. But with a force of will, she shook her head and gripped reality hard. No escaping to a mystical land now. *Maybe another day.*

Like a loving mother, Variant brushed David's hair back from his eyes and smoothed the perplexed frown on his face. "It's my friend, Clare. Your dad's partner at work, remember? We have to go somewhere, but I'll be back soon, don't worry."

As he gazed at the young woman with mismatched eyes and mottled skin, David's face lit up with the most adoring expression Clare had ever seen.

Variant kissed his cheek and then gathered her winter coat, scarf, and gloves from the back of a plush chair. "All set." She studied Clare. "You?"

There was nothing to do but shrug. No words would come. How could any mother be prepared to see her son tried for such grievous crimes? She shoved all thought of Herson's recent funeral from her mind. There was only so much she could handle.

Before she got to the door, Variant grabbed her arm. "Before we head out, there's something I need to tell you. And a favor I want to ask."

Since her leggings didn't allow for nervous foot-tapping, Clare made do with wringing her hands. She waited impatiently on the threshold, praying that Variant would be quick. She hardly wanted to show up late at the courthouse and make a bad impression on the judge.

Variant waved toward the bathroom. "It joins another room on the other side, you know."

Clare hadn't known, and she wasn't at all sure she cared. She tried to keep her expression interested, but it was becoming a serious challenge.

"Well, since I've been helping David so much, the other nurses started asking for help with simple chores, stuff that doesn't require real training but needs to get done. They're terribly understaffed, you know."

A squeak was rising from her throat, but Clare fought it manfully.

"So, it turns out that we could make a deal, kind of a work for lodgings and food sort of thing. Since I'm here at all hours with David, I practically live in the unit, they decided to make it official." Her face glowed. "I'm now a resident worker of the Vandi Long-Term Care Unit!"

If Variant expected applause, Clare must have been a disappointment. She couldn't imagine anyone wanting to live in a hospital. But then, she had to consider, not many people wanted to be a Human Services Detective. She rubbed her neck to manage the building strain. "You wanted to ask me something?"

"Oh, yeah." Variant leaned in. "I'm giving up my one-room studio, so that means I need to find a home for my piano, the one that Relevance gave me. I thought that maybe you could take it for a while. He wants to teach me a new song, but I figure he could do that at your place just as well." She glanced over her shoulder. "I play the one in the recreation room down the hall when they allow David to leave his room. He loves it."

A hundred questions ran over themselves trying to get first place in line. Clare held up her hand to stop the rampage.

"That's fine, though at some point, you'll move into your own place again, so it's just temporary, okay?"

Variant nodded like a happy schoolgirl who'd just won first prize.

Bafflement nearly made Clare see stars. *Would Variant and David ever…? Could he…?*

Refusing to even begin conjecturing, Clare turned abruptly and started down the hall. "Come by for supper some night this week, and we can get everything arranged." Her enhanced boots clip clopped authoritatively with every step.

Variant hurried after her, tugging on her coat and scarf as she went. "I want to cook supper, when I come. I've got a great new recipe I can try. You'll love it!"

Clare couldn't suppress a smile spreading over her face, warming her heart. No matter how terrible life could be, there were always odd jolts of joy mixed into the mess.

With explanations gushing from her lips, Variant rushed ahead and walked backwards, so she could speak directly. "I'm moving in because I love David, and I'm a better person when I am loving someone. I don't care what anyone thinks or that he's not perfect. He loves me for me, and I love him for him. That's how it is, anyhow, just so you understand."

Shaking her head, Clare knew that she couldn't, not really, but that didn't stop her from wrapping an arm around Variant and drawing her into a hug as they hustled out the door into a bright winter day.

—Vandi Courthouse —

Relevance stood off to the side of the judge's bench, his hands clasped and his head bowed. Dressed in a dark blue sweater and black pants, he couldn't think of any reason for mercy, but he didn't want pity. His legs felt stiff and his arms ached. Imagining a run through the park in the winter cold offered a dreamscape of relief but that would hardly happen any time soon. He may never see a park again for all he knew.

The judge, a Bhuac in fine elven form, with a strong jaw, a stiff spine, and eyes that harbored no sentiment, sat robed in a black cloak at a high table near the back of the room. Fingering his datapad, his gaze occasionally scrutinized Relevance as if he could ferret out the truth by studying the accused.

A bustle in the background arrested Relevance's attention, though he did not dare turn his head. He heard Taug's blustering apologies clearly enough, though.

"Oh, sorry, are you sitting there? A few seats together, if you don't mind?"

Grumbling and much harumphing suggested major seating rearrangements going on in the gallery.

Relevance almost smiled at the image of Taug's plump figure dominating the middle row, wrapping himself in proper form to avoid the embarrassing apologies when a stray tentacle crossed over approved territory and landed in someone's lap unexpectedly.

In his mind, Relevance followed the public gathering. The murmur of voices and pacing of footsteps had risen since he had arrived at the break of dawn. His long wait on a bench in the corridor, while people of all kinds—human and alien—defendants, prosecutors, witnesses, family members, and casual observers—marched with determined steps or strolled casually along with gazes fixed on inward concerns. With dispassionate distance in a mental orbit, he pictured professionals snapping orders to underlings, mothers wringing their hands, and fathers offering last-minute bits of advice to bored youth, irritated thugs with their cunning assistants—all passing by unaware of his anguish. No one wanted to look at him. They had troubles enough of their own.

Would his mother come? He shouldn't expect it, though he couldn't deny that his chest ached with the thought. *Has she given up on me?* Then he wondered if it was fair of him to want her to come. *Hasn't she been through enough?* But still the hope, selfish or not, burned inside.

A call, and someone in an almost familiar voice, made an urgent plea. "Could you please step aside? He's very fragile and needs a little space."

The urge to look around nearly mastered Relevance, but a deepening blush in response to the crowd who came to see him charged and sentenced kept his head down and his gaze fixed on the checkered flooring.

Finally, the court deputy rose and tugged Relevance to a large chair beside the judge's bench, facing the public assembly. He pressed Relevance's shoulder until he sat on the hard seat. Then, in a deep, rumbling voice, the deputy called everyone to order and formally announced the names of the judge—Sylvan, the defendant—Tribrid Relevance, the lawyer for the defense—a human named Mr. Frank, and the prosecuting attorney—a well-known Ingot with the appropriate name of Smash.

Daring to lift his head, Relevance surveyed the assembly, and his gaze at once fell on the plump, bio-suited form of Taug. Faye looked positively diminutive in her delicate elfin form next to his large bulk.

Directly in front of them, one row lower, sat Bala. He appeared to be munching on a candy bar. But what clutched Relevance's heart was the sight of Clare sitting between Variant and Gavin. *She came! And Gavin, too.* His gaze slid over Variant, not as unimportant but as a man blinded by the heart-stopping joy of seeing his parents seated companionably together.

Bala offered a fresh candy bar to Gavin on his left, but the heavily built man waved it away with a smile. Bala's grin faltered. An exaggerated eyeroll and Gavin snatched the bar, ripped the wrapper aside, and began to chomp. Smug, Bala pulled out three more bars and began offering them around like a kid at a school party.

Relevance shook his head, though his gaze roamed back to his mother who stared at him as if willing their eyes to meet. Once they did, a smile hovered over her face, and she lifted one hand, offering a timid wave. Nearly giddy with gladness, Relevance waved back. Then wondered if that was a good idea. *What if I end up in Bothmal prison? She shouldn't be seen waving to me.*

The next row down, a large man with a box in his arms shifted in his seat and adjusted a small blanket draped over the top.

Relevance leaned forward. *Max? What's in the box?*

As if in answer to his question, a small face with twinkling black eyes and a twitching furry nose peeked over the lid and glanced about.

His heart clamped in a vice; Relevance nearly yelped. *He shouldn't have brought Squire out in the cold. What if he gets sick?* The absurdity of that fear brought a derisive snort to his lips, while anxiety chilled his bones.

In the aisle, a shimmer of light sparkled, and Cerulean appeared out of nowhere, standing at the edge of Max's row.

I didn't know he could still do that. Or—?

Another flash, and a Luxonian, dark skinned, wearing a white robe suddenly appeared at his side.

His friend Roux probably. Moral support or as an official Supreme Judge? The sight of Cerulean comforted Relevance, but Roux's presence made him squirm uneasily.

The two squeezed by Max and found seats in the middle of the row. Cerulean was soon making formal introductions between Squire and his friend.

The scene reminded Relevance of a drama series he used to watch. He wondered if his head would explode. *Why have they all come?*

Official hammering, gavel on hardwood, and the crowd's murmuring died down.

Sitting as straight as only an Ingot can, one hand still clasping his gavel, Sylvan, in a tone as smooth as a still lake yet hard as a bedrock of granite, addressed the multitude of Humans, Luxonians, Bhuaci, Ingots, Uanyi, and Cresta. "Today's formal hearing will determine the guilt or innocence of Tribrid Relevance in the case of illegally experimenting on Newearth animals and bringing such innocents to sentience without any regard to their inherent rights as members of the Newearth planetary community. The fact that animals are generally considered lower life forms without self-awareness, advanced social constructs, and technological abilities, does not mean that they have no innate dignity or are less deserving of decent respect.

"Determining guilt will not be challenging as the facts have been assembled and are irrefutable. But the level of guilt and an appropriate response remains to be decided." He gestured to the prosecutor. "You may make your case first and then we will attend to the defense."

Smash rose from his seat and immediately lived up to his name. He held up a tomato and squeezed it in his grip until the pulp bled over his fingers and dribbled onto the floor. "This is what happens to an innocent mind under the influence of powerful drugs. There is no reconstruction possible. The unique being is destroyed by forces incapable of care or kindness."

He swerved and jutted a metal clad finger at Relevance. "Tribrid Relevance, well knowing the personal cost of experimentation on innocent life forms, himself being the result of such wanton overreach, showed little pity on the creatures he captured and caged, drugged, observed, and tossed out when their usefulness was over." His accusatory finger shifted to a large screen hovering in the center of the room, allowing for multi-dimensional images of the Animans in various stages of distress at Seth's Harbor. The pitiful pictures flashed relentlessly before the eyes of the assembly.

Gasps and startled commentary bubbled and spurted across the gallery.

Relevance closed his eyes as nausea rose and burned his throat.

"There is only one logical end to such a being!"

The prosecuting assistant handed Smash a clean white towel, whereby the attorney proceeded to wipe his hands with meticulous care. "Life Servitude on Bothmal Orbit at the Reclamation Harbor."

Nothing in his worst imaginings had prepared Relevance for such a fate. Bothmal Orbit was the largest garbage satellite in the known universe. Designated with the more dignified title of Reclamation Harbor, it was merely a sorting station for refuse found floating in space. No one actually lived there, so far as Relevance knew, though there were stories of criminals being sentenced to months on the satellite for grievous offenses while in Bothmal Prison, the largest Criminal Holding Center this side of the Divide.

The very idea of leaving a sentient being there for any length of time went against every code of ethics the Inter-Alien Correctional System professed. A life sentence in such a place was unheard of!

Relevance swallowed a lump in his throat and dared to glimpse the judge's face, hoping to see shock and perhaps even disgust. He was severely disappointed. Sylvan's face remained impassive, almost as if he had expected the demand and was seriously considering it.

Hope dwindling, Relevance shifted his gaze to the defense table. There, alone, sat Mr. Frank, a man he had met only once and who seemed as timid in the presence of Smash as a mouse facing a Uanyi Tigris. His hands clasped primly on the table, Mr. Frank said nothing, merely watched the proceedings as if he sat at home before his media screen.

In a rampaging conclusion, Smash brought to bear every known fact about LEAP Laboratory, Relevance's association with the disgraced scientist, Dr. Anzi, the unapproved use of an untested and unregulated drug called Dumplix, the capture and experimentation on ninety-seven known innocent animals, the unfortunate death of an assistant by the name of Jeremy Knowels…he rattled off a miserable list of further charges, but Relevance's mind stopped, frozen on the name of his former assistant.

Jeremy is dead? No one told me. He had visited Seth's Harbor several times, and Rachel had regaled him with the story of how Jeremy had assisted Cerulean with the information needed to obtain an arrest warrant for Dr. Anzi, forcing him to leave Newearth under the threat of a full investigation.

For the first time, the unfairness of the situation smacked Relevance in the head. *Jeremy is dead, Dr. Anzi escaped, and all that has happened—it's all blamed on me!*

Between memories of Jeremy's insensitive comments and the evolving sadness in his eyes, Relevance struggled to piece together the man within the clumsy assistant he knew. *He probably died from overexposure to Dumplix. Is that my fault? What about Dr. Anzi? And all the people who supported him, who supported LEAP Laboratory?*

A tug on his arm, and the deputy hissed, "Get up and come with me. We're taking a break before your defense starts."

Startled, Relevance stared at the nearly empty room. How long had he been staring into space?

Quiet pervaded the area, and though the deputy suggested a stroll up and down the corridor to stretch his legs and perhaps a bite to eat, Relevance refused. He couldn't face anyone, not now. Perhaps not ever. His doom was set, and all he had to do was endure the last scene, bitter as that would be. No defense in the world could save him now. He wasn't sure, given the hopelessness of his life, that he wanted to be saved. Perhaps a slow death on Bothmal Orbit would be better. At least he couldn't do any real harm, and no one could find fault with him. *Garbage doesn't complain. No moral outrage there.* He laughed so bitterly he could taste it. *I'm going insane.*

A bulky figure, his shoulders hunched protectively over a box, snuck into the empty room and trotted forward.

Max? Relevance had seen the cyborg man a dozen times in his life but rarely had any reason to speak to him. He could not understand why Max had come. *Unless…* With a spark alighting in his chest, he met Max in the middle of the room.

Dropping to his knees, Max set the box on the floor. "He's not doing well, so I have to hurry him back to Seth's Harbor, but he wanted to tell you something before we left." Max looked around. "I don't think anyone will mind. I'm just being sensitive to his last wishes."

A squeak piped up, "Don't put me in the grave just yet!"

Max turned back the blanket, and Squire's black eyes twinkled up at Relevance.

His vision blurring, Relevance knelt at Squire's side.

Squire lifted one shaky paw and pointed it at Relevance. "You asked me what makes humans human."

Relevance nodded as his heart writhed in his chest. He could barely coax out an affirming yes.

"You gave me a mission, Relevance. I've known wild, and I've known tame. They both have their merits but to have a mission is a great gift. One you gave me. No matter what else, remember this."

Guilt rending him to pieces, wishing he were already at Bothmal, Relevance gushed, "But I wronged you, gave you sentience only to have it taken away. You should have lived a long and happy life in the wild."

A wan smile and Squire's voice grew husky with weariness. "There's no saying how long or how happy for any of us. For my son...I hope so. Me? I've lived a lifetime in a few months."

"You don't hate me?"

"I hate no one." A smile spread over Squire's face. "My sentient, free-will choice." As if the sun had climbed through the window and wrapped the small Animan in a golden glow, Squire beamed as he lay back on his soft blanket.

Enraptured, Relevance sighed. A mountain had moved off his chest, and he could breathe again. "You are better than sentient, you are wise."

Voices murmured as people began to filter back into the courtroom.

In a moment, Max arranged the blanket, bundled Squire's box into his arms, stood, and trotted to the door. He spoke over his shoulder. "I'll take him home, but Justine's coming. So don't worry."

Relevance couldn't imagine why Justine's arrival should stop him from worrying, but he brushed that thought aside with the happy relief that no matter what else happened, Squire was well cared for.

Once the room had settled to a peaceful drone, Sylvan once again smacked his gavel and silence ruled.

The official deputy boomed, "Defense will now present its case."

Mr. Frank, looking a bit dazed, rose shakily to his feet. He swallowed and stared at the judge with an earnest expression. "I have little to say, your honor, as the facts of the case have been presented in detail by Prosecutor Smash. I can hardly deny a word of it."

Relevance dropped his head to his chest, the tiny flicker of hope now extinguished. He could hear the judge's sentence as a foregone conclusion.

Murmurs rippled through the crowd.

Mr. Frank's voice suddenly took on an authoritative tone. "But I do have a few witnesses, who would like to speak and one written testimony that will be offered into evidence."

Relevance lifted his head, positive that his heart had ceased to beat.

Mr. Frank gestured toward the gallery. "Taug, a well-known Cresta scientist, a specialist in the field of hybrids, will come forward now."

It took some doing, but Taug eventually made his way to the front of the room where he was offered a chair in the witness box. The deputy swore him in using every ounce of his official authority. "By your honor as a Newearth citizen in the face of this assembly, you swear to tell us the truth to the best of your ability?"

Taug's head bobbed. "Yes, certainly."

Mr. Frank paced forward and directed his witness. "Please tell us what you know about Tribrid Relevance and what conditions led to his committing such violations as have been leveled against him."

Unexpectedly, the defense attorney ambled across the room to the south wall where he proceeded to stare out the window as if he had nothing better to do than listen to a story told behind his back.

A few bubbles rising, Taug got comfortable and clasped his tentacles over his broad lap. "As most of you know, I designed Relevance and his brother Herson in my laboratory in response to a desire to help a childless woman. To me, it was a simple affair intended to solve several problems at once. I wished to help a friend, and in the case of Relevance, I saw a unique opportunity to assist the Ingot race, which, if you remember, was suffering from a severe reproduction crisis at the time."

Taug blinked as his gaze roamed over the assembly. "Though I am not the one on trial here, I probably should be. I was found guilty of overstepping IAAC rules years ago, and I repented for my actions then and still do today. But the consequences are still unfolding."

He turned and pointedly faced Relevance. "This young man, and I may say *man* since he is the biological son of a human, though he also carries Tabunite and Ingot DNA, has only responded to a question implanted inside of him at his conception: He wanted to understand his true identity. By designing hybrids, animal-humans, he reflected the very forces that created him. In an ancient Bhuaci saying—hurt people hurt people—so he repeated the mistakes of his past to better direct his future. Or so he thought. Repeating past mistakes does not clear the way for understanding. But there was no way for him to know that."

Taug tilted his head to meet the pointed stare of the judge. "Tribrid Relevance is guilty of breeding hybrids, true, but his mistake was born from forces he could neither understand nor control. No one understood him, and his desire to understand himself was not a sin."

Silence reigned a moment.

Finally, Mr. Frank thanked Taug and pointed to another member of the assembly. "Will Clare Erlandson, the mother of the accused, please step forward?"

Taug and Clare passed each other with minimal interaction. Taug might have offered a wink of encouragement, but Relevance was certain that his mother kept her gaze down as she headed across the room and found her seat on the witness chair. She was sworn in, and Mr. Frank deemed it useful to step closer and offer his condolences. "I am sorry to have to call you forward to testify on behalf of your son, but you have unique insight that may shed light on a difficult matter."

Her lips pressed in a straight line, Clare merely nodded.

"Can you expand on what the Cresta told us about Tribrid Relevance?"

Her face puckering in undisguised distaste, Clare glared at Mr. Frank. "I wish you wouldn't refer to people by their race. Any more than I would want to be identified by my height or shoe size."

Wide-eyed, but Relevance wondered if unsurprised, Mr. Frank bowed through a humble apology. "So sorry. I see that this is a sore point, and I've no wish to offend. I suppose you never think about the fact that your son is a tribrid?"

So smoothly asked, the question hung innocently in the air, but ears perked up and even the judge's eyes narrowed as he stared at the witness.

Clare cleared her throat, shifted in her seat, and then sucked in a deep breath. "On the contrary, it's all I thought about while he was growing up." She stared straight ahead as if refusing to see anyone in the room. "I wasn't used to children, and he was unusual to say the least. He did nothing like what the books said he should do. Even Kendra—" Her eyes focused, and she surveyed the assembly, searching. "Well, she is a friend who tried to help." A heavy shrug and Clare's hands strangled each other. "I was a hopeless case."

As if wanting to spare his witness any further suffering, Mr. Frank chimed in, "You mean because you didn't know how to raise children?"

A dead expression arrested all vitality, and Clare's voice dropped to a whisper. "Because I didn't love him."

Hardly moving a muscle, Mr. Frank urged further clarity. "I don't understand."

Squeezing her eyes shut a moment, Clare seemed to be gathering her strength. "I only asked Taug for one child. I never asked for two and certainly not a hybrid and a tribrid. I was overwhelmed. My heart clenched tight, and I refused to acknowledge Relevance as"—her gaze drifted over Relevance—"my son."

In a heartless move, Mr. Frank pulled out a datapad and flashed it before the murmuring crowd. "But the record clearly states that you were Relevance's mother."

Another whisper and Clare barely managed to shake her head.

Relevance's hands clenched with the desire to rip Mr. Frank's head from his shoulders. *What does he think he's doing?*

Pitilessly, Mr. Frank continued. "You hated your son, didn't you?"

At this, Relevance would have vaulted across the room and acted on his desire, but Clare's pitched cry nailed him in place.

"No! I loved him. I always loved him. In my terrible, frightened, hurt way, I didn't show it properly. I focused on his brother, poured my attention on him to make up for my…my emotional neglect. Both Herson and Relevance felt it, I'm sure. They knew something was wrong but they were children; they didn't understand. I was so confused! I needed help but didn't know who to ask. Even my friends couldn't save me."

His tone gentle, as if asking for forgiveness for his earlier harshness, Mr. Frank pursued his private purpose. "That's why you sent him away?"

Tears slipped down Clare's face. "Yes, I was wrong to do it, but I honestly didn't know what right looked like. I couldn't bond with a tribrid. He didn't look like me or anyone in my family. But the urgent need to get rid of him and focus on what I could handle didn't work either. It nearly destroyed me…"

"You tried to kill yourself and, as a result, severely damaged your body?"

Clare's head dropped onto her chest, her eyes squeezed shut.

As if all the air had been sucked out of the room, no one moved. Horror mixed with grief flooded the air, making it difficult to breathe.

Fury filled Relevance, but he wasn't sure who he wanted to kill.

His voice soft now, Mr. Frank moved forward. "You have suffered unendurable pain. And so has your son." Mr. Frank lifted his arms as if encompassing the assembly. "Is there anyone here you want to hold accountable?"

Gathering herself, Clare wiped her eyes and lifted her head. "I have made mistakes, as we all do. I'm not suggesting that Taug and other eager scientists didn't have a part to play, certainly the tragedies of my childhood shaped my thinking, but if I tried to weigh of all the wrongs done to me and the mistakes I have made in response, it would never be done. It's a fact; bad choices become evil in other people's lives. But Relevance is a human being with mixed DNA, unique and capable of free will. He has been hurt and hurt others. "She sighed. "What this court deems best is in the judge's hands, but I want to make it clear, it is possible to repent and make amends." Clare's gaze embraced Relevance. "No matter what happens, I am Relevance's mother, and I will always love my son."

Very much in need of a break to calm rattled nerves and wipe teary eyes, the judge called for another recess. "We will break for a mid-day meal and reconvene this afternoon."

Relevance wasn't sure he would live that long. This process was soul-wrenching, even a tribrid body could only take so much. A cry rose from deep within to he knew not who. *Please, no more!*

To his relief, it was Cerulean, this time, who kept him company through the lonely wait. The idea of eating made him nauseous, and the Luxonian-man didn't seem to mind missing a meal. They stood together facing the south window, watching a breeze scuttle snow across the courtyard. A large fountain with a leaping fish sculpture stood prominently in the middle of the space. Two weights hung in perfect balance from the fish's gaping mouth. As the snowy mounds had heaped up unevenly, it seemed that the fish ought to fall over, but it stayed in place, frozen in winter's tight grip.

His voice a deeper baritone than expected, Cerulean spoke without turning his head. "You heard your mother?"

Relevance had to stir his mind to come up with any semblance of an answer. "She said many things."

"One of them more important than all the rest."

He couldn't risk being wrong, exposing his soul and be crushed by cruel reality once again. He studied Cerulean and asked his own question. "Why do you care?"

A smile and the Luxonian finally turned his head and met Relevance's inquiring eyes. "About humanity?"

Relevance waited. What would be would be.

Turning completely around, Cerulean leaned on the window sill and folded his arms over his chest. "Your mother is a descendant of a very kind man, a principal in the last primary school on OldEarth, Mr. Erlandson. He tried to protect the woman I loved, Anne Smith, who was the last of her kind before the exile to Lux and your subsequent resettlement on Earth…Newearth, I should say."

His confusion turning to irritation, Relevance snapped. "Why say, 'your,' as if I had something to do with it? I'm hardly a member of the human race despite what my DNA may say." He snorted. "Ask Dr. Anzi. The one who got away free and clear."

A shake of his head and a soft smile spread over Cerulean's face. "If for no other reason than your stubborn thinking, I would know you are Clare's son. Deny it at your peril, Relevance, but you are a member of the human race; you are a part of a long lineage that goes back before recorded history. Humans were on this planet, living and dying, hurting and helping, long before I came. All of that history is inside you, in the fiber of your being. Some of your ancestors were probably villainous. But some"—Cerulean pushed off the window sill and faced the fountain again—"were remarkably good in terribly hard times." He paused as he looked back. "As for Dr. Anzi, trust me, he isn't getting away from anything. He's stuck inside his own deranged mind and that will haunt him for the rest of his days in bitterness and grief."

Three sparrows huddled on the snowy basin of the water fountain. They fluffed their feathers but didn't appear unduly concerned by the fact that there were no berries to eat and no water to drink.

Shifting the conversation onto safer territory, Relevance asked an obvious question, as he pointed to the birds. "How do they survive such a bitterly cold winter?"

"They help each other. Huddling for warmth and finding old stores of seeds and grain, even bugs." Cerulean shrugged. "It's a mystery that's solved when you consider that even with all *our* intelligence, friendship makes survival possible."

"We can be pretty deplorable friends when we have a mind to be."

"The price of free will. But, in my long years, I have seen the worst situations bring out the best in people. Something more is at work than our minds can comprehend. I've learned to accept that."

Horrific images swamping his mind, Relevance had to clutch the sill to keep his balance. "What if I go to Bothmal? Will that bring out the best in me?"

Cerulean reached over and pressed Relevance's shoulder, a boy being comforted by his father. "Did you hear your mother?"

Relevance nodded.

"She loves you. And no matter what else, you need to remember that."

The rest of the midday break passed in quiet. Cerulean stood staring out the window, communing with whom, Relevance could not imagine, though it seemed clear to him that Cerulean was not alone.

Finally, the assembly shuffled back into the courtroom, sleepy with the weight of a full meal and anxious about testimony that few had the heart to hear.

It was Roux who spoke next in a coordinated statement between the Luxonian Supreme Judges, the Ingot High Command, and on behalf of Song, and Walking Flower, lead representatives of the Bhuaci and Insectine peoples.

Sitting in the witness booth, with the standard swearing-in dispensed with, Roux cleared his throat, drew out his datapad, introduced himself and named those he represented, and then read in formal style.

"In the case of Tribrid Relevance, after a careful review of the complex situation, in the understanding that he will desist from ever participating in any experiments on sentient life in the future and will make reparation by assisting the Newearth Docking Bay managers—Max Omega and Justine Santana—in the establishment of the Right from Wrong Center of Healing, we hereby grant full pardon for his misinformed participation in the development of LEAP laboratory."

Roux lowered the datapad and locked his gaze on Relevance. "Should you ever be tempted to experiment on animal, human, or alien life, again, this pardon will be revoked and the prosecutor's plan will be carried out with our full approval."

Relevance held the Luxonian's gaze without wavering.

Once Roux had returned to his seat, Judge Sylvan lifted his hammer as if to make his final pronouncement.

A woman stood up, one hand stalling the judge. She lifted her datapad. "I have the written testimony of Squire, one of the most successful of all the Animans. May I have your leave to read it aloud? Since he has suffered the effects of the experiments directly, I believe his testimony is worthy of our respect."

The judge nodded, and the clerk announced her name as she descended the steps, "Justine Santana, Manager and Security Officer of Newearth Docking Bay."

Clearly, Justine didn't need to read the statement as it passed before her eyes. She had probably memorized it the second after it was written.

"Salutations Vandi Court Officers and all concerned Newearth Citizens,

I, Squire, being of sound mind, if not of body, do declare that though Relevance's experiments on animal life forms were poorly considered and caused great suffering, his intention was to determine the true worth of humanity, in answer to Dr. Anzi's despairing conclusion that the human race was virtually dead.

"As a humble servant who wished to serve well, I considered this question throughout my sentient experience,

even when my son was born a wild creature who could never understand his father.

"Our sins are doorways to redemption, and redemption is the window to the soul. Being able to admit a mistake makes room for forgiveness of self and others. I, who was most wronged by Relevance and Dr. Anzi, forgive them freely. In this, I believe, lies the greatest proof that humanity yet lives. If you would respect my short life as an animal-human hybrid, you will respect my forgiveness."

Eternally,

Squire

All eyes locked onto Relevance. He could not see them, but he certainly felt them.

Judge Sylvan dismissed Justine and cleared his throat noisily. "Tribrid Relevance, have you anything to say in your own defense?"

As if he had been run over by a thousand autoskimmers and dragged through oceans unending, Relevance staggered to his feet. Uncertain whether his voice would rise above the tumult of his mind, he heaved a deep breath, looked over the assembly, met his mother's firm gaze, and attempted to speak.

"I am a mistake. Ill-considered and unwanted, I should never have been conceived." His gaze wavered to Variant, whose eyes engaged his in sympathetic understanding.

"But I *was* conceived. My tribrid DNA directed flesh, bone, and blood to shape the unique being that is me. When I was born, no one knew what to do with me. As I grew, my differences became my downfall. Unacceptable to some" —his gaze roamed to Clare— "but loved by others"—he shifted to Gavin—"I discovered that I could harden my body, my mind, and my heart. The idea of revenge, making others see and feel what I saw and felt, encouraged my scheme to design hybrids. I planned to create a world within a world, one where I would rule with benign authority. Among hybrids of my own making, I would finally fit in. I would have a home." He sighed and his shoulders sagged. "Dr. Anzi was an answer to a prayer and an unremitting curse. I wish now that I never met him."

He swallowed a sharp pain rising in his throat. "I am most sorry for the suffering I have caused to innocent people, including my assistant, Jeremy, who died, probably in reaction to overexposure to the Dumplix drug."

Surreptitiously, he wiped his blurry eyes and forced himself to maintain his focus. "I swear by all that I hold dear to never experiment on any life form for the rest of my existence. I would be honored to serve Max Omega and Justine Santana in their efforts to assist those suffering from addictions in the Right from Wrong Center. Most of all, I would like to say that I am sorry, and I hope that you will forgive me."

It took a moment, but finally Sylvan found the power to smack his gavel and end all testimony. He scraped back his chair and stood. "I need a brief moment, and I will return with my final judgment."

No one moved from their seats. Relevance saw nothing, heard nothing, cared for nothing. If he had been frozen in time, he could not have been more still.

When Judge Sylvan reappeared and the clerk told everyone to rise, a hushed expectation held the room in a tight grip.

Judge Sylvan thrust back his shoulders and stared pointedly at the accused. "Tribrid Relevance, I find you guilty of the crime of experimenting on innocent life and assisting in bringing animals to sentience without IAAC approval or official Newearth regulation of any kind." He exhaled. "That being understood, you are sentenced to serve full time at the Right from Wrong Center for Healing for fifteen years, monitored by the managers, Max Omega and Justine Santana, who have agreed to report to the IAAC concerning your behavior on a yearly basis for the term of your sentence." He gazed around the room with a weary smile. "You are free to go."

Chapter Ten

Home

—Seth's Harbor—

March, Year 75, Newearth Reckoning

Bala set a loaded picnic basket just inside the massive door and followed Kendra into the great hall.

Rachel stood by the large window, morning light streaming in, a violin resting on a table with a music stand next to it, nearby.

A head taller, Relevance stood beside Rachel, their hands together, fingers intertwined.

Kendra halted, taking in the sight. Bala came alongside of her and clasped her hand. A brief squeeze to reassure her.

She squeezed back.

Uncertain how to break the moment, Bala reverted to his standby humor. "Spring certainly has sprung. Anything exciting out there we should see?"

With a start, Rachel twirled around, almost letting go of Relevance's hand, but he held firm. She smiled up at him and then returned her gaze to her parents, blossoming suddenly from studious quiet to exuberant joy. "Oh, good, you made it!" She bounded across the room and flung herself at her mother, wrapping her arms around her as if they hadn't seen each other in years rather than a couple of weeks.

Kendra laughed as she pulled back and peered at her daughter. "You feeling all right? I haven't seen you this excited since your promotion at Vandi Hospital." Her brow furrowed. "You're still taking the promotion, right?"

Rachel laughed as she hugged her dad in turn. "Yes, of course! It's perfect. I'll be able to coordinate medical personnel and materials between the hospital and the Right from Wrong Center on the Docking Bay." She glanced over at Relevance who stayed quietly in the background. "Relevance really likes working with Max and Justine." A smile quirked on her lips. "Max is a hoot and a half!"

Nearly choking, Bala spluttered, glancing from his daughter to Relevance. "What does that mean exactly?"

A grin spread over Relevance's face. "It's an OldEarth expression I came across while reading one of Rachel's vintage books." He shrugged, abashed. "It fits."

Kendra's eyes softened as she stared at Relevance. She came forward, her hands extended. "How are you doing, Relevance?"

As if caught unprepared for a sudden speech, Relevance shifted gears and pointed to the stairs. "Uh, I'm fine. They're all upstairs waiting for you." His face tightened. "It's near time."

All laughter smothered in remembered grief, Bala heaved a sigh and led his wife forward.

The four climbed the winding staircase in respectful silence.

Once in the room, Bala nodded to his two sons.

Seth stood on one side of the small bed where Squire lay, his breath rattling in his chest, his life hanging by the merest thread.

Barni knelt on the floor rolling acorns to Inheritance, who seemed to be making a game of the twirling nuts.

He doesn't understand. The fact that the young squirrel had never reached sentience felt like a blessing. Bala sighed. It was when Relevance knelt at Squire's bedside and lifted his tiny paw in his hand that Bala feared his heart would break.

A tiny sob escaped from Kendra, but Rachel, well trained in the art of mercy in painful situations, stood by, one hand resting supportively on Relevance's shoulder.

Seth watched; his face etched with the grief of too many goodbyes.

Barni scooped the young squirrel into his arms and carried him to the bed.

Inheritance scrambled to run free.

Relevance opened his mouth to speak but no words came. A stifled sob and he just held the little paw until the ragged breathing came to final rest.

Squire lay still, his body unmoving. Life as he had known it was over. What came next for such as him, no one knew.

Bala and Kendra murmured their prayers in quiet unison.

Reaching over, Rachel lifted Squire's limp paw from Relevance's fingers and laid it gently over the white sheet. She tapped his paws into place, his eyes already closed, and stepped back.

Swallowing convulsively, Relevance struggled to regain his footing.

Inheritance, seeing an opportunity, leaped from Barni's hands onto Relevance's shoulder.

The motion was so smooth and skillfully done that everyone's attention was immediately riveted on the small squirrel.

Seth snorted a laugh. "You'll be the wonder of the woods, little one!" But then his gaze darted to Relevance's face. "Oh, I didn't mean. You'll take him, I expect. He'll live with you and…" His words trailed to a confused end.

Like an anxious uncle, Barni hovered at Relevance's shoulder, watching Inheritance's every move, ready to catch him should he fall.

With great care, Relevance reached up and drew Inheritance from his shoulder and cupped the squirming critter in his large, powerful hands. He met Seth's direct gaze. "He's a wild one all right and he belongs with his own kind. A city is no place for a spirit such as his." He reached out, offering, toward Seth. "Please take him to where his father roamed in happiness and allow him to live as free as his spirit."

A nod, and Seth accepted Inheritance in his arms. He glanced aside at his brother. "Guess you'll believe me when I tell you about my next adventure in the woodlands."

Cracking a smile, Barni quipped back. "I'll still want to see for myself!"

Kendra linked her arm through Barni's and drew him toward the door. "So, how is it going with the Healing Center? I hear they've had some new admissions?"

His shoulders straightening in his professional mode, Barni dropped his tone and began to fill in the details.

Bala watched as Seth set Inheritance among the acorns again, the two joining in youthful fun.

Rachel's gaze adored Relevance as they clasped hands and headed for the door.

Bala didn't know what else to do with the fullness of his heart, so he pronounced his conviction. "Squire was the best Animan I ever knew, and I'll miss him forever."

Everyone stopped in place, frozen.

With the relief of released grief, he pointed to the door. "He'd be the first to tell us, 'Get the picnic basket and go eat!'"

—Aram County, Woodlands—

Bala walked with Kendra through the evening woods to Cerulean's cabin where they would spend the night, and then in the morning, they'd head to the transit that would take them home. The rising moon lit a brilliant path before them. He wrapped his arm around her waist, holding her close.

She looked up at him, her eyes glimmering. "Will they be happy together, you think?"

The image of Variant feeding David with peaceful devotion flashed in his mind. Then he saw Rachel's sparkling eyes as she faced Relevance, whose reflecting love radiated like the sun. Bala sucked in a deep breath of pure woodland air. "Not all the time. But will they love each other even when they aren't happy? Yes, I believe so."

Accompanied by the distant hoots of communing owls, they wandered along the well-worn trail between Cerulean's cabin and Seth's Harbor. Relevance's house was not far away, and Bala knew, with the certainty of his soul, the trail to that young man's home would be worn smooth before the season was out.

—Waukee, Clare's House—

Clare answered the door and was not surprised. She was pleased. A gentle thrill ran down her spine.

With a courtly nod, Gavin stood in the doorway and held out a bouquet of spring flowers. Where he managed to get them this early in the season, Clare could not guess. It didn't matter. Delight brought a smile to her face. "Come in. Variant is in the kitchen, and Relevance will be here shortly. He had to stop by the market to pick up some juice for dinner. *Knowing him, he'll probably pick up a variety pack to make everyone happy.*

To the tune of Variant's humming in the background, Clare led Gavin to the big double-sided couch and took a seat facing the open kitchen. At her right stood a table, loaded with a half-finished birdhouse project, an assortment of nail polishes Variant had brought over "for fun," a water bottle long drained and in need of a good wash, and one thick, old-fashioned album.

Gavin picked up the album, set it carefully on his lap and opened it. He studied the first pages with concentrated attention: Clare as a baby…Clare's mom and dad hugging…Clare taking her first steps…Clare and her best friend at school…

Her heart jumping into her throat, Clare's immediate thought was to grab it away, saying that it was nothing, just a silly memento of the past. But a twinkle shining in Gavin's eyes arrested that idea. She leaned over and tried to see what he was grinning at. Little girl Clare dressed in a ballerina outfit, holding a wand, her head poised artfully. A hot blush worked over her. *I remember that day. I was so proud of myself!*

Tapping the picture, Gavin's grin turned into a laugh. "So beautiful, so innocent, and proud." He looked aside and embraced Clare with his eyes. "You were a good girl, Clare; you tried so hard."

How can he know...from a picture? Tears unbidden pooled, blurring her vision. Her voice rose in a husky whisper, "I did."

As if he had just given her an actual hug, Gavin returned to the book and continued turning the pages, fascinated by details she had hardly ever noticed.

Still embarrassed, Clare tried to affect indifference. She directed her gaze around her familiar home, the place she had lived in for so many years, which now felt so new and different.

Humming a lullaby, serene and peaceful, Variant chopped vegetables at the counter, then paced to a shelf where she retrieved a handful of spice bottles.

Variant's piano stood pride of place on the south wall. Gleaming in high, polished redwood, it, along with Relevance's violin, which rested on a stand beside the piano, brought an air of dignity to the space, a claim to more than mundane routine but a mystical passage to the spiritual world.

For the first time she could ever remember, Clare felt at home in her home. *I like it.* She paused and continued her survey, soon pausing on the bookshelves full of OldEarth finds—some gifts from Cerulean, others cookbooks that Bala thought might inspire her toward greater culinary adventures.

She sighed as she considered how long she had ignored Bala's many attempts to widen her narrow world.

Her art station, dusty with long neglect, held the remains of a pottery project she hadn't thought about in years. She frowned. *Why did I give it up?* But deep inside, she knew. *I almost gave up on everything.* Visions of a shapely flower vase challenged her to try one more time. A spark of gladness filled her.

A work desk, tucked into the northwest corner with a slim new com unit, reminded her of a half dozen cases that needed her attention. They were important, just as worthy as the Hogsworth case years ago, back when she first met Justine. *What an adventure that was!*

Finally, her gaze settled on the big bay window. Her cat sat primly outside on the porch railing, no doubt expecting savory leftovers as soon as dinner was over. With a happy sigh, Clare considered her miniature world and knew with contrite honesty that she had never fully appreciated it before. *I love my home.*

The door swung open, and Relevance, carrying a large case of colorful fruit juice bottles and an overfilled grocery bag, strode straight into the kitchen. He bypassed the large wooden table and set his parcels on the counter with an "Ooff!" that brought a smile to Variant's face.

They chatted playfully, Relevance insisting that Variant didn't really know how to cook, and he'd have to see if he lived through the meal first to pass judgment on her skills. Swatting him like the brother she never had, Variant mocked outrage, and then offered him a hot pepper to chew on as an appetizer.

Clare shook her head at the marvel that, suddenly, she felt as if she had two teenagers in the house, and with a shock, realized that was exactly what she had. Delight filled her. Only the image of Herson's grave shook her smile. *My dear boy, wherever you are, I still love you.*

Finally, Gavin closed the album and leaned back, one arm reaching around the top of the couch, almost touching her shoulder. He was so close; she could feel the warmth of his body and smell the scent of his cologne. *Or does he exude a natural spice?*

She wanted to ask what he thought of her family album, but shyness clamped her mouth shut.

Until dinner.

Sitting around her large wooden table in chatty companionship, Variant's supper delight was eaten to the accompaniment of laughter, teasing, and a fruit juice contest—first place going strawberry-cherry-pineapple. The bottle was given pride of place in the center of the table.

The dishes soon cleared and loaded in the washer, Relevance wiped the table; Gavin swept up nonexistent crumbs from the floor, and Clare packed the meager leftovers in the cooler for tomorrow's lunch.

As Clare resituated herself on the couch, Gavin sitting even closer, Variant took a seat at the piano, and Relevance drew forth his violin.

As The Moonlight Sonata rose gloriously into the air, the harmony of the two young people who had suffered and overcome so much filled Clare with divine joy. *I wasn't looking for love—I was looking to love.*

Relevance's heart swelled. The violin tucked under his chin in proper form, he played as if his heart depended on each beautiful note. His gaze slid from Variant's cheery face to Gavin's fatherly nod, and then, as the final chord vibrated into the greater universe, he embraced his mother. *I'm home.*

A. K. Frailey

A. K. Frailey has written the historical sci-fi *OldEarth Encounter* series, a contemporary first contact novel, *Last of Her Kind*, the *Newearth* sci-fi series, an *OldTown* series, short story collections, a modern parent's reflection on J. R. R. Tolkien's works in *The Road Goes Ever On: A Christian Journey Through The Lord of the Rings*, personal and introspective *My Road* books, children's books, and a poetry collection.

She taught in Milwaukee, WI, Chicago, IL, Los Angeles, CA, and Wood River, IL, as an elementary education teacher.

She also trained teachers in the Philippines for the Peace Corps and later earned a Master of Fine Arts Degree in Creative Writing for Entertainment from Full Sail University.

Ann homeschooled all her children and currently manages her rural homestead with her family and their numerous critters. In her spare time, she serves as an election judge and secretary/treasurer of her small town's cemetery.

A. K. Frailey Books QR CODES

A. K. Frailey Website

Translated Books Page with Links

A. K. Frailey Interviews Page

A. K. Frailey Amazon Author Page

www.ingramcontent.com/pod-product-compliance
Lightning Source LLC
Chambersburg PA
CBHW070615310726
48982CB00001B/83

* 9 7 9 8 9 9 9 8 2 4 1 3 4 *